SHIP OUT OF LUCK

NEAL SHUSTERMAÑ

DUTTON CHILDREN'S BOOKS
AN IMPRINT OF PENGUIN GROUP (USA) INC.

Dutton Children's Books
A division of Penguin Young Readers Group
Published by the Penguin Group
Penguin Group (USA) Inc., 375 Hudson Street, New York, New York 10014, USA

USA / Canada / UK / Ireland / Australia / New Zealand / India / South Africa / China
Penguin Books Ltd, Registered Offices: 80 Strand, London WC2R 0RL, England
For more information about the Penguin Group visit penguin.com

Text copyright © 2013 by Neal Shusterman

Printed in USA   First Edition   1 3 5 7 9 10 8 6 4 2
Designed by Kristin Smith

Library of Congress Cataloging-in-Publication Data

Shusterman, Neal.
Ship out of luck : a companion to The Schwa was here / Neal Shusterman.
pages cm
Summary: Brooklyn-native Antsy Bonano embarks on the largest cruise ship in the world,
where mischief, adventure, and deportation await.
ISBN 978-0-525-42226-6 (hardcover : alk. paper)
[1. Cruise ships—Fiction. 2. Adventure and adventurers—Fiction.
3. Caribbean Area—Fiction.] I. Title.
PZ7.S55987Sm 2013
[Fic]--dc23
2013000031

The publisher does not have any control over and does not assume any responsibility
for author or third-party websites or their content.

For Keith, Thresa & Jordan

CHAPTER 1

MERMAID SUSHI, EXPLOSIVE RAINBOWS, WORLD POLITICS, AND OTHER THINGS THAT GIVE ME GAS

DON'T ASK ME BECAUSE I DON'T GOT AN OPINION.

I'm not red, I'm not blue; I'm not an elephant or donkey; I'm not left or right; and I ain't center either. I'm not even in the ballpark. If it's a ballpark, then I'm playin' hockey.

The way I see it, politics is like a broken thermostat: all hot air, all the time, no matter how sweltering it is, and don't even get me started on the humidity.

Bottom line: I don't believe anyone who says they got the answers to society's ills because society's ills mutate faster than the flu, and no amount of Purell is gonna protect you from that juicy sneeze. So I don't make my decisions based on what some whining loudmouth with an ax to grind says. I go by my guts, when I got enough of 'em. I guess that makes me independent.

You want to talk "public policy," then talk to my mother, because she's got policies enough to sink any peacetime economy. The "No Shoes in the Living Room" policy. The "No Un-showered Friends in My House" policy. The "Get Up and Get Your Own Freakin' Drink" policy.

Put all these policies together and you got yourself a

1

platform. The "WOULD IT KILL YOU TO SHOW A LITTLE COMMON COURTESY?" platform—which, if you ask me, oughta be how we run the country.

What happened on the boat—excuse me, I mean "ship"—had nothing to do with making a political statement, and if I had known I was gonna be thrust onto the national stage like a piñata in headlights, I woulda stayed home.

It all started, as so many things seem to start, with Old Man Crawley . . .

"You will take this invitation to your parents and get an immediate RSVP," Mr. Crawley said. He handed me an envelope, but when I tried to take it from him, he wouldn't let go. It stuck tightly between his fingers, kinda the way money usually does.

"Your parents' answer," Mr. Crawley said, "shall be 'yes.'"

I tugged harder on the invitation until I finally pulled it out of his vise-grip claw. "If their answer has to be yes," I said, "then it's not an invitation, is it?"

Mr. Crawley's response was a scowl that made the wrinkles on his face become deeper, which I didn't even think was possible. Old Man Crawley is kinda like a living legend in Brooklyn, although I use the word "living" loosely. He's the reclusive owner of Crawley's Lobster House and lives above the restaurant with fourteen dogs. Fifteen if you include the guide dog. That's not for him, it's for his granddaughter, Lexie. Trust me, Old Man Crawley doesn't need a guide dog; he has perfect vision. He's got eyes in the back of his head, and maybe in some other people's heads, too, because I swear he can see everything.

My relationship with Old Man Crawley is this long, involved story. All you really need to know is that (a) he's filthy rich from a life of scrooge-like living; (b) he and my dad are business partners in a restaurant called Paris, Capische; (c) Old Man Crawley hates me less than he hates most everyone else, which I guess makes me the closest thing he has to a friend.

So I leave his place with the invitation, and as I'm walking down the street, I open it. Crawley musta known I'd do that, because inside is a second envelope that reads *Open this one, Anthony, and there will be severe consequences.*

Fine. I brought the thing home and put it in my mother's hands. She looked at it like it might be a bad report card or a telegram telling her that someone's dead like they did back in the days when death notices came by telegram and not by e-mail.

"It's from Crawley," I told her. "Just open it, say yes, and let me get on with my life."

She opened the envelope, pulled out a fancy-looking card, then looked at me like she was gonna kill the messenger.

"Is this some sort of joke?"

"Why? What's it say?"

"See for yourself." She handed it to me and I looked it over.

The "honor" of your family's presence
is requested on Saturday, the 29th of June,
on board the Plethora of the Deep
for seven days
to celebrate the 80th birthday
of Mr. Charles Jameson Crawley.
A suitable gift is expected.

Okay, so my experience with cruises is limited to the Circle Line. That's the boat that goes around Manhattan while some underpaid high school dropout points out all the tall buildings as if you can't see them for yourself, and if you're lucky, you ram into a careless speedboat, adding some actual excitement to the tour. But this invitation was for the real thing. And not just any cruise ship—this was the *Plethora of the Deep*, the largest, most luxurious ship in the known universe.

I saw this whole thing about it on TV, and how Caribbean Viking cruise line had to build new docks in every port just to fit the *Plethora*. It's got a Junior NASCAR go-cart speedway, the infamous Cavalcade of Waterslides, an underwater lounge with glass walls so you can watch the propellers make sushi out of any passing mermaids, and a world-class roller coaster. Just the thought of it makes me drool like a knuckle-dragger from the Jersey Shore.

And my mom says, "Forget it. I don't do boats."

I opened my mouth to protest, but realized even before a word made it from my brain to my vocal cords that protesting would be no use. My mother does not make decisions; she makes proclamations. The kind that guys on horseback posted in kingdoms of old to subdue the peasants.

"Tell Mr. Crawley 'thank you, but we respectfully decline.'"

I closed my mouth, realizing this would take a peasant revolt. The kind with torches and pitchforks.

"Okay," I said to my mom. "I'll tell him," and then added, "I don't want to miss the Fourth of July anyway." That got her attention.

"Why? What are you planning?"

I shrugged. "Nothing much." Then I left her to the darkness of her own imagination.

Last year, the Fourth of July was a blast. My friends Howie and Ira and I got our hands on some real fireworks that the Sheepshead Bay Rotary Club had purchased but couldn't get permits to use, on account of they don't officially permit anything in Brooklyn.

In *my* neighborhood, however, the Fourth of July is all about broken rules and losing fingers. Not that we were stupid enough to do anything dangerous. We hadn't had a Roman candle fight since, like, the third grade. We took every precaution with the fireworks. We figured we could set it off from my front porch and light up the sky above the whole neighborhood like they light up the Statue of Liberty. And the best part about it was that we only had to light one fuse, because the thing was automated. Once you started it, it cycled through like some sort of explosive computer system. To be extra safe, just so that we didn't set my house on fire, I angled the fireworks away from the house.

Here's something I learned about fireworks last year: If you don't aim them straight up in the air, they take on this trajectory called "gravity's rainbow." In other words, they go up in one place, arc across the sky, then come down somewhere else, blowing up the pot of gold at the far end.

Have you ever seen those war movies where the enemy relentlessly bombs the good guys in their foxholes and the good guys all form lasting friendships that eventually threaten their marriages? Well, let's just say that us kids on East 56th Street made the folks over on East 53rd Street bond in ways that could be considered unnatural in certain religions.

With my mom attempting to sink our all-expenses-paid cruise, I went looking for an unlikely ally in my father, who, after his heart attack this past year, shed his workaholic ways and had finally given himself permission to speak the word "vacation." Not that he's actually taken one, but at least now it was in his vocabulary. The thing is, he and Mom had been talking forever about going somewhere, but whenever it came up, it was like, "Where do you want to go?" "I don't know, where do *you* wanna go?" I think the fear is that someone's going to suggest visiting relatives in Italy who we don't know but feel some genetic guilt about.

I presented the invitation to my father later that afternoon. He was out back tending to our yard. A few months ago, I killed all the plants in the yard and half the plants in the neighborhood in a tragic gardening accident. His doctor suggested he turn our dead yard into a Zen garden to help him relax. So now our backyard is all volcanic rocks, bonsai, and sand that gets pushed around by a rake. It's really cool, for like the first ten seconds.

I crossed the garden, ruining the pattern of sand with my footprints, and handed him the invitation. My dad's easy to laugh but slow to smile, so I know this smile is genuine.

"Well," he says, patting his newly slimmed waistline. "I guess I'm gonna need a new bathing suit!"

To which I reply, "Mom says we're not going."

Dad's smile fades, and he hands me back the invitation. "Well, it was a nice idea."

"But—"

"No buts. Your mother and I have an agreement: We don't go anywhere as a family unless we both agree to it."

In the past, this has served our family well, on account of the time Mom wanted to take a walking tour of Amish covered bridges and the time that dad wanted to follow Bruce Springsteen on a six-city tour. These are examples of what we call "midlife crisis," which is when parents go temporarily insane because they realize how boring prime-time TV has gotten, and a crisis at least makes things interesting.

"The Caribbean's too humid anyway," Dad says, and returns to his raking. Watching him reminds me that things have not been normal in our home—and by normal, I mean loud. See, one thing you need to know about my parents is that they love yelling at each other. Even when they're expressing affection, they do it at a volume that can bring down enemy aircraft. *Whadaya mean you love me? I love you more! What are you gonna do about it, ha?* But ever since my dad's heart attack six months ago, it's all been daisies and sunshine. Any conversation that might raise blood pressure is avoided like the plague.

"We've become very midwestern," says my sister, Christina. "It's disturbing."

My brother, Frankie, is convinced it will pass, and normal volume will return. Frankie just finished his second year of college and works selling time-shares in the Bronx to really, really stupid people—because

7

anyone who would buy a time-share in the Bronx has got dog intelligence, at best.

"You can't pass up a deal like this," Frankie tells them. "It's a full-service resort—and subway convenient." One thing I can say about Frankie: He could sell anything to anyone. He's the number-one salesperson at Bronxe Pointe Vacation Villas, so I figured he could tweak Mom just enough to get her aboard the *Plethora of the Deep*.

"I'm not a miracle worker," was all Frankie could say.

I convened that evening with a few of my friends in my attic, which had become a hangout spot in our neighborhood on account of the little attic window has a very revealing view of Ann-Marie Delmonico's bedroom. This was not something I advertised or took advantage of much, but word got around anyway. What also got around was that Ann-Marie Delmonico's attic window has a very revealing view of my bedroom, too. For reasons that should be obvious, both Ann-Marie and I now follow a strict closed-curtain policy. It's what you call a mutual understanding, like the way most nations, except the crazy ones, promise not to nuke each other.

That being the case, any view from my attic is entirely in the imagination of the viewer. Which leaves my friend Howie out in the cold, since his imagination is a field of tumbleweeds, without even a breeze to make 'em roll.

So there we were in the attic, me, Ira, Howie, and this new guy, Hamid, all of us comparing and contrasting various complaints we had about our parents. While the others seemed to have plenty of gripes, I only had one at the moment: my mother's inconvenient cruise-a-phobia.

"That stinks, right?" Hamid said when I told him. "My father hates flying, so we never go anywhere we can't drive. I've never even met half my relatives, right?" Hamid ends most of his sentences with "right?" as if he needs to double-check with you to make sure he actually has an opinion.

"You don't know how lucky you have it," Howie says. "Not meeting my relatives is not an option, and there's no end to it not being an option."

Ira, by the way, was videotaping the whole thing. He had taken to making a video log of his entire waking life and then editing it down to webisodes that he posted online. At the last count, they've been viewed twice, both times, I think, by him.

"I'll get more people watching once I get to Israel," Ira said. "People like controversial places."

"When are you going?" I asked.

"Next week," he told us. His family was going on this big Holy Land extravaganza with their temple that would end with his sister having her bat mitzvah at the Wailing Wall, with like fourteen thousand other Jewish-American kids whose parents opted out of the big gigantic party thing in favor of something more meaningful and less expensive.

"My parents are all freaked out," Ira said. "They think we're going to get blown up the second we get in the shuttle bus from the airport." Then he turned to Hamid. "No offense."

Hamid is Muslim—half Palestinian, in fact. His parents and Ira's parents are part of an ethnic dinner group.

"No offense taken," said Hamid. "As long as you promise to give the finger to some random soldier in Gaza, right?"

"Good as done," said Ira. They tapped fists and all was well. This is why I love America. No matter what our cultural upbringing, we can all be equally idiotic in peace and harmony.

"So that leaves three of us stuck in Brooklyn all summer," Howie said, a bit satisfied with the fact.

"Actually," said Hamid, "my family won't fly, but we're driving up to Niagara Falls and taking a train across Canada."

Howie's all disappointed. "Y'know, more people die on trains than in airplanes."

"Or by being blown up," added Ira.

Hamid sighed. "I know, right?"

"Well," says Howie, "at least we got each other, Antsy! We're both in the same boat."

"Yeah," I said, "which is no boat at all."

Just so you know, Howie's had a rough year. First, his dad gets arrested for tax evasion and thrown into jail. Then, while stripping down for his prison jumpsuit, the guard notices a weird lump on his back that no one saw before, because no one in Howie's family looks at his dad that closely. Turns out he had a tumor that would never have been discovered had he not evaded his taxes and gone to prison.

"The good Lord works in mysterious ways," my mother said when she heard, "but more so, the IRS."

Long story short, Howie's dad was now in some super-experimental prisoner-only treatment that involves baboon glands. So far it's had a high success rate in lab rats, but his family is understandably stressed. All that, plus his mom's spectacular failure in anger management therapy, has left Howie one taco short of a basket case.

For these reasons, Howie must be handled with less abuse than we normally give him. I usually don't mind hanging with Howie when there's someone else around, but one-on-one, he'll drive a person nuts.

"Spending quality time with Howie is a mitzvah," Ira once said. "Like giving soup to lepers."

Still, the idea of Howie turning up on my doorstep every morning was not my idea of the perfect summer experience—but clearly neither of us was going anywhere.

I got indigestion even before dinner that night, thinking about yet another summer with nothing to do. To be honest, my stomach hasn't been right since spring break, when I visited some classmates in Sweden. Who knew not to drink the water? So now, thanks to my own personal "Stockholm syndrome," my rumbling stomach registers on the Richter scale, and I half expect the guy from Caltech with the bowl haircut to come on TV and announce the magnitude.

Anyway, it was while we were eating dinner that night that everything changed, and all because of my father. See, usually my father is a straightforward kind of guy, like me. He says what he thinks, even if it's moronic and causes him a world of pain. My mom, on the other hand, has got this

11

internal filter that screens out the stuff she'd eventually regret saying. I think Frankie and Christina inherited the filter gene, but I didn't—which I guess has left me in a special bonding situation with my father. We spend so much time together in the doghouse, we can never get a dog because there'd be no room, except for maybe a Chihuahua, but have you ever seen those things? They're vicious. Our neighbor got one, and it scares off the Dobermans.

My dad's neither a Doberman nor a Chihuahua. He's more like a German shepherd. Smart, loyal, doesn't take anything from anybody, but does not get subtlety, and is easily manipulated.

So that being the case, Mom was totally unprepared for what Dad did at dinner that night.

Dinner was going along fine until about halfway through the meal, when my dad reached up and scratched his chest right in the middle. It was such a slight gesture, you'd never notice it, unless of course you were my mother, who, like an eagle, can spot a sardine from a treetop a mile away and then intentionally ignore it because sardines are disgusting.

She didn't say anything about it the first time, or even the second time—but the third time my dad touched his chest, she said, "What's the matter, Joe? You want me to get you some water?"

"It's nothing," Dad answered too quickly. "I'll be fine." He cleared his throat, coughed a little, and shrugged.

"Did you take your pill?" Mom asked.

"What am I, a child? I don't need you to remind me to take my pill." He sounded irritable. My dad rarely sounds irritable over such little things—and this was another red flag for my mom.

Through all of this, Christina and I were looking back and forth between them, wondering where this was going. Frankie, who loses brain function while eating, just shoveled down his chicken tetrazzini, oblivious to the unfolding drama.

Dad took a few more bites of food, then put down his fork and looked at his hand, clenching his fingers into a fist a few times—kinda the way you might if you felt your fingers going numb.

"Joe, you're scaring me," Mom said.

"I told you, it's nothing."

From there, the whole thing slipped into the standard "you're-working-too-hard-you're-not-taking-care-of-yourself" lecture, which my dad gets about every second Tuesday and which has probably kept him alive for the past six months since my mom is absolutely right. My dad usually listens to her when she tells him he needs to slow down. This time, however, Dad didn't give in. He started making excuses and rationalizations. The manager's just not pulling his weight at the restaurant, Frankie's college tuition has gone up, and so on and so forth.

By now even Frankie had looked up, probably because they mentioned his name. We now all realized that this was a duel. A line had been drawn in the sand of the Zen garden.

"You need to take some time off," my mom said, "period, the end."

"We cannot afford a vacation right now, so it's out of the question."

"So spend some time around the house."

"Yeah, right, because that's not stressful, is it?" My dad took a deep breath and let it out. "I'm fine. It's nothing. Drop it."

The rest of the meal went on in silence. Just clattering forks, my mom slapping my hand for reaching over her plate for the salt. The usual.

It wasn't until we brought our plates to the sink that Mom said, "Antsy, tell your father about Mr. Crawley's invitation."

I had already told him about it and was about to say so—but I stopped myself, because maybe I got a little bit of that mental filter after all.

"Maybe we can go on that cruise after all," my mom said.

That's the moment I realized that, for the first time in history, my dad was engaging in a secret, underhanded ploy. I gotta tell you, I was proud of him.

CHAPTER 2

VELVETEEN HOWIE, WARM NUTS, AND MY FIRST FEDERAL OFFENSE

THE WAY I SEE IT, THE BEST NEGOTIATIONS ARE THE kind where everybody wins, and no one realizes they've been tricked. Take the sale of the island of Manhattan. The Dutch got themselves a whole island—which they needed because the Netherlands is sinking—and in exchange, the Indians got a bunch of beads.

Okay, maybe that's not a good example, but the point is, my mom got more than beads. Sure, she hated boats, but she hated the idea of Dad dying even more. In the end, she got to feel like she was saving his life, and, as long as he didn't croak on the ship, everyone got what they wanted.

When Ira left for Israel and Hamid for Canada, Howie showed up at my door at eight in the morning and rang my bell repeatedly until someone answered it. The second I heard his voice downstairs, I got out of bed and hid my half-packed suitcase. I hadn't told Howie we were going on the cruise. I mean, I didn't want to burst his bubble on account of he had so few bubbles to begin with. So he thundered up the stairs and into my room with a notebook that was filled with scribbles I doubt even he could read.

"I've been planning the Fourth of July," he told me. "I found some recipes online for building your own fireworks out of everyday household items."

Although part of me thought it was tempting, I knew it wasn't gonna happen. At least not with me.

"Sorry, Howie," I told him, "I kinda got other plans."

"Okay," he said. "What are we gonna do?"

"Well . . . you know that cruise on the *Plethora of the Deep* I said I wasn't going on? Well, it turns out I'm going after all."

"Oh," Howie said, slowly getting it. "Oh . . . so then you won't be here for the Fourth of July?"

"I'll be back, though—and there are other kids around for the Fourth of July, so who cares that I won't be here; you've got the whole neighborhood, right?"

Now he looked like one of those sad clown paintings on velvet.

"Uh . . . Yeah, yeah. It'll be great." Then he glanced at his wrist like he's got a watch and said, "I better go. I've got some fertilizer to buy for the fireworks."

He left, and suddenly *I'm* feeling like fertilizer.

I thought about it for a few minutes, then went to see my mom, who was in the master bedroom, also packing.

"I've got to get a new bathing suit," she said.

"Yeah, you and Dad."

"I've gained all the weight he's lost."

"Conservation of matter," I told her, which was something I got wrong on my science final, proving that

16

we learn from our mistakes, but do we get any do-overs on finals? No! So what's the use?

My mom then noticed the way I stood in the doorway, not coming or going.

"Spill it," she said.

"Spill what?"

"Either you did something or you want something. I'm sure either way it will cause grief or cost money, so you might as well spill it now and get it over with."

I paused for a second. "We got a big family cabin on the *Plethora*, right?"

"With a balcony," she said, "for when I vomit."

"And Frankie can't go 'cause he's gotta work, right?"

My mom stopped packing and turned to me. "So?"

"So . . . what if I brought a friend?"

Mom figured it out before I said another word. I could see her playing mental Ping-Pong with the idea, then she said, "As much as I love Howie, you know I can't stand him."

"Trust me. I know exactly how you feel."

She shook her head and sighed. "Sometimes I worry that I've instilled too much Catholic guilt in you."

"You have," I tell her, "and you should feel guilty about it."

She grinned at that, then she came over and grabbed me in a one-armed hug that could barely reach around me now that I've gotten taller than her. It's the kind of hug that still feels good as long as it's not in public.

"If he snores," she said, "he's going overboard."

. . .

Howie, of course, was thrilled and did everything short of pledging me the life of his firstborn.

"You're a great friend, Antsy. Everyone else in the world sucks compared to you."

This kind of exaggeration is what you call *hyperbole*, and Howie's got a zillion of 'em.

He went off to tell his mom, who was happy for him but furious that she didn't get invited, and Howie had to work with her on some anger management techniques.

The decision to take Howie on the cruise opened up a can of worms that had no bottom. First I had to convince Crawley to take Frankie off the ship's itinerary and replace him with Howie.

"Out of the question on all counts," Crawley said. "There's a sizable fee for changing guests on a cruise, and on top of it, your ingrate of a brother's plane ticket to Miami is nonrefundable. I won't throw away one plane ticket just to buy another."

"Hey, I don't mean to punch a gift horse in the mouth," I told him, "but I already promised Howie he could go."

"Then you pay for his ticket."

And that was that. So now I was stuck with one of four miserable choices:

1. I could pay for Howie myself, which, unless I won the lottery, was not gonna happen.
2. I could tell Howie he had to pay for it, which was not gonna happen either.

18

3. I could renege, say sayonara, and leave
   Howie waving good-bye at the airport.
4. I could pawn it off on my parents and ask
   them to pay for it and make my grief theirs.

I knew they'd do it because they got big hearts, although my dad's got a pacemaker to keep his going. But before I could even break it to them, I was blindsided by the Birth Certificate Fiasco.

I will say right up front that I do not habitually break the law unless you count jaywalking and using the handicapped stall in public restrooms, because, face it, they're the only ones big enough and clean enough to make public restrooms bearable.

I knew that forging Howie's birth certificate was not exactly legal—but to travel internationally on a ship, you need a passport and/or a birth certificate. Howie had neither.

"Whadaya mean you don't have a birth certificate?" I yelled at him when he told me. "Everyone has a birth certificate—what, were you hatched?" and for a crazy moment, I entertained the thought. Howie, however, had a more rational explanation.

"My dog ate it."

Sadly, this was true. His schnauzer, Nixon, had a taste for legal documents. It had gotten into the family's filing cabinet and chewed its way through the birth certificates, the mortgage, and several years of tax returns. (This is what made it so hard for Howie's dad to defend himself against the tax evasion charge, and the "my dog ate it" defense doesn't fly well with Uncle Sam.)

"You make my life miserable," I told Howie, "but I'll take care of it."

And then I had the big idea. The idea that would solve all my problems in one fell swoop. I dug out my brother Frankie's birth certificate, went to my computer, scanned it in, and got to work on a digital cut-and-paste. First I changed the date of birth so that it was closer to mine but more than nine months away, because having a brother born four months after me was physically impossible in most humans. Then I changed the *middle* name on the birth certificate so instead of "Francis Vincent Bonano" it now read "Francis Howard Bonano." That way it wouldn't be suspicious when everyone called him Howie. I even duplicated the official watermark that says "Do Not Duplicate," then painstakingly embossed the official state seal into the paper with the prong of a fork. It was masterful if I do say so myself. In the end, no one would have guessed this wasn't Howie's real birth certificate and that he wasn't a Bonano. Unless of course you saw there was no resemblance, but that happens in lots of families for various reasons.

No one really cares, I told myself. After all, it was just so the cruise people could cover their butts in case some Caribbean nation's government gets overthrown while we're on a shore excursion or something and we have to prove who we are to avoid firing squads. The cruise being just a few days away, a fake birth certificate with a fake name was the only way to get Howie on board.

"We gotta slip this past my parents without them knowing, or my life is nil," I told Howie when I presented him with his new official identity. He stared at the thing, like maybe it was legitimate and there was something about his past he didn't know about.

"But Crawley's gonna know," Howie said, "because the tickets are still in Frankie's name—and he knows I'm not Frankie."

"Don't worry, I'll deal with Crawley."

My only concerns now were keeping my parents out of the loop and getting the whole thing past Crawley. As for the larger issue of this being not technically legal, I didn't give it a second thought at the time. Why should I? You don't give jaywalking a second thought until you're hit by a truck.

We flew out of JFK, an airport designed by Satan, and began our adventure.

Crawley arrived at the airport by limo, accompanied by his granddaughter, Lexie, and Moxie, her guide dog. Lexie and I have been good friends since eighth grade, but I hadn't seen her for a while, and I was surprised to see that she had her hair curled.

"It looks nice," I told her.

"So I've been told," she said. "I like the way the curls feel around my face."

The limo driver pulled out their luggage and a wheelchair from the trunk, which Crawley immediately sat in. He doesn't actually need a wheelchair, but he uses it when it serves his supervillain purposes. "When you're in a wheelchair, people move out of your way," he once told me. "And if they don't, you can hit them and they won't hit back." I know his preference would be one of those sedan chairs carried on the shoulders of Philistines. He also wore dark cataract glasses, as he always does on the rare times he's out in public. Not because he has cataracts but because they hide his eyes. "Eyes are very communicative," he once pointed out. "And I have nothing to say to these people."

He nearly blew a gasket when he saw Howie with us. "What's he doing here? You had best tell me he's here to see us off!"

I took Crawley aside so that no one else could hear us.

"Actually, no . . ." I began, figuring I'd double-talk my way out of it, but Crawley didn't let me say another word.

"No? Do you have any idea what's going to happen when they see your brother's name on the ticket once we reach the security check? They'll boot Howie from the flight and probably do a cavity search on the rest of us. So unless you've got proof that Howie Bogerton is actually Frankie Bonano, this promises to be the stupidest in a long line of stupid things you've done."

"Uh . . . well, I actually *do* have proof."

He wasn't expecting that. He took off his dark glasses and glared at me. "Are you telling me you falsified his ID?"

"Birth certificate. So it'll also get him on the cruise."

Crawley scowled at me a moment longer, then the corners of his mouth turned up in a twisted smile and he released a single, loud guffaw. Crawley's laughter was a rare event. Leap year comes more often.

"Clever boy!" he said, then added, "Don't expect me to visit you in jail."

We managed to get through the security check by

means of distraction. The TSA agents were focused on Lexie and Moxie, while my parents were focused on the sign that warned against pacemakers in the metal detector. And the one time they happened to look Howie's way, my sister dropped her carry-on bag on purpose to draw their attention. (Christina later charged me ten dollars for her services as a covert operative.) The guard accepted Howie's birth certificate without a hitch, and once we were on the other side of security, Crawley congratulated me on "scamming the Man."

The plan was to fly to Miami, stay overnight at an Embassy Suites, then board the *Plethora of the Deep* in the morning. Crawley had bought us all first-class tickets because he wanted insulation from strangers.

"Two degrees of separation from the unwashed masses is sufficient," he said as he took his seat. I pointed out that in first class, most masses would be washed, to which he replied, "You never know who'll get upgraded from coach."

Lexie sat beside me. She was already wearing a Caribbean sundress, full of both color for others and texture for her. We sat in the front row, which they call the bulkhead, with Moxie at her feet. I thought it was really cool that the airline allowed guide dogs. Crawley did not bring "the sins and virtues"—that is, the fourteen afghans that ran rampant around his huge apartment. Not that he didn't try. He fought bitterly with Caribbean Viking cruise line, but the only pets allowed on the ship were guide dogs. To be honest, I don't think he really wanted to bring them, he just wanted a good fight.

"My grandfather told me what you did for Howie," Lexie whispered to me shortly before takeoff. "Forging that birth certificate was deeply thoughtful and profoundly misguided. That's what I love about you, Antsy."

"The fact that you love anything about me is what I love about you," I told her. She smiled and gently rubbed the hairs on my arm, which was Lexie's version of a kindly glance. Still, such intimate physical contact always gave me goose bumps, which I'm sure she could read like Braille.

Just so you know, I used to date Lexie back in eighth grade. Now we're just really good friends, except when one of us starts seeing someone else. Then we're just annoyed with each other.

"I'm looking forward to seeing my parents," Lexie said. "I haven't seen them since Thanksgiving, if you don't count Skypeing. It's nice that they'll be meeting us on the cruise."

"There's nothing 'nice' about it," Crawley growled. "They just want to suck up to me for my eightieth birthday."

I've only met Lexie's parents a couple of times myself. They're real jet-setters, spending months at a time in Paris, or Monaco, or wherever rich Americans who think they're European go. They'd prefer Lexie be in some fancy boarding school overseas, but such places don't really cater to the blind, and besides, Lexie didn't want to leave Brooklyn.

"My relationship with my parents is complicated," Lexie once told me. "But I know they love me."

I often wondered what it would be like to spend months

at a time away from your parents rather than having them breathing down your neck on a daily basis. Lexie didn't seem to mind the distance. But then, Lexie liked to keep her feelings to herself.

There were several things I discovered on the first leg of our journey:

1. Bad food tastes good when served by flight attendants.
2. You can never have enough warm nuts.
3. Flight attendants do not like being called "the help," which is how Crawley addressed them.
4. Airplanes make a whole lot of noises that I don't think have anything to do with flying, and maybe I don't want to know what those noises are.
5. Landing in Miami is a lot prettier than taking off in Queens.
6. Embassy Suites has no actual ambassadors.

Then at 11 A.M. the next morning, we were shuttled along with a bus full of Crawley's "unwashed masses" to the Port of Miami. Everyone was brimming with anticipation. Howie was nervous, but not because of the passport thing.

"The Caribbean is a very dangerous place," Howie said. "I mean, there being pirates and all."

"That's just a movie," I pointed out. "A movie based on a ride."

"A ride based on reality!" he said, raising one eyebrow to appear wise. "And there's longpork, Antsy. Longpork!"

"So what?" I told him. "I like pork."

Then he got in close and whispered like there was anyone around who cared. "Longpork is people! They got people who eat people!"

"Great," I told him. "Can I send them Wendell Tiggor and a few other choice morsels from our neighborhood? My dad can provide a recipe that works with beef, chicken, or people."

He looked at me like I was serious, and since tormenting Howie was like a national pastime, I had to keep it going.

"It's a pretty exotic ship," I said. "Maybe they'll serve longpork in the dining room one night."

His face filled with an expression that was half horror, half disgust, and half excitement, which, if you know Howie, is mathematically correct. "Probably not," Howie said. "It's more of a room service kind of thing." He thought about it and bit his lip, maybe trying to taste himself.

Finally our shuttle bus got off the freeway, and the ship came into view.

Okay, so now comes the part I'm sure you've been waiting for. The description of the one, the only *Plethora of the Deep*. But you know what? I'm not even gonna bother. Just go online and type in "big honking boat" and you'll find everything you need to know. I mean, take the biggest

26

freaking thing you can possibly imagine and then triple it. As Howie put it, "It's the closest thing on earth to an Imperial Star Destroyer." It's so big, even the inside cabins have balconies, which to me implies that alternate dimensions are involved, but what do I know?

Even the brand-new cruise terminal looked like something right off the cover of a sci-fi novel. I nearly got hit by a taxi staring up at it as we got off the bus.

I can't really say the weird stuff started at the cruise terminal, because weird stuff has been sticking to my heels like toilet paper for as long as I can remember. Not just weird stuff but weird people with weirder problems. I'm like a magnet for the normality impaired. So naturally, I'm the one who sees something freaky.

See, inside the cruise terminal, there's this big floor-to-ceiling glass wall, designed to give you a spectacular view of the ship—but the ship's so big, all you can see is this endless wall of balconies eighteen stories high. At this point, we're all waiting in line to check in, and I'm sweating because, unlike airport security, these cruise line agents are chatty, and what if they want to match us up with our birth certificates and my parents find out that Howie is suddenly my brother.

Then, out of the corner of my eye, I see movement. I turn to the window, and someone's falling from the ship.

I've seen people fall before. First, I saw a guy fall from a bridge—although that time it was just a dummy and we had thrown it on purpose. The second time, though, it was a real guy falling from a parade balloon that got stuck on the top of the Empire State Building. I'm sure you've seen it a million times online, including the version with added sound effects that make it obnoxious instead of tragic.

This time it happened so quickly, I couldn't be exactly sure what I saw—but I was pretty sure it was a person. The faller plunged past the balconies, but instead of hitting the dock, he disappeared in that narrow gap between the dock and the ship, which was maybe twenty feet wide. I didn't hear him hit the water because the cruise terminal was playing a loud steel drum version of "Hot, Hot, Hot" on endless repeat.

I shouted out something that my teachers would call an "expletive," which in turn brought a head smack from my mother, which the security guard next to us seemed to approve of.

"Did you see that?" I said, my voice about two octaves higher than normal. "This guy . . . the ship . . . he fell!" My brain couldn't quite put the words in order.

Howie shrugged. "I didn't see anything."

My dad turned to look at the ship like he's gonna see the instant replay. I looked around, but no one else had seen. The other cruisers were too busy fussing over their paperwork or complaining about security confiscating their hidden stash of alcohol.

"Come on, somebody has to have seen it." But apparently it was just me.

"It was your imagination," grumbled Crawley. "Move along."

But I'm too much of a moron to let it go. I ducked under the velvet rope and left the line. "I'll be right back."

A cruise terminal is not like an airport; it's more like a warehouse. Downstairs, all the luggage that just came off the ship from the previous cruise was organized in a massive room full of sunburned people futilely trying to find the pieces that belonged to them. Guards who looked like they might Taser you for sneezing in their direction were everywhere. But one thing I've learned in life is that if you act like you know where you're going and you mumble a heartfelt but meaningless excuse without slowing down, they usually let you pass.

"Hey!" a guard said. "You can't go that way!"

"Yeah, but I gotta get my thing from the guy, because he forgot," I told him in a heartfelt way, and breezed right past him, no problem. I feel confident I could escape from a maximum security prison should it ever become necessary.

So I got out onto the dock, where a forklift was loading massive crates full of luggage through the ship's huge cargo door. I reached the edge of the dock and I peered into the water. No faller. No body. Nothing.

Finally, two guards came after me. "Hey—this is a restricted area!"

I tried to explain what I saw, but they weren't buying.

"Fine. We'll file a report," one of them said, but we all knew no one was gonna file anything but their nails.

Then I looked up at the cruise terminal and saw my parents looking down on me, my mother's eyes melting

29

holes in the glass. Meanwhile, right next to them, Howie was holding up his room key and giving me a thumbs-up. It turns out, me running off had flustered my parents just enough that they didn't notice when Howie presented himself to the cruise agent as Francis Howard Bonano.

The guards escorted me back into the terminal, and that was that. Since nobody else saw anything and there was no evidence, I had to reluctantly conclude that it was my imagination. At any rate, I wasn't going to let it mess with my good time. Besides, there were plenty of other things about to mess with it.

CHAPTER 3

DISTRACTIONS ABOARD THE LARGEST FLOATING OBJECT EVER CONCEIVED BY THE MIND OF MAN

THERE'S THIS THING CALLED ATTENTION DEFICIT disorder. They used to call it hyperactivity. We all know kids like this. They bounce around from one thing to another like a Super Ball—which, by the way, can actually embed in the ceiling if you bounce it on a tile floor hard enough. I know, 'cause when I was younger, I got three of them stuck in the ceiling of our downstairs bathroom, and to this day my mother refuses to remove them because she claims they're evidence. Evidence of what, I don't know, but like most things, I'm sure it'll come back to bite me.

So I've been told that maybe I got borderline attention deficit, on account of the way I got trouble sticking to a single subject. But the way I see it, I'd rather hit three walls and get stuck in the ceiling than stand like a lump in the middle of the room staring at myself in the bathroom mirror.

My point is that on the *Plethora of the Deep*, *everybody's* got ADHD. You can't help it. It's like Las Vegas without the sleaze. There's too much to look at, too many people handing out rainbow-colored drinks, too many glittering chandeliers, too much weird artwork by famous artists, and way too many string bikinis, although, to be honest, you really can't have too many of those.

My parents were not immune to being dazzled. They were so dazzled, in fact, that they got lost with Christina trying to find the cabin. "They'll find it eventually," Crawley announced, insisting that Howie push him onward.

As it turns out, our cabins weren't "cabins" at all. We had two adjoining "sky suites." One was for Crawley, Lexie, and Lexie's parents, who were going to board when the ship got to the Cayman Islands. The other suite was for my family and Howie. Each suite had two stories and was like a loft apartment. They must have cost Crawley a small fortune.

"Wow . . . this is too much, Mr. Crawley!" I said.

Crawley stood out of his wheelchair and examined a silver platter of chilled sushi, compliments of Caribbean Viking cruise line. "You're right, it is too much," he said, "but I've decided to spend as much money as I can before I die so that neither the government nor the various vultures with my last name will be able to pick over my rotting carcass."

And Howie says, "You won't have that problem if you get cremated."

Crawley got this look on his face like he just swallowed bad sushi and turned to his granddaughter. "Why do I surround myself with imbeciles, Lexie?"

"Well," said Lexie, with an indignance that only she could deliver, "as one of 'the vultures with your last name,' I'm sure I don't know. Now if you'll excuse me, Moxie and I are going to explore. Perhaps we'll visit the petting zoo." Which made sense, considering she's tactile and all. I offered to go with her, but she declined. "I'll find my own way. Asking for directions is a good way to meet people."

I gotta admire Lexie. She's got it nailed. I was sure by the end of the week, she'd know everyone on the ship. Crawley, on the other hand, had no such desire. He went to the huge two-story windows and closed the curtains.

"It's too bright in here," he said. Then he turned on the TV and swatted Howie and me away when we reached for the silver platter. "Go eat your own sushi. I ordered a bon voyage platter for your suite, too."

We went to our own suite to find the front door open. I figured it meant the rest of my family finally found their way here, but no such luck.

While I scarfed down all the sushi without octopus, Howie flipped through a big book on the coffee table that told everything you ever wanted to know about "The Largest Floating Object Ever Conceived by the Mind of Man."

"Hey, look here, Antsy," said Howie. "It says 'the *Plethora of the Deep*'s twenty-one mineral-rich Jacuzzis are oxygen enhanced to provide a soothing massage with patented therapeutic bubbles.'"

"Yeah, I got your therapeutic bubbles right here."

With the sushi inhaled, I was now ready to explore. "So what do you want to check out first?" I asked him. "The roller coaster? The Cavalcade of Waterslides?"

"Neither. I want to find the ghost."

I sighed. "Not that again!" Since the moment he found out he was going, Howie had been harping on this. According to Howie, this ship was the lifelong dream of

Jorgen Ericsson, the founder of Caribbean Viking cruise lines, but he died before the *Plethora* was completed. There was a rumor circulating that his ghost haunted the ship.

"What, do you think he's gonna be posing for photo ops?"

"People have taken pictures," Howie said. "But he only shows up on iPhones."

"Yeah, right," I said. "I'm sure they're as fake as your birth certificate—which I'll regret I ever made for you if you spend the whole cruise ghost hunting."

He pulled out his iPhone. "Not the whole cruise . . . just a day or two."

I pushed him out of the room. "I am not wasting my time looking for Jorgen Ericsson's ghost," I told him. "But if I was, where do you think we might find it?"

I got a big mouth. I don't deny that. Sometimes it's a good thing, like the time I stopped some moron from falling into an open manhole by yelling "hey, moron, that's an open manhole!" But other times, it sets me up for a world of trouble, like just before we left the suite, when I had announced to anyone who might be listening, that I made Howie a fake birth certificate.

Okay, so as I was heading down the hall, I realized that I forgot my camera, so I went back to the suite. Keep in mind that I had just left it less than a minute ago. No time for anything to happen, right? I opened the door and standing there was a beautiful girl taking something out of a backpack.

"Whoops, sorry," I said, because my first thought was that I stepped into the wrong room. But no—because not only did my key work in the lock, but the backpack she was dipping her hand into was mine.

I'm stunned by this, so my brain can't access the full menu of appropriate responses. It's more like the children's menu, and I'm playing connect-the-dots with my mental crayon. All I could say was, "What the heck . . ."

Then I saw what she had in her hand. It was my wallet.

Finally my brain engaged, and at last I uttered something useful. "That's my wallet!" Okay, maybe not useful, but at least informative.

She didn't act like she'd been caught red-handed. She didn't act freaked or surprised at all. She just glanced at the wallet in her hand and said, "Piece of garbage. Not even real leather." She had a Spanish-sounding accent, but her attitude was more French. It made her seem exotic. But exotic or not, her hand was in my cheapo wallet, which didn't have much money in it, but that didn't matter. It was the principle of the thing.

"Put it back, or I'm calling security," I told her. "On second thought, I'm calling security anyway." I stood there, blocking her exit, wondering how I could get to the phone without letting her escape and wondering how to make a citizen's arrest, and if you could even do such a thing on a boat. She didn't act like she was going to bolt at all. Instead she took a five-dollar bill out of my wallet, then returned the wallet to my backpack.

"Go call security," she said. "You can tell them I stole five dollars, and I can tell them that you made your friend a fake birth certificate."

Now my brain flipped the children's menu over and was doing the word search.

"You should close your mouth," she said. "You could swallow a fly." Then she brushed right past me and left.

I saw this thing on TV once where a guy comes into a criminology class, throws something at the professor, then runs out. It's all part of the lesson, though. Each student is asked to fill out a police report of the incident, and then they compare them. It turns out that none of the reports were the same. Some people said the guy was wearing a green shirt; others said it was blue. Some said he had glasses, others said he wore a hat, and some were fairly sure it was a girl and not a guy. The point was to show how unreliable eyewitnesses can be.

After the burglar girl left, I tried to play the whole thing over in my head so I could remember every little detail. By my own unreliable eyewitness account, she wore jeans that were torn at the knees and shredded at the cuffs. Her pale pink T-shirt had stains on it—or it might have been a logo that was so worn out, you could barely see it. People pay a lot of money to look that poor, but that wasn't the case here. This girl was not fashionably frayed; she was the real thing— which made me wonder what she was doing on this ship at all.

I wanted to report her, but what if I did and what if she got caught and then she squealed about how Howie's birth certificate was a forgery? A federal offense like that is worse than petty robbery—so even though she was the real criminal here, I could have ended up like Howie's dad, getting injected with baboon hormones in federal juvie, if there is such a thing. At the very least it would have gotten us all booted off the cruise. So I had no choice but to keep my mouth shut.

And then I realized something: The only way she could have known about the birth certificate was if she heard me say it. Which meant she had been in the room all along—that's why the door was ajar when we first went in! Where had she been hiding? The closet? The shower? Underneath one of the beds? It creeped me out. I felt violated. It was worse than when Ann-Marie Delmonico watched me undress the one time I forgot to close my curtains.

I went out to meet Howie, who was now riding the glass elevators up and down in search of ghostly reflections in the glass—but I couldn't say anything to him about the girl. That was okay, though, because it meant I could at least try to put it out of my mind. The suite door was locked now, and she couldn't have a key, right? But then, how did she get into the room in the first place? Maybe the cabin steward let her in! Maybe it was a conspiracy! My God, I was starting to sound like Howie!

"What's up with you?" Howie asked. "You look like you've seen a ghost. Did you? Did you get a picture?"

I have to admit with so many things to do on the ship, I was able to put all the weirdness out of my mind. The faller had been my imagination. And the girl? She only got away with five bucks. What was five bucks compared to a roller coaster that dipped to the surface of the ocean, and a zip line longer than a football field, and an entire laser-tag deck? "Distractions," the cruise director had called these things in his welcome-aboard announcement. "I'm sure you'll find a hundred different distractions on board to make this the best vacation of your life."

That's what makes up a big part of our lives, y'know? The distractions. Lots of times, we're like moths fluttering around a porch light. Bugs'll swarm around that bulb, all distracted, forgetting in their minuscule insect brains that there's something else they should be doing, like biting people or making more bugs. We're like that, although our brains are generally larger, Wendell Tiggor being the exception that proves the rule.

Human distractions are bigger, better lightbulbs. We got TVs and computers. We got blinking casino lights and live bands on cruise ships playing yet another version of "Hot, Hot, Hot" until you wanna puke, but in the end, they're all just porch lights. So we go from one bright bulb to another until we hit the bug zapper, and it's all over.

I'm not saying it's a bad thing. What fun would life be without our chosen porch lights? But every once in a while, we get these moments where we look away from the lights, and it scares us, on account of there's nothing but darkness until our eyes adjust. And that's when we get to see the stars!

You don't see many stars in New York City. Sure, everyone knows that they're there, but knowing and seeing are two totally different things. I can honestly say that, had I not met Tilde, I might never have seen the darkness. Or the stars.

CHAPTER 4

THE PRINCESS OF THIEVES PAVES MY ROAD TO A HIGHLY UNPLEASANT PLACE IF YOU BELIEVE SISTER MARY MARLENA

I DIDN'T SEE MY PARENTS UNTIL AFTER THE LIFEBOAT drill, which took place right before we set sail. Let me tell you, it's a real skill whipping a shipload of clueless people into a well-oiled machine of disaster readiness. Howie and I tried to hide in a bathroom, just to see if we could get away with it, but we were flushed out, so to speak, and handed dorky orange life preservers by a guy who had, ten minutes before, been handing out dorky drinks with umbrellas.

They packed everyone like sardines in neat orderly rows on the lifeboat deck, which you can also play shuffleboard on when the ship isn't sinking. "These are your 'muster stations,'" a crew member in a neon-green baseball cap loudly announced. "This is where you will come if you hear the emergency signal sound." He then told us that we should not blow the whistles attached to our life preservers, which was like telling little kids not to eat the chocolate. Dozens of whistles blew.

Now that they had a captive audience, an announcement came on telling us all not to sit on balcony rails, and not to throw burning material overboard, and a dozen other prohibited things that stupid people have done and probably sued the cruise line for when they either died or got horribly maimed from their own stupidity. The announcement would have been fine, except that it was repeated in six different languages, one of which may or may not have been Klingon. All the foreign announcements begin to lull my brain into a Zen-like trance, like my dad gets when he's raking sand, and I realize that the life preservers are so stiff, and we're packed in so tight, I might actually be able to fall asleep standing up and no one would know.

In this state of altered consciousness, I began to think about that balcony-sitting rule, and it reminded me of the guy I thought I saw fall. I never actually saw a face—and the mind can make you think you saw something you didn't. Before getting on board, I did see pelicans soaring low across the bay. Those things have a pretty huge wingspan. So, what if one of them dive-bombed some fish next to the boat, and I looked out just in time to see it? That was a much more logical explanation than some poor schmuck falling off a balcony.

By the time the announcement had switched into pig Latin, or whatever, I was totally over it and was one hundred percent convinced the faller was all in my imagination. The girl in my cabin, however, was very real . . . but I could live with the loss of five dollars and was determined not to let it ruin my good time. But then, what if she came back to steal more?

The horn blasted, concluding the lifeboat drill and waking me out of my stupor. The neat orderly lines of emergency-prepped passengers now became a slow herd of bright orange cattle. I found my parents in the crowded stairwell. Apparently they had finally found our suite in time to be rushed out for the drill.

"Did you have to eat all the good sushi?" Christina asked. I pointed out that I left her all the octopus, but like me, she won't eat things with suction cups.

"Listen, there's a safe in the closet," I told my dad. "When you get back to the room, make sure you put all your valuables in it, because I hear there's already been a theft on board."

"Where'd you hear that?" my dad asked.

"I don't know. Around. Just make sure you put your stuff in the safe and lock it, okay?"

"Stop worrying your father," my mom said. She tried to smack me, but the life preserver was too tight and she couldn't get any leverage.

Of the ship's gazillion Jacuzzis, the best one by far was way out on the very tip of the bow, like a foaming zit on the tip of the ship's nose. The bow Jacuzzi was a little bit of genius because it allowed you to be King of the World while still being massaged by patented therapeutic bubbles.

This was where I went as the ship set sail. It amazed me that so few people took advantage of this prime location as we left port—just me, a middle-aged couple covered in so much sunscreen, they looked like they had been dipped in Cream of Wheat, and some buff guy with more body art than the Sistine Chapel.

41

The ship was one big party now. Confetti was flying everywhere like it was New Year's, and a live band played reggae that was pumped through speakers all over the ship. The burglar girl and the phantom faller were fading into the past as I luxuriated in the Jacuzzi while sipping a virgin piña colada.

After a few minutes, the sunscreen couple went to find some shade, and the tattooed guy went to get himself a bucket of beers, leaving me alone in the bubbling water.

So there I was, up to my chest in hot water, looking out beyond the front of the ship, and when I turn back around, there's someone else slipping into the tub. Someone in a faded shirt and torn jeans. She's actually wearing jeans in the Jacuzzi!

"Hello, Enzo," she said "Nice day for a soak."

I'm speechless, which is unusual for me and usually the sign of a fever—but the only heat I'm feeling is from the Jacuzzi. Was the burglar girl following me all this time? And if so, why?

"It's Antsy, not Enzo," I told her.

"Antsy is a stupid name. I like Enzo better."

"There is obviously something very wrong with you," I told her. "Do you even have a bathing suit?"

She shrugged. "I don't need one. Besides, I have to wash my clothes eventually, *verdad*?"

"Are you even a passenger on this ship?"

"The fact that I'm on this ship makes me a passenger, doesn't it?"

"Yeah, but I mean a paying passenger." The question was

only half serious. It was meant as more of an insult than anything until she said:

"Why pay when you can travel for free?"

Now my annoyance with her was being replaced with a sick sort of curiosity.

"You can't be serious . . ."

She just smiled.

"You're a stowaway?"

She lifted a finger to her lips "Shhh," she said. "Loose lips sink ships."

I was struck with fever-like speechlessness again. I used to daydream about stowing away. Sometimes on a plane, sometimes on a boat, sometimes on a spaceship. I'd make up some adventure, then slip past authorities, which I could always do, because in your own head you're always smarter than the goons trying to stop you. But this girl was the real thing, and it scared me, because to successfully stow away, you had to be a whole lot smarter and a whole lot crazier than me.

"I want you to stay away from me," I told her.

Her response was to move across the bubbling foam of the Jacuzzi and sit right next to me.

"Is this far enough?"

I couldn't tell if she was flirting or just being obnoxious, and before I could figure out which I would prefer, the Sistine Chapel guy returned with his girlfriend, Rosetta Stone, who had words on every part of her body that her string bikini didn't cover and maybe beyond. It occurred to me that neither of them could see that the girl with criminal intents sitting beside me was fully dressed beneath the foam.

"I like your ink very much," Crime Girl said to Rosetta. "*¿Es bíblica?* Is it biblical?"

"No," the girl said, looking at her arms and whatever part of her midriff she could see beneath her bikini top. "It's the lyrics to all of Madonna's hits." Which explained why her belly button was labeled LA ISLA BONITA.

"Hi, I'm Tilde," said Crime Girl. "And this is my boyfriend, Enzo."

I suddenly started to gag on my virgin piña colada.

"Nice to meet you," said the illustrated couple.

"Yeah, right," I said. "I better get out of here before I puke and make the bubbles less therapeutic."

"*Espérame*, Enzo," said Tilde. "Wait!"

She followed me, revealing her soaking wet jeans for all the world to see. When we were finally far enough away from the reveling masses so that no one else could hear, I turned to her and gave her one of those loud *I mean business* whispers.

"I told you, it's Antsy, not Enzo, and I don't want to have anything to do with you from now until the end of time. We never met; I never saw you. We're done. End of story."

Then she crossed her arms and got way too smug. "According to US documentation laws, the penalty for forging a birth certificate or passport is a fine of twenty thousand dollars and up to three years in prison."

I just stared at her, increasingly aggravated that she could throw me so off balance. "How do you know this?"

"That is my business," she said.

"Fine. Turn me in. I don't care anymore. Just leave me alone."

44

"I don't want to turn you in," she said gently. "I just want your help."

I told her something I won't repeat, then tried to escape, but she wasn't done with me.

"The difference between you and me, Enzo, is that I don't care if I get put off the ship."

That stopped me cold, because if that was true, then she could blackmail me, and I had no defense. She smiled, knowing she had me. "Meet me in the Neptune Lounge after dinner," she said, "because we have a lot to talk about."

"Why me?" I asked. "Why not some other idiot?"

She shrugged. "Because you're the idiot I met."

I know how to play chess, but I'm not very good because I don't have patience, and I take things personally. There was this kid I knew—star of the chess team. Joey the Chin, we called him on account of he didn't have much of one; he was all overbite and Adam's apple. Anyway, he challenges me to a chess match and on, like, the second move he threatens my queen with a measly bishop. I'm ticked off at being threatened, so rather than running away, I capture his bishop for spite, and he's all, "What did you do that for? Now you lose your queen!" And he takes it with a pawn. I lost the game, of course, but not before making him chase my king around the board like a spider on the kitchen floor that you just can't kill.

My point is that I tend to go kamikaze if anyone gets in my face and threatens me—even if it makes the situation ten times worse for me. So, if you follow my habitual pattern, you'd expect me to expose Tilde the second she tried to blackmail me, no matter what the consequences.

But I didn't do that, because deep down there was a part of me that found her interesting, and a little dangerous—like maybe *she* was this year's illegal firework, ready to blow something up spectacularly on July Fourth.

Everyone's luggage arrived at our suite before dinner except for mine. "They've got a lot of luggage to sort," my father said. "It'll show up eventually." But that was little consolation. All I had to wear to dinner was the bathing suit I was smart enough to pack in my carry-on and the clothes I came on board with. Well my bathing suit was wet, and my clothes stunk to high heaven because in my excitement that morning, I forgot to put on deodorant.

Howie was still out ghost hunting, so, still in my wet bathing suit, I wandered into the adjoining suite, figuring I could hang a little bit with Lexie. Her luggage had arrived, and she had already dug out her flute and was playing. She plays really well for a first-year student, and I figured the music might lighten me up a bit and get my mind off of blackmail and my own desire to either strangle or make out with the blackmailer.

As much as I tried to slip in without being noticed, few things slip in under Lexie's radar.

"How was the water?" she asked. "Warm enough?"

I couldn't help but smile, because I knew her MO so well. She could smell that there was someone in the room who had just been in a chlorinated situation—but she didn't know who it was or what the situation had been—pool, spa, or waterslide. Only when I answered would she know who was in the room and where I'd been—but Lexie is masterful at hiding what she doesn't know and making you think she's the blind Sherlock Holmes.

"Let's just say someone turned up the heat in the Jacuzzi," I told her.

"Better hot than tepid," she said.

"Right, tepid," I repeated. Lexie had a habit of teaching me vocabulary words I wouldn't use except in a conversation with her.

"Do you like this piece of music?" she asked. "Do you think it shows off my skill as a flautist? I want my parents to see how much I've learned already."

"Even if you weren't a beginner, I'd think it was impressive."

"Then you're too easily impressed." She returned to practicing, determined to knock her parents' overpriced European socks off when they arrived.

Lexie's great, but she hasn't been able to escape her own lap of luxury. Even the flute her parents got her is gold plated instead of silver like a normal one. And because her parents are never around, her grandfather has treated her like the center of the universe all her life. I guess it's hard not to fall into that gravity. She tries, but in the end everything is always about her.

I guess that's natural to an extent. I mean, we can't help but be at the center of our own worlds. But every once in a while we gotta see the bigger picture. I know, I should talk, right? I'm always the center of some stupid drama. The thing is, though, I tend to shove myself into other people's dramas and then don't know how to get back out again.

When my suitcase hadn't arrived by dinnertime, my father took pity on me and offered me what may have been the ugliest shirt in the history of man-made fabric. I didn't even know there were such shades of brown or that they could be tortured into such painful paisley shapes. I decided BO was less assaulting on the senses and stuck with my Neurotoxin T-shirt—which, under the circumstances, was appropriate since I was close to being declared a biological weapon.

Dinner on a cruise ship is old-school eating: multiple courses served over two hours in a grand five-story dining room as opposed to my usual five minutes of snake-like inhaling. I might have had patience for a long, drawn-out dinner if I didn't know I was expected in the Neptune Lounge by a girl who was admittedly cute but probably a sociopath—which is like a psychopath with enough social skills to form a cult or become class president. Whatever the case, I knew this girl was not going to be good for either my health or my sanity.

Our table was for eight, but Crawley never showed, because he hated the concept of crowds almost as much as he hated the people in them.

"My grandfather has opted for room service in our suite," Lexie said as she arrived with Moxie. Then, as she sat down, she took a dainty little sniff of the air, wrinkled her nose, and I thought maybe I should have gone into the

Jacuzzi with my clothes on like Tilde, because maybe the chlorine would have de-stenchified me.

"Sorry," I said. "I'm perspirationally challenged today."

She found my hand and patted it. "I usually like the way you smell, Antsy. But today, not so much."

Howie grinned with contentment, because for once the complaint was not about him.

"It's not his fault," my mother said. "Antsy's luggage is missing."

Having your mother explain to your friends why you smell has gotta be pretty high on the list of life's most miserable moments, ranking right up there with elevator crash and bus plunge. Fortunately, though, once the appetizers came, there was plenty of garlic in the air to hide behind.

"I run a restaurant," my dad told the waiter, to all our embarrassment. "This better be good."

"Not to worry, sir! Da *Plethora of da Deep* has werry werry good food." His name was Igor, pronounced like "eager," which he was—but he also pronounced "plethora" "ple-THOR-a," so all his stressed syllables were suspect. Igor had a weird little smirk on his face, like he knew something about the food that we didn't—but then again, maybe it was just a cultural smirk, because his name tag said he was from Belorussia, which I assumed was below Russia.

"Try everything," Dad instructed us. "This is your chance to have foods you'd never order in real life, like frog's legs and rabbit."

To which my mom said, "If any of you order rabbit, I'm disowning you."

I had the venison and told her I was eating Bambi.

After the main course, music began to play, and the waiters left everyone's desserts melting at the serving stations. Then, standing in the aisles, they led the whole dining room in what must be a cruise ship's version of the seventh-inning stretch. In other words, they did the Macarena.

The Macarena is one of those things that has fallen into that funk-filled purgatory of purged pop culture. You know the place—it's a pit of eye-rolling despair filled with all the stuff that's too worn out to be trendy, but not old enough to be nostalgic, so it's just plain embarrassing. But few things could be more embarrassing than my parents getting up to do the Macarena with the waiters.

"Shoot me now," said my sister. "In the head, so it's quick."

I pantomimed blowing her brains out, which both of us found disturbingly satisfying, and, with an end to the Macarena nowhere in sight, I decided it was time. I excused myself and left, in search of the Neptune Lounge.

The Neptune Lounge was beneath the waterline on Zero Deck. It was a bar with dramatic lighting and floor-to-ceiling windows that looked out under the sea. I suppose while in port, you had a great underwater view of fish and dolphins and stuff, but while the ship was moving, it was all just churning water—which I found hypnotically cool.

Tilde was already there, sitting at a little table, eating wasabi almonds out of a glass bowl. She was still wearing the same clothes she had worn in the Jacuzzi—air dried now, and I wondered how she had the nerve to sit in a lounge where everyone else was dressed fancy.

I sat down across from her. "So I'm here," I said. "What do you want?"

"Relax," she said. "Enjoy the view." She held out the bowl to me. "Nuts?"

"Yes, you are."

Insulted, she pulled the bowl back. "None for you."

I leaned a little bit closer and kept my voice down. "I don't get it. Aren't you worried that you'll get caught?"

"The bartender and I have an understanding. He doesn't tell on me, and I don't tell about the liquor I saw him sneaking back to his room."

"What, are you blackmailing the whole ship?"

She tossed a couple of almonds into her mouth instead of answering me, then tilted her head to one side. "You smell *como una mofeta*, Enzo. Like a skunk."

"Never mind that."

She smiled. "I like it. It means you are living a full life. Lots of action!"

"Yeah, I'm a regular action hero. Are you gonna tell me why I'm here?"

She paused for a moment, studying my face, then finally she got down to business. "I need a lookout. Someone to make sure the coast is clear when I go into cabins."

"An accomplice, you mean. To help you steal."

"Call it what you like, as long as you do the job."

"No!" I said. "What, are you crazy? No!"

I had raised my voice, and a couple drinking martinis a few tables away glanced over at us.

Tilde threw an almond and it hit me in the eye. "*¡Idiota!*" she said—a word that probably sounded the same in every language. "Didn't your mother ever teach you to use your indoor voice?"

I just stared at her, my eye watering from the wasabi, so it looked like I was winking. "Didn't your mother ever teach you not to steal?"

"Consider my proposal," she said, winking back, then leaned in and whispered in my ear, so close her lips were practically touching it. "You have a day to change your mind, or you fail."

I got goose bumps for two totally unrelated reasons. "Wait! Do you mean twenty-four hours or tomorrow morning? And what happens if I fail? Do you turn me in?"

But she just stood up and walked away. I tried to follow her, but by the time I got to the lounge entrance, she was gone.

It was after ten when I got back to the suite, and, as if I wasn't already frazzled enough, my suitcase still hadn't arrived. My dad and I went down to the purser's desk and waited in line with a bunch of spoiled people who were complaining about things like how the cushions on their balcony chairs weren't plush enough or that their cabin was too close to the elevators, or too far from the elevators, or unacceptably equidistant from the elevators.

When we finally got to the front of the line, my father

explained the situation, which I could have done myself, but I knew I wouldn't get any respect in brown paisley. (Yes, I finally broke down and put on the shirt.) The assistant purser sent us to the Land of Lost Luggage at the very bottom of the forward stairwell, but we found nothing resembling my suitcase.

"There's a logical explanation," my father said. Howie had suggested that it was taken by Ericsson's ghost, which, as it got closer to midnight, was looking more and more logical.

Back at the purser's desk, the head purser apologized over and over again.

"So very sorry for your inconvenience."

I thought we were going to be given the brush-off, like we would have back home. In fact, back home, the guy would have blamed us for having a bag that was so easily losable. But instead the guy offered me fifty bucks in credit at the ship's clothing boutique. My dad, however, was able to negotiate fifty dollars a day for every day that my suitcase wasn't found, since I'd need a new outfit each day. It was a pretty impressive piece of negotiation, I have to say, although I think it helped that we were in one of the most expensive suites on the ship. Money talks, as they say, even though the talking money was Crawley's and not ours.

All night long I tossed and turned thinking about Tilde and her threat to turn me in. She could do it without getting caught. She could write an anonymous letter and drop it in the suggestion box. Or maybe she had some "arrangement" with one of the security officers, like she did with the bartender.

By morning, without my suitcase, I was going through "stuff" withdrawal. You know, when you're away from your stuff and you not so much miss it as you feel incomplete without it.

"Take it as a spiritual lesson," my mother told me. "It's God's way of reminding you not to rely on material things."

"Of all the people on this boat, why am I the one who gets the spiritual lesson?"

"Maybe it's because you haven't been to confession since the ice age."

I knew I wasn't getting any parental sympathy, especially with fifty bucks a day to spend on clothes. The thing is, the clothes on the boat were so expensive all I could afford was a T-shirt and socks. My dad had to kick in some extra so I could get a pair of shorts.

I never really considered myself materialistic, but I do like my stuff just like anyone else. My electronic stuff, my music stuff, and the stuff that I wear. Suddenly I realized that I was like Tilde now. Stuff-less. The only difference was that for me, it was a temporary situation. But even so, I was not digging it. I tried to imagine what it would be like to be stuff-less indefinitely, but thinking about it made my brain hurt.

"You can wear my clothes," Howie offered, but he'd barely brought enough clothes for himself—and besides, his shirts all had dumb slogans on them like I'M WITH STUPID with the arrow pointing to himself.

"It's called 'self-defecating' humor," Howie once told me. "Because if someone's gotta take a dump on you, you might as well do it yourself."

I knew he must have gotten the expression wrong, but you don't argue with Howie on these points. He marches to the beat of a different drummer. The kind who plays air drums.

Anyway, our second day on the *Plethora of the Deep* was what you call a "sea day," which is exactly what it sounds like. People lounge around by the pools or the sundecks or play bingo or whatever. Christina got sucked into the "Junior Adventurers Camp" like it was a black hole, and we barely saw her for the rest of the cruise. They've got a program for kids my age, but I've got ongoing issues with organized activities—especially when the organizer is an Australian survivalist dude in short-shorts with legs so obnoxiously muscular, he looks like a human frog. Howie bonded with the guy immediately, though, on account of Howie had so many questions about wallabies and dingoes.

"Lance is pretty cool," Howie insisted. "He says he's gonna teach us how to survive the end of the world by eating cockroaches and stuff."

I told him I never associate with anyone named "Lance" on principle, then I took off on my own.

I went out to the bow Jacuzzi, again telling myself I was just there for a soak and wasn't looking for Tilde. Then I wandered around the ship telling myself I was just exploring and not looking for Tilde. Until finally I was up on the sundeck, and I heard this little kid say, "Mommy, that girl's gonna fall and die!"

"That's nice, Billy," said Mommy, without looking up from her Kindle.

I looked to where the kid was pointing, and there was Tilde. She was not where she was supposed to be. She was not where *anyone* was supposed to be.

The bright yellow lifeboats on the *Plethora of the Deep* are designed to withstand nuclear Armageddon. They've got a hard-shell top, propellers that mean business, and a water-sealed entrance that looks like an air lock. Tilde was sitting on top of one of the lifeboats, like she wanted to get caught—but on a ship where everyone was into indulging themselves, no one but little Billy and me were looking.

"What, do you have a death wish?" I shouted out to her.

She looked up at me, grinned, then jumped from the top of the lifeboat to a balcony, and she was gone.

I was furious—mainly at myself for not just letting it go. Thinking quickly, I backed up and started counting paces from where I stood on the sundeck to the nearest elevator. I took the elevator down two decks and measureed the same amount of paces down the starboard hallway. It left me right between two doors, and I thought of that old story "The Lady or the Tiger." But in Tilde's case, it could be both. I knocked, and she opened the door.

"Aha! So you *are* a passenger!" I accused.

"Says who?"

Then she pointed to the heart-shaped announcement pasted on the door that said HAPPY ANNIVERSARY, BERNIE AND LULU, 13 YEARS OF WEDDED BLISS. She closed the door behind her. "Keep walking, Enzo—who knows when Bernie and Lulu are coming back."

We walked down the narrow hallway, with me constantly bumping into the wall, because this girl has got me way off balance. "Where are you from, and what are you doing here?" Two simple questions. I knew she wasn't going to give me straight answers, and I was really curious to see how crooked they would be.

"Why is it your business?" she said.

"It became my business when you stole money from my wallet."

She looked away from me at that. "I come from Quintana Roo, Mexico," she said. "And I'm here because I choose to be. Is that good enough for you?"

"Not really."

"Well, too bad."

"They're going to catch you and throw you off of the ship; you know that, don't you?"

"They haven't thrown me off yet." Then she stopped and looked me in the eye. "Are you here because you want to help me, or are you just afraid I'll turn you in for your friend's birth certificate?"

"I don't know," I admitted.

She studied me for a moment, then said, "I won't turn you in. You're free to go."

But I didn't leave. I should have, but I didn't. "I'm not gonna help you steal."

"Taking money from people on this boat is not stealing. It is the redistribution of wealth."

"Yeah, into your pocket."

"¡*Idiota!* The money is not for me. And don't ask me who it's for, because I'm not telling you. Just know that it is needed more by them than the people who have it now."

"Don't you think they'll miss it?"

"No," said Tilde, very sure of herself. "I never take more than five dollars no matter how much they have. And believe me, some of the people on this boat have more money than God." Which is an expression that never quite made sense to me, because if money is the root of all evil, how could God be rolling in it? It's what you call "flawed logic."

"So will you help me?" Tilde asked.

"No," I told her. "No way." And then I added, "Let me think about it."

Then she handed me a key card. It just looked like a blank, white card, with a magnetic strip. None of the fancy designs that the other key cards had. "This is a passkey," she told me. "It will get you in any room on the ship. If you decide you want to do something more in this world than get fat and sunburned, come to Bernie and Lulu's room, then climb from their balcony to the lifeboat. Just make sure Bernie and Lulu aren't around." Then she pushed open a door that said AUTHORIZED PERSONNEL ONLY.

I looked at the passkey like I was holding something I could be executed for. "Where did you get this?"

She reached into her pocket and pulled out a second one. "Same place I got this one." Then the door closed behind her.

58

• • •

You can't throw a stone in this world without hitting someone who's doing something they're not supposed to be doing—such as throwing stones. Most of the time we either don't notice what other people are up to or we don't care. It falls into that industrial-sized "not my problem" bowl where we stash stuff like Ebola outbreaks, Japanese earthquakes, and African genocide. It's a nasty vat of soup.

I guess it's a defense mechanism. I mean, we all can't be Mother Teresa, so instead of filling our heads with other people's problems, we opt for our own problems, which are never as big as we make them out to be. Then, if we start to feel guilty that we're insensitive boneheads, we go and adopt some orphaned kitten we see on the news because it's easier to save a kitten than it is to save the entire Sudan and because kittens are cute, but starvation and/or genocide is not. In fact, it's disturbing and who wants to bring that kind of grief into their comfortable living room? So we keep on saving cats and throwing a few bucks at telethons, and we feel good about ourselves.

Meanwhile, we ignore that vat of really bad things in the world—a vat that ain't smelling any sweeter the longer it sits. We can live with it, as long as we never dip our ladle into the soup. We can die happy, because, as they say, it's blissful to be an ignoramus.

I admit to being an ignoramus for most of my life, but not all the time.

So there I was, on what was supposed to be the best vacation of my life, and what do I do? I start chugging from the nasty vat.

I knew that whatever world Tilde came from, it was nothing like my own. Clearly, she had a life harder than I could probably even imagine—because how desperate do you have to be to stow away aboard a cruise ship?

At first I couldn't bring myself to break in on Bernie and Lulu, but I didn't have to. Tilde found me that afternoon in the arcade. She didn't say a thing, just caught my eye, and I followed her.

I went with her from cabin to cabin, deck to deck, and I stood lookout as she went in with her passkey and a special security key that opened room safes.

In my whole life I have never stolen money, unless you count that time the vending machine at school broke and started dumping quarters in the coin return like a slot machine. (I was there; it happened; I took advantage of a good situation, so sue me.) But agreeing to be Tilde's partner in crime, that was a whole new level of criminal activity.

At first, I was really paranoid about it, until I realized I was now in everybody else's nasty vat, and they didn't want to taste it. People are always told to "report suspicious activity." Well, between you and me, it only works in airports. Everybody gets reported in airports. The guy picking his nose will get reported, because what if the nose pick was signaling a guy with a shoe bomb that the coast was clear to blow himself up? But everywhere else? Forget it. If you're not at an airport, suspicious activity becomes someone else's problem.

Tilde and I managed to hit dozens of rooms that afternoon. Just like she promised, she never took more than five bucks from any one wallet, so no one noticed, or if they did, they probably figured their kids took it to use at one of the various money-sucking locations on the ship.

I made lots of excuses so that I'd feel okay with being a part of this.

Rationalization #1: Tilde was like Robin Hood, stealing from the rich and giving to the poor, which I guess made me Friar Tuck. And since a friar is like a priest with a bad haircut, my mother would approve, right?

Rationalization #2: I didn't actually take the money, I just stood outside. I was what you might call a "facilitator," which sounds so much better than "accomplice."

Rationalization #3: I could be a positive influence on Tilde and eventually convince her to stop stealing. But this was stretching it, because the idea of me as a positive influence on anybody was higher fantasy than Lord of the Rings.

Did I feel guilty?

Yes.

Did I know that it was probably the second-worst thing I've ever done?

Yes.

Am I gonna tell you what the worst thing is?

In your dreams.

But here's the really scary part: Weeks later, after it was all over, and the media blew everything out of proportion—after all the crazy stuff that this day led to, would I take it back?

No, I wouldn't.

Which means that I committed a crime and I'm not repentant. According to Sister Mary Marlena, who taught catechism until I drove her into early retirement, non-repentant sinners get a first-class ticket to hell, where the nuts are more than warm and there ain't no upgrades.

As to whether I believe that, well, I guess it all depends on whether or not the road to hell is really paved with good intentions. But I'm hoping for the more logical possibility that it's paved with the same asphalt they use in my neighborhood—because those potholes come from a darker dominion than Brooklyn.

CHAPTER 5

A ROGUE WAVE OF RESTLESS LOBSTERS AND THE BUOYANCY OF MY BOAT

"WHERE HAVE YOU BEEN ALL DAY?" MY MOTHER asked as we all got dressed for dinner. I couldn't look her in the face because my mother reads faces likes it's an ingredient list on a food package, and if she sees something unnatural, she's not gonna buy it. And today, my whole face is unnatural.

But she didn't look at me. She was too busy worrying if her dress fit because it was formal night and we all had to look good, although the sleeves on the sports coat I borrowed from my dad were so short, I looked like a circus monkey.

Lexie had long since taught me how to tie a tie because she couldn't stand to be in the company of someone who didn't know how. "I'm sure you look dashing," she said, checking that my knot wasn't lopsided. "Just make sure you find your suitcase by the time my parents get here. They'll notice an ill-fitting wardrobe."

"You look elegant," my mother told me. "Fancy schmancy."

"Fancy Schmancy Antsy!" said my sister, thrilled with herself.

And then Lexie hesitated, still holding the knot of my tie, and asked, "What's wrong, Antsy?"

Lexie always knows when I'm not myself. She says it has to do with my breathing.

"My grandfather says everyone has a 'tell,'" she once said to me. "Most people are looking for it, but I'm listening for it. And you, Antsy, take deep breaths and hold them when something's wrong."

Even after she told me that, I could never catch myself doing it. I guess it's just my natural reaction to secret stress.

Now that Lexie had caught it, my parents began to pay attention. My mother looked at me and instantly saw that my ingredient list was full of red dye and questionable preservatives.

"What did you do? Did you break the boat? I'll bet he broke the boat!"

"Yeah, I dropped Crawley into the propeller to see if he would puree."

"I heard that," yelled Crawley from the connecting suite.

Even Howie was staring at me. "I didn't see you all day, Antsy. Where've you been?" Everyone waited for an explanation.

"What is it with you people?" I said. "We're on a cruise and there's lots to do. Am I supposed check in every ten minutes like a five-year-old?"

"Don't get all defensive," my mother said. "It was just a question."

"Maybe I was out sunning myself."

"Were you?"

"Maybe."

And then Christina smirked. "Or maybe Antsy has a girlfriend."

My mother sighed. "Wherever you were, I don't want to know about it unless you were doing something I don't want to know about. In that case—I want to know."

I took a deep breath and realized I was holding it again. I let it go and tried to make my breaths smooth and carefree, but it only worked when I concentrated.

Everyone else let it go, but before I left for dinner, Lexie whispered in my ear, "We'll talk later."

Everyone on the ship was dressed fancy schmancy on formal night. Photographers were set up taking photos everywhere with fake backgrounds, even though the real background was more interesting than the fake ones. Why would you go on a cruise and have your family photographed with a backdrop of a country garden?

My parents chose not to have our pictures taken, because a family picture would exclude Howie and make him feel bad, but a picture including him would make us feel worse.

In the dining room, lobster was the recommended dinner choice, and everyone ordered multiple plates. I think this ship will singlehandedly make lobster extinct within the year.

Crawley, who dressed in a tuxedo, stayed in his room for formal room service, and Lexie stayed with him, both of them refusing to have cruise ship lobster on principle, because it couldn't possibly be as good as the lobsters he serves in his famous seafood restaurant.

After dinner, I went back to the suite to peel off my monkey suit.

"You oughta come with me to the Sports Deck," Howie said. "Lance is gonna teach us to play rugby. That's Australian football."

I told him I like my football American, like my cheese.

It was after he left that Lexie came in from the adjoining suite.

"Escort me on the roller coaster, please," she said. "I've never been on a roller coaster at sea before."

"Neither has the rest of the planet."

"Not so," she said. "The *Plethora* has been sailing for almost six months, which puts us behind the curve of cutting-edge experience."

We both knew that this wasn't about a roller coaster, though. This was her opportunity to have "the talk" about why I was breathing so irregularly—and needless to say, there was a long line to ride the "Rogue Wave" roller coaster, leaving us plenty of time to talk.

"It's a lovely night," Lexie said, not minding the wait. "I love the sultry Caribbean breeze."

"Sultry. Right."

The line moved quickly, so she dispensed with the small talk. "Won't you tell me what's wrong?" she asked, in her most sympathetic, understanding voice. "You've been awfully quiet . . ."

"What do you mean quiet?" I said a little too loudly,

because I find it insulting to be told I'm quiet. Behind us, a group of foreigners looked at me severely for being loud and American.

Lexie sighed. "Is it something I did? Or maybe you're worried about seeing my parents again? They dislike you less than they admit, really."

Lexie has a tendency to think any strife in other people's lives must somehow be about her. I could have said that she got it right, but I couldn't do that in good conscience, so I said, "It's not about you, and it's not about your parents."

"Aha! So I'm right! There *is* something wrong!"

I cursed and she laughed. It made me feel cornered. "Why can't you let my situations be mine?"

"Because you're my friend and I care about you."

We were at the front of the line now and took our places as the previous riders, now soaking wet, exited the roller coaster.

"If you care about me, then you'll respect me enough to stop asking."

Then she got all bristly. "Fine. If you don't want my help, then you won't get it."

We rode to the peak of the ride in silence, then after an insane drop, we spun through loops and corkscrews and twists and a final plunge right to the surface of the waves that drenched us in tepid—did you hear that—*tepid* Caribbean water that felt cold at sixty miles per hour. Then the ride brought us back to where we started.

Although I love roller coasters, I had just eaten half a

dozen lobsters, and my stomach was now trying to push my lungs out my ears, and Lexie says—

"Let's do it again!" She tries to drag me back to wait in line, but I won't budge, because if I ride again, I know those lobsters are gonna come a-calling.

"Maybe tomorrow," I tell her. "Right now I gotta lie down."

"You're such a lightweight."

And then I hear, "Excuse, please. You like up-down fastness? I ride mit you, ya?"

I turned to see one of the guys who had been behind us in line—he was about our age, although it's sometimes hard to tell with foreigners.

"You no eyes, so I touch you," he said, and he took Lexie's dainty hand in his large one to guide her. "You safe, ya?"

Lexie giggled. "What a charming invitation. I would be honored," she told him. He nodded, clearly not understanding her words but getting that she meant "yes." Then she dismissed me with a wave of her hand. "Go Pepto-Bismol yourself into a pink stupor. Whatever your troubles are, you can share them with the bottle." And she went off for more up-down fastness.

From there, I went up to the buffet—which is where all the people went who either didn't want to dress up for dinner or couldn't wait to be served. Food was the last thing I wanted to think about, but I wasn't there to eat. When no one was looking, I filled a few plastic bags with food. I had a sack of garlic shrimp, beef broccoli, and an entire breast of turkey with all the trimmings.

68

I'd like to say that sneaking into Bernie and Lulu's cabin and climbing into Tilde's lifeboat was dangerous, but it wasn't. Bernie and Lulu apparently spent all their waking hours either in the casino or at the buffet, so they weren't in their cabin when I used the passkey to break in. And climbing from their balcony to the lifeboat, well, the way the ship was designed, even if I slipped in between the two-foot gap, I'd only fall onto someone's balcony one deck below.

Tilde was in the lifeboat, as I suspected she would be.

"Hey," I said, "I brought you some food."

When I showed her what was in my backpack, she laughed. "You didn't have to do that. It's not like I'm going to starve without you."

I shrugged. "If you got caught taking this food, you'd get arrested or beheaded or whatever they do to stowaways. If I get caught, they'd give me silverware to take with me."

But then, when I took in the bigger picture, I saw that she had canned food stockpiled in the lifeboat. Much more than she even needed. Still, she ate what I brought her.

"So what's your deal?" I finally asked her. "If I'm helping you, then the least you could do is tell me why I should."

"You tell me," she said, "because it sounds like you have me all figured out."

This, I knew, was a setup. It's like the old question, "Do I look fat in this?" The answer, in any conceivable situation, is always "no." Basically, she was sitting me down in a minefield and seeing if I could get through it without death or hospitalization.

"You're smart," I told her, which I think was true, and it

was a good place to start. "Not just smart, but street smart. You know how to make things happen and how to get what you need."

"*Sigue*," she said. "Continue."

"You don't have much. Maybe you got nothing at all. Poorer than dirt. Somehow you saw an opportunity to get on this ship and took it. I'd probably do the same."

"Dirt isn't poor," she said. "It must be rich to grow anything." Then the ship hit a swell, and the lifeboat rocked like a Ferris wheel car. "Don't worry. It's safe," she said.

"I wasn't worried."

"Continue."

"Okay, so you've got this whole thing wired: how to stay out of sight while in plain sight. I know about that on account of I had this friend who could stay hidden without even trying. He could probably walk right onto this ship and no one would even notice. But you're not like that. You have to work hard at not being seen. But like I said, you're smart. You've got it wired."

"Anything else?"

"Oh yeah. The money. You're probably giving it to your family, which is back wherever you come from. Or maybe you're saving it to bribe whatever crewman finally catches you."

"And you think that's clever?"

"Very." And then I added, "You figure the worst that can happen to you is you're put off the ship. You're too young to go to jail for something like this, and the cruise line doesn't want that kind of publicity, so they'd keep it quiet, and you'd get sent back home. For you, it's a good deal no matter how you look at it."

Then she smiled and moved closer to me.

"So now it's your turn. What's your 'deal'?"

I shrugged. "I'm just a guy from Brooklyn."

"In a sky suite?"

"Yeah, well, I have a rich friend."

"The old man with the cane?"

"Bingo." Then I added, "Better not let him catch you. Believe me, he will find a way to make your life a living hell." Then I felt bad, because maybe her life already was a living hell. And then I said the stupid thing that I had thought about but promised I wouldn't say. "Listen, you can hide out on my balcony. I won't tell anyone."

She just laughed at that. "Why would I want your balcony when I have this luxury yacht?"

At the time I thought she was talking about the lifeboat, but later I came to realize she meant the entire *Plethora of the Deep*, which she saw as her own personal playground.

She kept on smiling. "I appreciate your offer, though." Then she moved closer and said, "We can kiss if you like."

This I was not expecting.

"That's why you're helping me, isn't it? So go ahead. We can kiss, but that is all. Nothing more." And she puckered her lips in anticipation.

Okay, I have to admit, I was feeling stirrings. Let's just say that the ship wasn't the only thing that hit a swell. And she was right—I wanted to. She was beautiful; she was mysterious; she was so unlike anyone I knew in the real world. But she was wrong about one thing: I didn't help her because I wanted to make out with her, and if I did that now, it would make me feel like a creep—because what if, in that secret place where my subconscious makes its sneaky little plans, what if that really *was* the reason why I helped her after all?

I could hear all my friend's voices in my head screaming, "Do it! Do it! Do it now, before she changes her mind!" I could even hear Ira saying , "Get it on video!"

"No," I told her, even though I knew I'd regret saying it in ten minutes. "I'm not gonna kiss you."

She looked at me like I had slapped her in the face.

"Why not? I know it's what you want."

"First of all, you just ate a pound of garlic shrimp," I told her. "And second, you're not my type."

"Oh . . . so then you like boys?"

"What? You think any boy who won't kiss you must be gay?"

"Pretty much, yeah."

I was about to deny it, and then I realized something. She had been in control of everything from the moment we met. This was my chance to be in charge of the situation. To control the controller.

So I looked her square in the eye and said absolutely nothing, neither confirming nor denying the suggestion.

Her eyes went wide at my silence. "I'm sorry," she said, looking away. "I didn't realize . . . Forgive me, I didn't mean to hurt your feelings."

And so by not saying a thing, I suddenly had the upper hand.

. . .

I have no experience playing for the other team—and wearing a dress on Halloween doesn't count. There are some guys you kinda know what their deal is and others who you'd never know unless they told you, like my cousin Benny, who evades gaydar like a stealth bomber.

Guys at school use the "G" word as an insult. I don't know why that is, but it just is. I admit that I've been guilty of that—but I also know I'd never treat a guy bad if he really was. Only the real lowlifes pick on guys or girls for being gay.

As for me, I got no problem with all the variations of humanity. As long as no one's making me do something I don't want to—like the one time we played spin the bottle at a party. Spin the bottle is not a smart game unless you bend the rules, because the bottle don't know the concept between male and female, and my bottle landed on Vinnie Bamboni. Have you ever seen Vinnie Bamboni? Calling him ugly is an insult to ugliness, and to top it, he's got breath like used dental floss.

Neena Wexler, class president and an iron-fisted enforcer of rules, was running the game, and she insisted you play by the book or you don't play. So rather than get anywhere near Vinnie Bamboni's butt-ugly lips, I left to go play Grand Theft Psycho with all the other guys whose bottle had landed on Vinnie. This does not make me homophobic. It just means I got standards.

The way I see it is this: The whole sex thing is pretty weird to begin with. I mean, do you remember the first time you learned about it? (And if you haven't yet, my apologies.

73

I won't give out spoilers.) I mean, we start to hear about all this stuff way back when we still think kissing is gross. At first we think somebody's got to be pulling our leg, until we realize that it's all true, and more. Then somewhere along the way, we put two and two together and realize that our parents must have done the deed to get us, and maybe they're still doing it right now. At this very moment.

Then we get a little older and boom! Suddenly we got these hormones that make us want to do the freakiest things, and we wonder, "Where did these feelings come from? Why do I want to do *that*? And how can I get my homework done with that stuff filling up my head?"

So if all of these desires are kinda freaky, what makes *my* freaky stuff any better than the freaky stuff that gay personages feel? And don't they got the right to do what they gotta do as long as they're not doing it in my kitchen, like the way my mom and dad French kiss while making dinner, which erases the very concept of my appetite?

"Whatever makes your boat float," as they say, be it fresh water, or salt water, or, as in Peter Pan, a little bit of fairy dust. And if Tilde wanted to think my boat floated a little high in the water just because I refused to kiss her, well, that was her problem, not mine.

CHAPTER 6

SECRET CONVERSATIONS ON A SHIP IN A BOTTLE WITH A DEAD GUY IN THE DARK

WE WERE HEADED TO JAMAICA, AND ALTHOUGH the ship boasted speeds much faster than any cruise ship afloat, it wasn't speeding anywhere just yet. Instead it was taking its sweet time. The next day was another sea day. The captain, who, like much of the crew, had some unidentifiable European accent, came on like an airplane pilot to announce our position like every ten minutes. He kept saying his name, but I never quite got it.

"I think he said 'Captain Feety Pajamas,'" Howie said, which would have been moronic, except for the fact that it's exactly what I thought he said, too.

I forced myself not to look for Tilde. I figured now that I had a little bit of control of the situation, I could let things simmer. I sat out on the sundeck for most of the day, with a lot less sunscreen than I needed, and soaked up enough rays to roast a turkey. It made going down the waterslides very painful.

All day they had contests and competitions around the main pool. Howie entered himself in the Hairy Legs Contest. So did my dad.

"If you win the Hairy Legs Contest," my mom told my dad, "we might get invited to the Captain's Table."

The Captain's Table was this big, round thing smack in the middle of the first floor of the dining room, beneath the giant chandelier. On the first two nights, Captain Feety Pajamas, all dressed in a brilliant white uniform, greeted those elite people who got mysteriously selected to sit at his table. My mom had now made it her personal mission to dine at the Captain's Table before the end of the cruise.

Word to the wise—if they have a hairy legs contest on a boat that you're on, abandon ship. Don't wait for the seven emergency blasts—just jump.

Howie and my dad lost to a caveman in a Speedo. Don't try to imagine it; it will only bring you pain.

It was as I was still basting in my own juices that a shadow fell over me, and when I looked, I saw Tilde silhouetted by the sun. "Hello, Enzo. Meet me on Deck Zero, by the aft elevators after dinner. I'll show you something very few people get to see." And she left before I could say yes or no.

At dinner, however, I had a conflicting invitation, somewhere between the consommé and the escargot.

"They're having a midnight seventies party out on the Lido Deck tonight," Lexie said. "I'll forgive your prior insolence if you dance with me!"

Okay, so I want to be clear about this: I like being with Lexie, and I do like dancing with her. When she dances, her movements are from the soul. She dances like no one else is looking. Under any other circumstances I'd jump at the opportunity, but I was too curious about what Tilde wanted to show me.

"Sorry, Lexie," I said. "Maybe another night."

"Antsy, stop being a snot and go," my mother said.

And in the awkward silence that followed, Howie raised his hand. "I'll go."

"Well," said Lexie, "at least there's one gentleman in our party."

It occurred to me that I was choosing to spend my time with a girl who was ridiculously poor instead of a girl who was ridiculously rich, and I wondered what was wrong with me.

When dinner was over, Lexie left with Moxie to give her grandfather some attention before the dance. As usual, Crawley had dined in his suite and showed no sign of coming out unless we hit an iceberg. Once Lexie was gone, Howie began to sweat.

"I shouldn't a done that!" he said, staring sullenly at his cherries jubilee. "My mom made me take all these dance classes when I was little, but the girls I danced with always got hurt. I tell you, I'm cursed!" I could see the horror in his eyes as his challenged imagination worked overtime. "What if I dip her and her head cracks open on the railing? Or what if I spin her off the ship and I gotta go in after her and we both drown or get eaten by sharks or worse? I don't know what's worse than getting eaten by sharks, but whatever it is, *that's* what's gonna happen!"

"Well," I told him, getting up to leave. "You'll just have to cross that bridge when you fall from it."

As it turns out, the Howie Danger Dance was never gonna happen, but I didn't know that yet. All I knew was that another Tilde-themed mystery was waiting for me in the ship's nether regions.

Usually the cheapest cabins were on the lowest decks, but this ship had "Atlantis Suites" with big underwater windows like the Neptune Lounge—and some of them supposedly had balconies, although I still can't grasp the concept.

"About time, Enzo," Tilde said to me when I showed up on Zero Deck. Then she took me through a No Admittance door and we were off into the mysterious bowels of the *Plethora of the Deep.*

Below the passenger decks, there's a whole hidden world on a cruise ship that most people don't get to see. The secret corridors of service. Gray walls, linoleum floors—nothing like the shiny brass and glass and glitz of the passenger decks. On the gunmetal-gray walls were postings in various languages instructing the crew on proper behavior. Hands must be washed, uniforms pressed—that kind of thing. Violations were to be reported. From down here, the *Plethora* looked more like a military vessel.

We kept out of view of any passing crewmen, then Tilde slipped down a smaller hallway, pulled a blue crewman's jumpsuit from a closet, and handed it to me.

"The blue ones are the uniforms of the engine crew," she told me. "Put it on quickly."

I slipped the jumpsuit over my clothes and zipped it up. As I looked out of the small connecting hallway, I could see other crew members passing by. They didn't take any notice of us, because we were in the shadows.

"When they see me, they'll know I'm not one of them," I pointed out.

"There are more than two thousand people in the crew and many of them do not look any older than you. You will have no problem."

"What about you?" I asked.

"I have an understanding with the crew," Tilde told me. "They don't see me, I don't see them . . . but if you see a ship's officer, warn me. Then I need to hide."

Reluctantly, I followed her out into the main hallway. It was just as she said: No one looked at me or at her. She took me down a gangway and then another, then we wound through a maze of narrow steel hallways that seemed to have no purpose other than to be generally confusing. Finally we came to a steel door that looked entirely unremarkable except that it had a digital keypad lock on it, like a vault door.

"You must not tell anyone about this," she said, then reconsidered. "On second thought, tell anyone you like. They won't believe you anyway." Then she tapped a series of buttons on the keypad. I heard a whoosh of air and she pulled open the heavy steel door.

People do weird things. Especially when they're rich, although when people are rich, it's not called weird, it's called eccentric. Or maybe it's not that the things they do are weirder than what everyone else does—maybe they're just bigger and harder to ignore. For instance, there's that Winchester Mystery House in California, where some nutty lady spent her whole life building a house full of stairways that went nowhere and doors that opened onto nothing but empty air. The mystery wasn't so much that she built it, but that she could stand being around contractors for that long. We had this guy put in a skylight once, and by the end of the week, we were worried we'd have to start hiding the knives from my mom.

Then there's the guy who started Aflac Insurance—he built an entire mansion on the roof of his company's six-story parking structure, complete with trees and a swimming pool, because he wanted to live at work.

I suppose if I was rich, last year's Fourth of July mishap would have taken out half the Eastern Seaboard, so maybe it's a good thing that I'm not.

Jorgen Ericsson, the founder of Caribbean Viking cruise line, like so many super-rich people did some things simply because he could.

When I first saw what was on the other side of the steel door, I didn't quite get it. We were now in a huge chamber, maybe a hundred feet long and twenty feet high, housing a single large object. At first I thought it was another lifeboat—the old-fashioned, wooden kind, but much bigger. It was really run down, and it had a strange shape—both the bow and stern pointed up into the air. Then I realized that the huge chamber had no other door—which meant there was no way to get the big wooden boat in or out. It was like a ship in a bottle—which meant that it was here from the beginning. The *Plethora of the Deep* was actually built *around* this weird wooden boat. But why?

"Jorgen Ericsson believed he was a direct descendant of Leif Ericsson," Tilde told me. That's when it all came together in my head, and I realized what I was looking at.

"Is that . . . a Viking ship?"

Tilde nodded. "Ericsson always made sure that each of his cruise ships had a piece of an old Viking ship somewhere inside it. Maybe a mast or a beam hidden deep inside. Sometimes in places no one would ever see, but he always made sure it was there. For the *Plethora of the Deep*, he bought an entire Viking war ship from a museum in Oslo and set it right here, in the *Plethora's* center of gravity."

I walked over to the ancient boat, amazed by the idea that at the heart of the world's greatest ocean liner was this humble boat from who knows how many centuries ago. The ancient Viking ship was still sailing the seas!

"That's nuts," I said, "but also it's kind of . . . genius!"

"I thought you'd like it."

In the center of the Viking boat was the remains of a mast—not much left of it, just a broken bit of wood—but that didn't take away from its impressiveness.

"How do you know about this?" I asked her.

Tilde shrugged. "I have become an expert on the *Plethora of the Deep*. Very few people know this exists, and only the ship's captain knows the code to get in."

"The captain and you," I pointed out.

She grinned. "I am very good at cracking codes." Then she went over to the Viking boat, which I was afraid to even touch—and she climbed into it. "Come on," she said. "I still have to show you the best part."

Although I was afraid my weight might break it, it was much sturdier than it looked. I climbed in after her, and it was like stepping into a different world. I already knew I was trespassing in a place I wasn't supposed to be, which was never usually a problem for me, but now I felt like I was also trespassing in a whole other time.

Tilde led me to a big wooden crate in the middle of the boat that seemed to be made of the same dark, ancient wood—but I could tell that this was not an original part of the Viking ship.

"And there he is!" Tilde said.

I did not like the sound of that. "There who is?"

"Jorgen Ericsson, of course."

Another moment looking at the box and I realized it wasn't just a box—it was a coffin. Maybe not like the kind most people use, but Ericsson had a theme going here. I guess he didn't want to ruin it.

"His wish was to be laid to rest right here when he died. Isn't it poetic?"

"Yeah," I said, fighting a sudden shiver, "in a mega-creepy kind of way."

I guess I shouldn't have been surprised. Some people were freakish about the way they wanted to be buried. There was this guy who insisted on being buried in his Ferrari, defying the expression "You can't take it with you." And that guy who created *Star Trek*? He never got buried at all. Instead, he had his ashes taken up by the space shuttle and

82

released into space, which, I guess, was the next-best thing to being "beamed up."

I thought about Howie and all his claims about Jorgen Ericsson's ghost. I don't know if his spirit really walks the halls, but in a very real way, his spirit was built right into his ship.

When I looked to Tilde, she had moved to the bow of the Viking boat and was lying on her back.

"What are you doing?"

"Looking at the stars."

"We're inside," I pointed out. "There are no stars."

"Yes, there are." Then she patted the space beside her, waiting for me to lie down next to her.

"Sorry," I told her. "Lying down in some guy's Viking tomb is probably not a good idea. We might get our heads smashed in by the hammer of Thor or something. Those Norse gods are nasty."

"You don't know the code to get out," Tilde said. "So you might as well come over here, because we don't leave until I'm ready to go."

And so I made my way to the bow and lay down beside her, looking up at the steel ceiling. The way the Viking ship was shaped, the only way we could lie side by side was if our heads touched. I could smell her hair now, and it surprised me. I figured a stowaway might smell a little bit sour this close up—I mean, didn't she wash her clothes by sitting in the Jacuzzi? I figured at best she'd smell like pool chlorine. Instead, her hair smelled like coconut and cherry shampoo. I took a deep whiff, enjoying the aroma.

"Cozy," she said.

"Yeah," I told her. "I'll bet Jorgen Ericsson is real cozy."

I began to squirm at the thought, but she grabbed my wrist. "Stay still," she said in a whisper. "Don't move a muscle."

"Why not?"

"You'll see."

In my life, I had never lain down, alone, right next to a girl, and all my proximity meters were flying into the red zone. This place, I knew, in spite of the dead guy, was the ultimate make-out spot. I toyed with the idea of just going for it, but then she said,

"If you were any other boy, I would not have brought you here. But because you're—you know—not interested in me, I know I don't have to worry about you taking advantage, the way another boy might."

Again I said nothing, neither confirming nor denying. Funny, but I felt that I was now taking advantage of her by *not* taking advantage of her.

"Your heart beats so fast," she said.

"Uh . . . I guess I'm just afraid of Ericsson's ghost."

And that's when the lights went out.

"Whoa!" I said.

"Don't worry," Tilde whispered. "The lights are controlled by motion sensors. As long as we stay still, they will not come on."

While I didn't like the idea of being in the dark just ten feet away from Jorgen Ericsson, I did like being there with Tilde far more than she realized—and if the lights came up, she might just figure that out, so best to stay in the dark.

84

"Look! Do you see?" Tilde said.

"There's no light. What would I see?"

She didn't answer me. She just waited. And then, in a moment, I spotted a tiny bit of light right above me. Then another and another as my eyes began to adjust to the darkness.

"You see?" Tilde said. "Stars!"

"That's impossible."

"Nothing's impossible," she told me, and explained that Ericsson had thousands of tiny lights embedded in the ceiling of his burial chamber.

"It matches the visible sky in Oslo at nine fifteen P.M., March 4, the date and time of his birth."

Time seemed to stop as we looked at the stars. In a while, I almost forgot they weren't real. With the gentle rocking of the *Plethora* and the feel of the old wooden boat against my back, it really did feel that we were at sea on a Viking ship, looking up at the stars.

"This is a good place for forgetting," Tilde said after a while. "Do you have many things you wish to forget?"

"Who, me?"

"No, Jorgen Ericsson. Of course you."

I racked my brain thinking about it. I wanted to forget the grade on my science final. I wanted to forget that time I won a dinner date with the most popular girl in school at the spring fund-raiser, then during the date, I managed to sneeze lettuce out of my nose onto her blouse—and no small piece either; this was like an entire side salad—and although I really wanted to believe it was honey-mustard dressing making it stick to her blouse, we all know it wasn't.

"Yeah," I told Tilde. "I guess there are things I'd rather forget."

"Me too," she said. "There are many, many things. When I come here and look at the stars, I forget those things for a while."

"That's good," I said. I didn't want to ask her what those things were. Somehow, I doubted they were about grades or about her most embarrassing moments. Whatever Tilde needed to forget, it was far more in need of forgetting than anything in my life. So I wished on a fake star that her memory would fail in all the best ways.

Tilde shifted closer to me, not moving enough to trigger the light sensors, but enough for me to feel her hip against mine. I tried to control my heartbeat. There's this creepy story by that Poe guy about a heart beating beneath the floorboards of a house, and I could swear I now heard my own telltale heart echoing in the wood of the Viking ship.

"So do your parents know?" she asked me.

"What, about you?"

"No," she said. "About you."

"Oh, right." I cleared my throat to stall. "I've told them exactly what I've told you."

Somehow, she still hadn't figured out that I'd told her nothing.

"What about your friend, Herbie? Are you two a couple?"

I decided right then and there that it was time to put a pin through her ballooning assumptions. "It's Howie," I corrected. "And no, we're not. To be honest, you're more my type than he is."

"So you're saying if you liked women, you would be attracted to me?"

"Yes. I mean I do, and I am."

She shifted very slightly closer. "You say this to make me feel good, but you don't have to," she said. "It's nice to be this close to a boy without him expecting more and more."

That's when I realized that this balloon wasn't popping no matter how much I tried to puncture it, because Tilde didn't want it to. It made me wonder how many guys had taken serious advantage of her in her life. She needed Enzo the Rainbow Warrior, not Antsy the Italian Stallion. I wondered how much she'd hate me if I took Enzo away from her now.

"Are you ever going to tell me something about *you*?" I asked, trying to shift the attention away from me.

"I'll make a deal with you," Tilde whispered. "If you tell me your darkest moment, I'll tell you mine."

"Darkest moment?" That was easy. It was still pretty raw and close to me. "My dad's heart attack. Those first few hours when we thought he wasn't going to make it." Yet as I thought about it, I realized that as dark as it was, I didn't want to ever forget it. It brought out the worst in me, but it also brought out the best in me and in my whole family. Sure, I wished it had never happened, but I wouldn't want to forget that it did.

"I'm glad your father is all right," she said. "Heart attacks are like earthquakes. They come suddenly and with little warning. But for my mother, it was more like a hurricane. I had warning, because I knew she was dying for a long time.

87

Still, nothing prepares you for the shock when it happens."

"I'm sorry," I said. "That's a pretty dark moment."

"That's not it." Then she paused. "My darkest moment came in the weeks after. When I realized that there was not another human being on earth who loved me."

Wow, I thought. I couldn't even imagine that feeling. What do you say to something like that? "That sucks."

"Yes and no," Tilde said. "Because it made me strong, and I realized *I* could love me and it could be enough."

"I don't think I could ever be that strong," I confessed. "I mean, half the time, I don't even *like* me."

"You don't always have to like yourself to love yourself," she said. Which didn't make much sense to me, but I was willing to go with it.

"Do you know what, Enzo? I feel safe with you."

For a guy, that can be an insult as much as a compliment. "You shouldn't," I told her. "There's nothing safe about me. Ask anyone who knows me." But it was like she wasn't listening . . . or she just didn't want to hear.

"I feel safe with you . . . and I need your help tomorrow. So I'll feel safe."

"What's tomorrow?"

"Jamaica," she said.

"You're going off the ship? You can't go off—you'll never get back on."

"Let me worry about that."

"No more stealing," I told her. "I'm done with that."

"No more stealing," she agreed. "Tomorrow, we'll be buying something."

88

"Is it something legal?"

She sighed. "Don't ask a question you don't want the answer to."

So I didn't ask anymore questions about it. I'm no fool. I knew Tilde was using me—and I knew it probably wouldn't land us anywhere good. But for some reason, I was okay with that. Somehow I trusted that whatever she was up to, it was in a big-picture kind of way, worthy of my limited attention.

Did she really feel safe with me, or did she just say that to get me to go along? In the end, it didn't really matter, because whatever she baited her hook with, I had already chomped down and wasn't getting free anytime soon.

A COUPLE OF MORONS AND LEXIE'S PARENTS, WHO ARE ALSO A COUPLE OF MORONS

AFTER OUR VIKING ADVENTURE, I WALKED AROUND the ship's promenade deck alone before going back to the cabin. It was hard to shake the weird feeling I had while lying beneath the stars with Tilde. It was like I was living two lives now. I was two people, Antsy the kid I always was and then this new guy, Enzo, who was breaking laws left and right and enjoying it. Not that the real Antsy doesn't mind bending the rules now and then, but this other guy, he was out of control.

There's this thing they call "folly-o-duh"—although since it's French, it's probably spelled with lots of silent *e*'s and *x*'s. Roughly translated, it means "a couple of morons." It's when two people get together, both feeding off the same bad idea, and since they keep agreeing with each other that it's not a bad idea at all, it spins out of control, and they lose all touch with reality. It's the principle that explains pairs like Bonnie and Clyde or Penn and Teller.

I was beginning to wonder if I was spinning into a folly-o-duh with Tilde—but if I was, I was enjoying it too much to stop.

Twice around the promenade and I felt more like me and less like Enzo. When I went into the cabin, Howie was there, sitting on his bed, looking dejected. Now I began to wonder what I missed in the real world.

"How come you're here?" I asked him. "Weren't you taking Lexie to the seventies dance?"

He shrugged. "She didn't wanna go. She said she's seasick, but the ship's barely moving." Then he sighed. "It's okay. Had we danced, we might have died."

I went through the connecting door into Lexie and Crawley's suite. Crawley was there watching the crawl of some financial news network. He pointed to the balcony, and now I could hear Lexie crying through the open balcony door. Moxie was lying on the ground trying to disappear into the carpet, whimpering like he did during thunderstorms.

"Your conspicuous absence in this entire situation has been duly noted," Crawley said.

"What happened?"

"If she wants to discuss it, she will. But for now, I suggest you get out there and make her happy. If you don't, I'll have your citizenship revoked and leave you in Jamaica or whatever godforsaken island we're on tomorrow."

"Not even you can do that, Mr. Crawley."

"Perhaps not, but I'll have fun trying."

I went outside. Lexie sat on the large balcony, her shoulders shuddering with her sobs. I'd seen her cry before, but never like this. Her flute was in her lap, and she gripped it with white-knuckled intensity.

"Lexie . . ." I said gently.

"Go away!" she yelled, caught off guard that I was there. Then she said more gently, "Just go away."

91

Of course I didn't go. Now I really felt like a creep for not taking her to the dance. "Hey," I said. "I'm really sorry I hurt your feelings."

"Don't be stupid," she said through her tears. "This isn't because of you." Then she wiped away some of her tears. "At least, it's only partially because of you."

"Well, I'm partially sorry," I said like an idiot. "I mean, I'm fully sorry for my portion of it."

Lexie took a deep, shuddering breath and another breath that was smoother. "I'm so, so tired of being 'the blind girl.'"

"Hey, technology is advancing and stuff," I said. "Maybe someday you'll be able to see."

"That's not what I mean!"

I didn't say anything else because if I was going to put any more feet in my mouth, I was gonna have to borrow someone else's from down the hall.

"Being blind isn't the problem," she said. "It's being seen as 'the blind girl.' When I asked you to take me to the dance, it was because you won't treat me like a china doll. You won't be afraid to bump into me or step on my feet."

"Yeah, I'm pretty good at that."

"Whenever I walk into a room of strangers, I feel all those eyes on me. I can't see, but I still feel those eyes; isn't that funny? People see me, and they automatically make assumptions that set me apart from anyone else in the room. I used to like that when I was younger, but now I see it's an awkward, lonely kind of attention. I want people to see *me*, not 'the blind girl.'"

"Even if you weren't blind, I think you'd stand apart,"

I told her. "But that's a good thing. I mean, blind or not, you're kind of . . . I don't know . . . remarkable."

"Remarkable," she repeated, but it came out bitter. "Yes, people make remarks about me all the time."

"That's not what I meant."

She reached over and put her hand on my knee, squeezing gently. "I know, Antsy."

We sat like that for a while listening to the whoosh of the ocean as the ship cut through the water.

"I think I get it," I said. "But I also get why it happens. It's like we have to put people into boxes, because our brains aren't big enough to make every person a person. So we put them all into boxes and then we get to decide whose box we're going to open. We gotta be careful, though, because if we open everybody's box, we'll go crazy. So yeah, you'll be 'the blind girl' and I'll be 'the obnoxious Italian guy' to like ninety-nine percent of the people we meet. But to the one percent that opens our boxes, they get to hit the jackpot. Although they'll probably return me for store credit."

She laughed a little, which was good. It meant there was another emotion there to fight against the tears. It occurred to me that she hadn't asked me about where I'd been. I could have avoided the subject entirely, but somehow, I felt I owed her an explanation.

"I couldn't go to the dance because I've been hanging out with someone whose been causing me a lot of grief," I told her. "But the thing is, this person needs my help."

She smiled, sought out my hand, and grasped it. "You're good at that, Antsy. Helping people."

93

"Yeah," I said. "Everybody but myself. Anyway, it's not what you think."

"You don't have to say any more. It's none of my business."

"Well, it kinda is. I mean you're expecting me to spend time with you on this cruise. Howie is expecting that, too, and I've been abandoning you both." Then I thought of something that was sure to cheer her up. "But hey, when we get to Grand Cayman, you'll get to hang with your parents, right? I know you're looking forward to that."

She took her hand back from me at the mention of her parents and began to run her fingers along the levers and valves of her flute.

"I *was* looking forward to it," Lexie admitted, "but we just got word that they won't be joining us. They had 'something pressing' in Paris."

"No way!" I clenched a fist, wishing I could give them a piece of my mind. Then it occurred to me that all the other stuff that Lexie just told me was small compared to this. Here was the real reason for Lexie's tears.

"Sometimes," Lexie said, "I feel like they just see me as 'the blind girl,' too."

"I'm sorry," I told her, for once glad that my parents were around to make my life miserable.

"Well, to hell with them," she said. "I'm having fun on this cruise in spite of it, and no one's going to stop me."

Then she stood and hurled her golden flute into the Caribbean Sea.

CHAPTER 8

RED, RED WHINE, WALL OF VOODOO, AND DEATH CAB FOR CUTIE

I DON'T LIKE BEING A TOURIST. MOST TOURISTS are loud, rude, clueless, and got no respect for the place they're visiting. The problem is, since I'm mostly loud, rude, and clueless, putting me next to a bunch of tourists makes me look like one of them. It's embarrassing. If I'm gonna visit someplace, I don't want to be clumped with some pasty-thighed retirees in sun hats. Lexie doesn't like being "the blind girl," and I don't like being "the ugly American."

Under normal circumstances, though, I would have given in and gone along with the herd, but I already knew there wasn't gonna be anything normal about my day on the island, with Tilde.

"What do you mean you're not going with us?" My dad was up in arms. "Do you have any idea how much we paid for the Deluxe Jamaican Island Tour and Snorkel Extravaganza?"

"So get a refund." My original plan was to tell them I was spending the day with Lexie, but then she left with Moxie for the spa, announcing that she was getting a three-hour seaweed wrap, which until then I thought was something you ate. It left me with no cover story.

"We made plans as a family," my mother said, wagging her favorite wagging finger. "The least you could do is follow them."

"If I have to go, so should he!" complained Christina.

"C'mon, Antsy," Howie begged. "It's an extravaganza!"

"I got your extravaganza right here," I said.

My mother threw up her hands and walked away. "I've raised a cultural imbecile."

I showed them my sunburn, which was still lobster red, and began to whine. "In case you forgot, I'm burned, and it hurts. I don't feel like going, so get off my back already!"

My dad shook his head, looking at me all disappointed. "Fine. Stay here and vegetate. I hope you and Crawley enjoy each other's miserable company."

"I heard that!" said Crawley from the adjoining suite.

I waited until they had all left, then watched from the balcony until I was sure all the tour buses were gone.

Crawley came up behind me, full of his usual suspicion. "What are you scheming?"

"Who says I'm scheming anything?"

He poked me on my sunburned chest intentionally, and I grimaced. "Don't insult my intelligence. You're always scheming something."

Which was usually true. But this time it wasn't. "I'm not the schemer," I told him. "This time I'm just the henchman."

Crawley nodded, somehow satisfied. "I always knew

96

you'd be a henchman sooner or later." Then he went back to his suite and closed the adjoining door.

As soon as I got off the ship, I found myself in Fake Jamaica. The pier was full of comfy gazebos in pastel pink and blue, sparkling-clean souvenir shops selling native crafts that all said "made in China," and an open-air stage, featuring yet another clone reggae band with regulation dreads playing "Red, Red Wine." It was all so controlled and sterile, it might as well have been Disneyland. I guess that's what some people want: a giant living diorama—because the real thing isn't always so pretty.

But if you don't get on the air-conditioned tour buses and actually have the guts to step out of the pier's security zone, you'll find a world that ain't so pristine but is tons more interesting.

First there's the guy who approaches everyone who looks under forty and asks them if they want to buy some prime *gancha* at discount prices.

"What's gancha?" a little kid asked his parents. "Can I have some?"

The father laughed and said, "Not till you're older."

The mother was not amused.

There were souvenir shops out here, too, but they were more run down and more packed with stuff. More real. The buildings themselves had a kind of crumbling character to them, like they barely survived the last hurricane but what hadn't killed them made them stronger.

"You scared me, Enzo—I though you changed your mind!"

I turned around to see Tilde. She was looking a little nervous and not at all her usual self. She gave me a hug, which she had never done before.

"Ouch! Careful—my sunburn."

"We should go now," she said. "We don't have much time."

I noticed she was gripping a paper sack a little too tightly. "Are you gonna tell me what we're doing? Does it involve the guy selling gancha?"

"*Idiota*. We're not buying weed or any other drug. What we're buying is much more valuable."

"Which is?"

Tilde put her hand in the air to hail a taxi. "Today, we buy freedom."

Kingston's cruise port had no shortage of taxis, and pretty soon a small car, billowing more smoke than my grandma's bridge club, screeched to a halt in front of us. The driver was all smiles. There was no shortage of friendliness in Jamaica.

"Hop on in," he tells us. "You want de island tour or beach? I know de best beaches."

Once we had gotten in, Tilde gave him an address scrawled on a piece of paper. "Take us there, please."

"Yes, yes," he said, without even looking at the paper, "but don't you want a tour first?" He addressed me instead of Tilde, figuring I was either the one calling the shots or the more likely sucker. "I give you and your cutie my deluxe island experience; how dat sound? Good? Betta believe it!"

"No," Tilde said sharply, gripping even more tightly to the brown paper bag in her hands. "Take us to the address and no more questions."

"Hoo hoo hoo!" laughed the cabbie. "Dat one knows where she is going! Betta watch yourself wit dat one, mon!" He actually said "mon." I wondered whether he really talked that way or just knew what Americans expected. Then he looked at the paper and that island-friendly expression on his face changed. "You kiddin' me?" he said. "You really want to go to dis place here?"

I didn't like the look on his face.

"Is it far?" I asked.

"About an hour. Why you want to go to dis place?"

"Not your business," I told him. "And if you don't want to take us, we'll find a cabbie who will."

He turned his eyes to the road and put the car in gear. "You say take you, I take you. Your money, your hides."

He stepped on the gas, spewed enough smoke from his tailpipe to kill a flock of birds, and we were off.

One thing's for sure, Jamaica is a beautiful island. It's got all these natural bays with clear blue water and white sand beaches—but if you have the guts to take your eyes away from the spectacular views, you see other stuff. Outside of the tourist zones there's so much poverty, it's hard to look at. I saw some kids playing in the street with a peeling, scuffed soccer ball that, in the US, would have been thrown out a long time ago. I had half a dozen balls in better condition in my garage. It made me feel kinda guilty to be complaining about my lost luggage when the stuff that I lost was probably more than these people even had.

The windows were rolled open, but the breeze did little

to ease the oppressive heat and humidity. Exhaust from passing cars spilled into the window—it wasn't just this car that had issues. At first, the cabbie whistled pleasantly as we rode through the busy streets of Kingston, but after a while, he stopped.

We turned down a rough road with much less traffic that led us away from the city. The road disappeared beneath the rain forest canopy.

"Everybody got good places and bad places where they live," the cabbie said as we wound deeper and deeper into the island. "But dis place where you're going, it's where you end up when you drop through de bottom of all de other places. Dis place, they call 'Hello-Hello.'"

"That doesn't sound too bad," I said.

"It means 'Hell of Hells.'"

We hit a pothole and the car took a nasty bounce. We would have lost a hubcap if the taxi had any hubcaps to lose.

"You two sure about dis?" the cabbie asked again.

"Yes," I told him. Then I looked at Tilde just to make sure she still wanted to go through with this, whatever it was. She nodded at me. I leaned over to her and whispered, "Whatever this is about, is it worth it?"

"Ten times worth it," she said.

"Okay," I said. "I believe you."

After about an hour, with nothing but winding roads and forests, we came to a crumbling village. I turned to Tilde, and I could see fear in her, *real* fear, and I realized that maybe she had told the truth yesterday. Maybe she *did* need me to feel safe, but who was going to make *me* feel safe?

There weren't many buildings. It wasn't much of a town. Most of the structures seemed to be made of parts of other things. A stone wall that was part of the foundation of an earlier building. Corrugated steel roofs covered with rust. Peeling doors that didn't quite fit into their doorframes. There were no children playing soccer here. No children anywhere. What few people I saw on the unpaved street seemed bone thin and ready for the town graveyard—which, by the way, looked a lot like the one we set up on our lawn for Halloween. Welcome to Hello-Hello.

The cabbie stopped the taxi but kept the engine running. "You pay for both ways now."

Tilde opened her bag, reaching in, and I saw a whole lot of green in there. As I suspected, it was a bag full of cash. I stopped her before she could pull any money out. "No," I told the driver. "We pay you when we get back to Kingston."

He wasn't happy about that but accepted it. "Fine, fine. But I see anyting I don't like, I'm gone. I don't need your money dat much."

The hairs on my neck started to bristle. If this place could scare a Jamaican cabbie, should I be scared, too? What kind of people, I wondered, would choose to live in a place known as the Hell of Hells, and why, in both hells, did Tilde want to go here?

We got out of the taxi, and Tilde looked toward a crumbling cinder-block bar. There were four guys out front who looked so shady, together they could form an eclipse.

"Wait for me here," Tilde said.

"Don't be dumb—I'm coming with you."

101

"No," she said. "I was told to come alone . . . and besides, you have to make sure the taxi doesn't leave us here."

"Yeah, that would be bad." I didn't even want to imagine being stranded here and having to spend quality time with the residents of Hello-Hello.

"But if you hear me scream," Tilde said, "come after me." Then she took a deep breath as if she was going underwater and strode toward the bar, ignoring the stares from the eclipsers. She pushed her way through the lopsided swinging door, and it swung shut behind her with an irritated creak.

I moved around to stand in front of the taxi so that the cabbie couldn't leave without running me over. Then I dared to look around.

There was an old, suspicious-looking woman slowly rocking on her porch, and in the next house over, a man peered out of a dark doorway, staring at me.

"You from the ships, then?" he asked, after about a minute of staring.

"Maybe," I answered.

"You got money?" he asked.

"Maybe," I answered.

And out of the darkness he gestured with his hand. "Come on in here; I'll show you what I got to sell."

"Leave da boy alone!" shouted the cabbie, suddenly all protective, like maybe he felt guilty for thinking of abandoning us here.

The man in the dark doorway pointed a bony finger at the cabbie like he was leveling a curse. "Not your business."

102

Then the cabbie turned to me. "Don't you go over dere, hear me? He ain't got nothing to sell you but misery."

"Yeah, I kind of figured."

For some reason, the old woman on the porch suddenly burst out laughing, and the man pulled back into his dark doorway, swallowed by the shadows of his house.

So now I'm feeling like I'm the first B-movie victim in late night voodoo theater, half expecting some guy with a python around his neck to do a cloudy-eyed dance around me, and I'm wondering if these people even know that they are, by their very existence, perpetuating a cruel stereotype. No wonder the people of Jamaica hate this place.

Now that I had a sense that the cabbie wouldn't ditch us, I marched toward the bar. Tilde had been in there way too long—but as I got close, the cluster of creepy eclipsers lined up like a human wall, blocking my path. They didn't need to speak because the look on their faces said all.

I was trying to decide whether I should batter my way through, thereby losing my miserable life, or try pointlessly to negotiate with them—but before I did either of those things, Tilde came out. I guess the wall of voodoo was like a one-way turnstile, because the creepy dudes allowed her to push through them. Then she grabbed my arm and pulled me back toward the taxi. She was shaking, but I knew better than to ask what had happened. Somehow I could tell she was shaking not because of what happened—but because of all the things that *could* have happened but didn't.

I looked down at the sack she held. It was a plain paper

103

bag but a different shade of brown than the bag she brought in, and it was a little less wrinkled. "Mission accomplished?"

She nodded but didn't utter a word.

"What did we buy?" I asked her.

"It doesn't matter."

"Hey," I told her. "I didn't just do the limbo through Jamaican Mordor to be told it doesn't matter!"

"All right, it matters," she told me. "But it's better if you don't know."

I could have pushed it but decided that this wasn't the time.

We got back into the taxi, and the driver took off even before I had closed the door, practically leaving my left leg behind—but I wasn't complaining. The dust from our wheels rose like a fog behind us, hiding the town as we left, and in a few moments "Hello-Hello" became "Good-bye, Good Riddance." Then Tilde reached over and grabbed my hand, holding it.

"I know this doesn't mean much to you," she said. "But I need it."

I squeezed her hand a little tighter. "It means a lot. I don't mind."

Maybe it was just my imagination, but the farther away we got, the less oppressive the heavy Caribbean air felt. The cabbie made chitchat, asking where we were from. I told him we were from California, and my name was Enzo Benini. That made Tilde smile. Soon the cabbie began to whistle again, and Tilde fell asleep with her head on my shoulder.

It seemed to take us no time to get back to Kingston.

Tilde jolted awake when the cab stopped, and we got out across the street from the cruise port. I gave the cabbie a good tip, or at least what I thought was a good tip, then, when I turned to look for Tilde, she was already gone. The cabbie gave a deep belly laugh.

"Your cutie is a handful and a half," he said. "You better not be nitro, 'cause she's a whole lot of glycerin."

I walked back to the ship alone. No one was in our suite when I got there. My family was still on their deluxe city tour and snorkel extravaganza, and Lexie was probably out charming her way to dinner at the Captain's Table. I could hear Crawley snoring next door so loudly, I was afraid a giant squid might attack the ship, thinking it heard its mating call.

I took a long shower, trying to wash away the memory of Hello-Hello, but no matter how much I scrubbed, there was one thing I couldn't send swirling down the drain.

Tilde's bag.

She had clutched it tightly on the taxi ride back to the ship, but she had also fallen asleep long enough for me to get a glimpse inside. I know what I had seen, but I didn't want to think about it. There's that expression about letting sleeping dogs lie, but like most expressions, it's got a hidden flaw. Because no matter what you do, the dog is eventually gonna wake up and demand to be taken for a walk at like five in the morning or relieve itself on your new living room carpet—which by the way, can never truly be cleaned on account of it gets right into the floorboards and delivers its aromatic gifts for many dog years after Fido has gone off to dog heaven. In other words, when it comes to sleeping dogs, letting them lie just postpones the inevitable. I couldn't avoid it: In the end I had to consider what I had seen in that bag and what it might mean.

Tilde had taken a bag full of stolen money . . . and she had exchanged it for a bag full of counterfeit passports.

CHAPTER 9

IS THAT A PASSPORT IN YOUR LEDERHOSEN, OR ARE YOU JUST HAPPY TO NOT SEE ME?

I HAVE A STUDENT ID. MY PICTURE STINKS. I DID that on purpose because there's nothing worse than a bad ID pic that looks bad by accident. Instead, it pays to take a meaningfully awful picture, twisting your face just a little bit so that the photographer, who doesn't care anyway, can't tell you're making a face because he doesn't know your real face from a hole in the wall, and maybe those buggy eyes and crooked smile are the result of unfortunate genetics or just because you're saying "cheese" with too much conviction. So now, when your friends look at the goofy picture on your ID and laugh, they'll be truly laughing *with* you instead of *at* you. Unless, of course, you're Mary Ellen McCaw, whose student IDs are always out of focus because her nose messes with the depth of field, leaving the camera convinced that there's got to be a second object in the picture, thus creating the kind of 3-D effect you need special glasses for.

Anyway, your ID represents you in all official ways. It gets you into school dances, it gets your grades, and it proves to the Attendance Nazi, that yes, you truly are present after you've been absent. Without it, you're a nonentity.

107

Eventually, that student ID evolves into a driver's license, which allows you a whole lot of other privileges as well as the supreme pleasure of speeding tickets and identity theft.

Passports are like ID cards on steroids. When I was younger, I always thought passports were mysterious documents that James Bond had in various different colors and with various fake names, like a magic ticket to get you in and out of anyplace in the world. Funny thing is, that's *exactly* what they are. A passport ties you to a place of origin, but by doing so it also allows you to go elsewhere, too. Of course, most of the time I don't know if I'm coming or going—but that doesn't matter, because I've got a passport. As long as your paperwork is in order, you can be clueless just about anywhere. I've never been to Japan, but I know if I wanted to and had enough money to buy a ticket, I could go. I've never been to France, but there are these study abroad programs I could sign up for if I wanted to. Once you've got a passport, you're free to roam the world.

But since we can, lots of times we don't.

It's like those movies in our movie collections. Why do we buy them? Because we love them—but then once we own them, we never look at the freaking things. So you got yourself a wall full of movies you take for granted, until you realize one of them was borrowed by your neighbor, who just moved to Armpit Fart, Indiana, and now that you know it's gone for good, that's the one movie you suddenly want to watch.

There are people who string together inner tubes and risk their lives to float to America. There are people who cross the border, sometimes disappearing in the deserts of New Mexico and Arizona, leaving nothing behind but bleached bones with no way to identify who they once were. These are people who not only don't own the movies, but they never even got to *see* the movies. Sure, they heard about them, and with that kind of word of mouth, they want, more than anything, to have a piece of the movies that you own but don't watch—even if it means going to Indiana to get it.

I was officially leading a double life now. Antsy Bonano, the regular kind of guy who got into just enough trouble to give the people who loved him indigestion, and Enzo Benini, international criminal—and not even criminal mastermind—no—just the underling of some misguided but intense stowaway girl with eyes that sucked you in like tractor beams.

This was undiscovered territory for me, on account of I'm not a follower. I'm the kind of guy who laughs at people who go around clinging to someone else, letting them call all the shots. I don't follow trends, and if some bozo at school develops an entourage, like Wendell Tiggor, whose cluster of Tiggorhoids swarm around him like flies around a warm summer turd, I march myself in the other direction. I learned early on that the kind of people who want followers got no business having them, and the kind of imbeciles who follow them got issues you don't want to know about.

So naturally, I was not prepared to find myself a follower when it came to Tilde. It was both scary and kind of fun to close my eyes and let go of the wheel.

Except that my eyes weren't entirely closed. I knew what I was doing, even if I wasn't willing to admit that to myself.

Jamaica was history. We were sailing away, and now it was nothing but pretty lights on a twilight horizon, separating the sky from the sea. I was beginning to think that Tilde was done with me or maybe she got caught when she tried to get back on the ship. I was worried about her and worried that maybe she was just using me, and now that she got what she wanted out of me, I'd never see her again.

So what? I kept trying to tell myself. So what if she just needed me for support when she made her trek into Hello-Hello. So what if I never saw her again? I'd probably be better off, right? And then on the other hand, what if *I* was the one using *her*? Using her to break out of my own comfort zone. I didn't deny that as dangerous as today seemed, it was exciting. Everything about our secret activities was charged up, and now I was hooked on my own adrenaline. The problem with adrenaline junkies, though, is that it takes more and more to get your heart racing. What starts as bungee jumping becomes skydiving, becomes base jumping, becomes a nasty red splat on the side of a mountain.

I was getting much better at keeping up pretenses. Not even Lexie could sense something was off about me. Of course that might have been because something was off about her. Ever since her crying jag, it seemed as if her radar for other people's business had been turned off.

We regrouped at dinner, and everyone told of their adventures. Howie, who had cut all of his jeans into

110

short-shorts, following the lead of Lance the youth counselor, claimed to have had a regular survivalist adventure. He snorkeled a little too close to the reef and got washed against some coral, which scraped up his arm. "It was a violent sea!" he insisted, with wide scary-story eyes and I swear a faint Australian accent. "The reef came out of nowhere. Suddenly it was there, and there was nothing I could do." To hear him tell it, you'd think he was attacked by a great white.

Christina's snorkeling experience was less dramatic. "I found Nemo," she told me. "Like fourteen thousand times."

My mother glared at her and told her she sounded like me. These are moments that make a brother proud.

"It was fun," my father said, "but the highlight of our trip will be in Cozumel, when we explore the Mayan ruins in Tulum!" Which was something he'd been talking about since he found out where the ship was going.

Lexie, who spent much of the day wrapped in seaweed, said she felt "reasonably detoxified," whatever that meant.

"How about you, Antsy?" my dad asked.

"I did nothing," I told him convincingly. "I laid around and did nothing, and it was the best day ever."

"How is that different from any other day?" my mom asked. I didn't answer her because my mom didn't really expect an answer. It's what you call a rhetorical insult.

As we left dinner, Lexie asked me to accompany her to the teen lounge. She didn't need me to—she had Moxie and knew the way there by heart already, but she asked anyway. "You don't have to stay," she said. "In fact, I would prefer if you didn't. I just want to arrive with you."

111

After we were away from my family, I thought she would ask me what I really did today—and if she asked, I would have told her—or at least part of it. I was dying to confess to someone. I mean, confession is genetic in my family. I needed someone to talk some sense into me so I could spend the rest of the cruise playing bingo, and tanning, and trying to surf the wave pool like a normal person instead of building the prosecution's case for a life sentence.

But she didn't ask. So I didn't tell. And she didn't talk about her parents, either—but I knew it was on her mind, maybe with a whole lot of other things I didn't know about. I had seen the way she threw that flute, like she was trying to get rid of something she couldn't stand anymore—but it wasn't something she could throw away that easily. She had said the seaweed wrap detoxified her, but there were still some dangerous toxins down there that no amount of seaweed could purge.

The teen lounge was intentionally retro but in a psychotic sort of way. One wall looked like a fifties diner, another area had sixties psychedelic beanbags beside floor-to-ceiling Lava lamps, and another section had a dark alien-industrial feel to it, complete with animatronic leather eggs that opened up to reveal slimy stuff inside.

Kids seemed to gravitate toward the corner that best suited their personalities. Hanging right at the border between Alien Creep Alley and Electric Kool-Aid Corner was a group of tall kids in muscle shirts, with haircuts that were just a little too short in some places and a little too long in others—a dead giveaway that they were European. The tallest of the three saw us and came over. I recognized him from somewhere but wasn't sure from where.

"Lexie!" he said.

"Antsy, this is Gustav. Gustav, this is Antsy."

Gustav grabbed my hand and firmly shook it. I wasn't expecting such a firm shake, so the bones in my hand kind of ground together.

"Hey," I said.

"Gustav doesn't speak much English."

Gustav smiled apologetically, but even with a pleasant smile, there was something that bugged me about him.

"Where is he from and why?" I asked.

"Gustav hails from Switzerland." Lexie patted him on a shirt that was irritatingly tight on his well-developed chest. They give chickens hormones to make them have chests like that.

Suddenly I realized where I had seen him before. This was the guy who offered to ride the roller coaster with Lexie when I had refused a second ride. I hadn't really noticed much about him or cared, because I was too busy fighting lobster Armageddon in my stomach at the time. Were Lexie and Gustav becoming more than just strangers on a train? Should I care?

"Zurich!" Gustav said. "I live Zurich!" Then mumbled something unintelligible to me in German, which I guess is what they speak in Switzerland. He knelt down to pet Moxie, talking to him in German, too, which I think freaked Moxie out, because he gave Gustav an "Are you talkin' to me?" look.

"Just...soon...minute," Gustav said. He gently touched Lexie's chin, then went back to his friends for a moment.

"Gustav and I have been spending time together," Lexie said. "He is the epitome of European chivalry. He's got good bone structure and a remarkable fat-to-muscle ratio." I didn't even want to consider how she knew that. "I feel like I can say anything to him."

"Yeah, but he can't understand you. It's like talking to a wall with chest hair."

"Exactly," she said. "What could be better?"

Meanwhile, Gustav stood leaning against a Lava lamp, talking to his friends in German. All three of them glanced our way and laughed.

Then Lexie leaned in and whispered to me, "Gustav thinks I can't understand German, but I can. Right now he's betting his friends that he'll have his way with me by the end of the cruise."

"What?" I clenched my hands into fists, ready to go over there and take a piece out of him. So what if he had more muscles in his neck than I had in my entire body. I'd get a few good punches in before he put me in the ship's infirmary—and then maybe by beating the living daylights out of me, he'd get thrown into the brig for the rest of the cruise.

Lexie squeezed my wrist, forcing my fist to open. "Don't," she said.

"Aren't you gonna smack him? 'Cause if you don't, I will."

Then Lexie said, "How do you know it's not what I want?"

I found myself opening my mouth to say something, but

I might as well have been trying to speak German because no words came out in either language.

"And," Lexie added, "how do you know *I'm* not the one using *him*?"

Finally, I found my words. "Lexie, you can't. I won't let you."

And she suddenly got bitter. I mean, weirdly so. "What are you going to do, Antsy? Tell my parents? Oh, that's right—they're not here, are they?"

"I'll tell your grandfather."

"Grandpa won't even leave the suite. What is he going to do?"

This was definitely not like Lexie. I looked over at Gustav, who gave me a muscular wave.

"This guy is international bad news. You can't see that— but I'm looking right at him, and I can!"

"Maybe I can't see him, but I can feel him, I can smell him, and—"

"Stop right there," I told her. "I don't want Gustav in any more of my senses or I'm gonna hurl all over one of those alien eggs."

Gustav came back over. He smiled at me with false politeness and touched Lexie's chin again to let her know he was back.

"It's my life, and I can take care of myself," Lexie told me. "And if there's a problem, I have Moxie to protect me."

Gustav just looked at us, oblivious. "Go now, Lexie? Dance with fun?"

I stood there watching as they left together, Gustav so

115

proper with the way he strode arm in arm with her. I was powerless to do anything about it. Lexie was right: This was her life and she had the right to make her own choices, even the bad ones. But wasn't it my job to protect her from herself? And if I couldn't figure out a way to do that, did that make me a lousy friend? Then I thought about Tilde's bag of passports, and my brain blew out like a transformer. On the one hand, I'm dealing with screwed-up everyday ordinary stuff, like my friend suddenly racing headlong down a path of self-destruction, while on the other hand, I'm dealing with screwed-up stuff that gets people killed by death squads in certain parts of the world.

"You want to order something?"

"Huh?" Then I realized I was sitting on a little red rotating stool in the fifties diner area, which was apparently a real fifties diner.

"Yeah," I said, "gimme a chocolate shake. No, make that two. No, make that three."

Then I spun myself in circles until I was so dizzy I couldn't drink any of them.

CHAPTER 10

ATLAS HURLED, AND AYN RAND AIN'T CLEANING IT UP

I'M VERY GOOD AT PRETENDING I DON'T CARE, BUT when it comes down to it, I do and it ticks me off. Why do I always, deep down, feel responsible for the people around me? For instance: Every time I see my dad eat something I know isn't good for him, I think it'll be my fault if he has another heart attack, because I didn't say something about it. Or how about when my sister picks the most sarcastic, unpleasant girls in her middle school to hang out with; I think it's my responsibility to make them unwelcome in our house, because if I don't, what if she becomes just like them? Would that be my fault?

"It's called a martyr complex," Ira once told me. "Since you're Catholic, you should probably ask yourself the Jesus question. You know, 'What would Jesus do?' And then decide based on your conclusion."

Well, I know what Jesus would do. He would suffer for everyone else's sins. So basically asking the WWJD question just makes a martyr complex worse. Believe me, I got enough of my own sins to suffer for; I don't need everyone else's.

· · ·

I wanted to talk to Tilde. I wanted an explanation about those passports—but who was I kidding? No explanation would have made me feel any better. So although I looked for her, I didn't do a good job of it. I didn't use the passkey she gave me to get into Bernie and Lulu's room, because I didn't want to find her in the lifeboat laying out the passports next to all that stockpiled food. I didn't sneak belowdecks to get into the Viking ship chamber. I didn't know the combination to get in anyway.

Instead, I went back to our suites to find Old Man Crawley having a late dinner all by himself again. Very suddenly and very unexpectedly, I wanted to keep him company, like maybe I was feeling almost as alone as him.

When I asked if I could join him, he looked at me like I must be pulling some kind of trick. Then he finally said, "Pull up a chair."

I sat down and looked at the spread of food. It was way too much for one man to eat. He had taken bites of several things, like the entire room service menu was his own personal box of chocolates.

"You can have whatever you like except for the crème brûlée. Touch that, and I pin your hand to the table with my steak knife."

I wasn't hungry, since I had already eaten a full meal, but I picked at a plate of fettuccini anyway, and started eating it.

"If you're here because you're feeling sorry for me, you can leave," Crawley said.

"Nah," I told him. "I got done feeling sorry for you

118

years ago. Right now, it's more like I'm feeling sorry for myself."

"That's even worse."

"Yeah, I know." I sucked in some fettuccini, then said, "Maybe not feeling sorry for myself, but dealing with too much stuff in my head. And since I know you couldn't care less, being here seems like the best place to be right now. Low pressure, y'know?"

The idea that dining with Crawley was a low-pressure experience almost made me laugh. I guess everything is relative.

Crawley ate an extremely rare prime rib without speaking for a while, then he looked at me as I continued to stuff my face. Somehow I managed to down the entire plate of fettuccini in like five minutes.

I'm not good with long silences, so once my mouth was done chewing, I started to talk but maybe got a little too revealing for comfort. Crawley was a man you didn't want to reveal anything to, since he could always find a way to use it against you at a later date, but I just couldn't shut myself up.

"Do you ever find yourself in a situation where all your choices suck, and there's nothing you can do about it?" I asked him.

"Yes," Crawley said. "It's called politics."

"Right," I said. "But I mean your personal choices."

"So do I." Crawley held up his fork and waved it as he spoke like it was a magic wand with meat stuck on the end. "Did you know I once ran for mayor of New York?"

"You're kidding, right?"

He glared at me. "You find it hard to believe I was once an idealistic imbecile like you?"

"No," I told him. "I find it hard to believe you'd get out long enough to run around the block, let alone run for office."

He shook his head slowly. "I so despise your impertinence."

"No," I reminded him. "You love it."

He weighed the idea, and the hint of a smile showed behind his perpetual frown. "I love despising it; there's a difference." He blotted his mouth with his napkin and continued. "The agoraphobia came later—but in my youth, I was foolish enough to think I could change the world, or at least the city. I thought I could fix things with an honest hand, telling people what they *needed* to hear, not what they *wanted* to hear."

He leaned back, thinking about a political campaign that went on long before I was born. "'You want strong unions and high wages?' I told people. 'Fine, then you have to be willing to pay a lot more for services. You want lower taxes and less government?' I told them. 'Fine—but you better be willing to live with lousy public schools and even longer lines at the DMV.' I painted for everyone–the left and the right—the best picture I could of the consequences of their choices."

"Did you win?"

Crawley shoved a miniature potato into his mouth and ground it down to nothing. "Of course not. The guy that told people what they wanted to hear won, and for the next four years the city went to hell in a handcart."

"Sorry," I said.

Crawley started in on his crème brûlée. "I wasn't. Because I learned a valuable lesson: Don't waste your breath on others because they will always disappoint you. Take care of yourself. And that's exactly what I did. I became a model of rational self-interest. Ayn Rand would have been proud!"

"Ann who?"

"She wrote *Atlas Shrugged*. Look it up."

"Not gonna happen."

"I'm not surprised. At any rate, my decision to invest in myself made me obscenely rich, and my success became my revenge."

"Revenge against who?" I had to ask.

"Everybody," he said, like it was obvious.

Crawley was always saying bitter stuff like this. It usually didn't bother me, but today I was feeling unsettled in more ways than one.

"Yeah, but what did all that money get you?" I asked. "Sure, you're rich, but you've gotta throw your own birthday party, because no one else will—and you have to make people come. And even then, you're sitting here all by yourself."

"Not by myself," he said, and then he leveled his spoon at me. "You're here."

Whether it was the conversation or the stuff in my head or spinning circles on the teen lounge bar stool, whatever the reason, I felt both my dinners deciding that they could do better than sit in my stomach and saw their golden opportunity for a grand exit.

It happened so quickly I didn't even have time to excuse

121

myself. I got up and raced to the bathroom, trying to push the door open and realizing a second too late that I needed to pull, not push. I only got the door halfway open before everything I ate over the past few hours came out the way it came in.

There are lots of cute euphemisms for puking your guts out—y'know, like "tossing your cookies"—but this was no cookie toss, let me tell you. It was more like when they yell *"Pull!"* at a skeet shoot. It was more like the Olympic discus throw, and this was a world record hurl.

I'd like to say it was, at least, in the general direction of the toilet, but the toilet was the only part of the bathroom spared. And it just kept on coming, wave after wave. Too much information, I know, but I'm all about sharing.

I was on my knees now. My vision was filled with black spots, because I hadn't been able to breathe for the longest time. Finally, when I stopped retching and began to catch my breath, I saw Crawley standing in the doorway behind me holding his cane and giving me a look. It wasn't the usual look. This was one I didn't know. I was ready to be cursed at and yelled at and told what a waste of biological material I was. But instead Crawley stepped in and handed me his glass of Perrier.

"Here," he said, "the carbonation will help settle your stomach."

"Sorry, Mr. Crawley," I said, still gasping for breath. "I'll clean it up, I promise."

"Don't be ridiculous. That's why we have concierge service." And he called for the suite attendant, while I did my best to clean myself up, at least.

"Now we're even," he said as I came out of the bathroom, putting his hand on his hip to remind me what he meant.

"Yeah, I suppose so."

Two years ago, he had fallen in his bathroom, almost breaking his hip. He was helpless and hated the fact that he was. Yet no matter how much he screamed and cursed at me, I still helped him. I had shown compassion, and he was furious—not because I had shown it, but because he had needed it.

The cabin attendant came, saw the mess, and called for an assistant because this was a two-man job. They made the place spotless and even sprayed some magic deodorizer so you couldn't even tell it happened. To my surprise, Crawley tipped the two suite attendants generously. "Less money for my son when I die," he told me.

I lay sprawled on the sofa, afraid to move for fear that some stray crouton that got left behind might suddenly want out, too.

"Thank you, Anthony," Crawley said to me after the attendants had left. "Thank you for the most entertaining evening I've spent on this cruise."

"You're welcome, I guess."

Once I felt I could stand without my legs giving out, I went back through the adjoining doorway to my own suite, which was still empty because everyone else was out having a good time. As I left, it occurred to me that what goes around really does come around. The compassion I showed Crawley two years ago had returned to me. I mean sure, in the moment, Crawley talked proudly about looking out for number one, but when it came down to it, it was kindness and generosity toward others that put some occasional joy in his life. He just needed a good excuse to show it.

And it also occurred to me how easy it was to overthrow life's most bitter lessons with just a little bit of compassion.

I will admit Old Man Crawley's advice on selfishness was very sound, if you wanted to end up like Old Man Crawley. I didn't. And I didn't think that was why Crawley liked to have me around. See, I was like his human Rubik's cube. No matter how predictable he said I was, he still couldn't solve me no matter how much he twisted me around. I was never afraid to tell him what I really thought, and sometimes what I thought was more on target than his philosophy.

"You have common grace," he once told me. "Accidental insight. And God help us all if you ever realize you're not as stupid as you think you are." He had only said that to me once. I think that telling me I wasn't as stupid as I thought was the closest thing to a compliment he ever gave me. I held on to that and brought it out on those occasions when I felt seriously dense.

I'm not as dumb as I think I am.

But if that's the case, why do I end up in such obnoxious situations?

After losing both my dinners, I went up to the highest point of the ship. It had to be close to midnight now, but the ship was still alive with activity. Way up here, though, I felt a little separated from it all. Above it all, in a very literal sense. The spot was a little outdoor sundeck wedged between the two giant spherical radar antennae that someone brilliant had painted to look like golf balls. I swear, they put lounge chairs everywhere on cruise ships, because any spot that got direct sunlight was a prime ray-soaking zone.

There were about a dozen lounge chairs on this little deck—totally empty except for a couple who were all over each other. I looked at them just long enough to determine that they were not Lexie and Gustav. Beyond that, I had no interest in them. They, however, seemed a little embarrassed to have me lying out on a lounge chair just a few chairs over from theirs.

"Do you mind?" they asked. "We were here first."

"Like I give a flying gerbil's butt," I told them.

Eventually they took their saliva wars somewhere else, leaving me alone with my thoughts.

My first thought was how great it would be to bring Tilde up here and do the exact same thing with her that the fluid-exchanging couple had been doing. It irked me that my thoughts went immediately there. People always say guys only have one thing on their mind. That's not exactly true. It's just that the "one thing" doesn't move out of the way for other thoughts. It's like a giant boulder in a river that everything else gotta go around.

My second thought was that maybe for just this week, I could take Crawley's advice and be small-minded enough to selfishly enjoy the cruise. I could forget about everything, hang out with Howie, and find ourselves a clique among the many other kids on board, being a blissful ignoramus until it was time to go home.

My third thought was how my second thought was making me want to throw up again. I'm very skilled when it comes to making things harder on myself.

"Aren't you cold without a jacket, Enzo?"

Very rarely am I caught completely off guard, but hearing Tilde's voice so close to me—and so close to the things I had just been secretly thinking about her—made me jump. The lounge chair fell back from the sitting-up position to the reclining position with a loud clatter, leaving me flat on my back. I lay there without moving as if I meant to do that.

"It's the Caribbean," I told her. "It's like ninety million degrees, even at night. Why would I need a jacket?"

"Because it's chilly in the wind, isn't it?"

And now that I thought about it, she was right. I was relieved that she didn't get arrested in Jamaica but angry that she was involving me in something that left me in way over my head.

"Thanks for your help today," she finally said.

I shrugged. "I didn't do anything. That's what I'm telling *you*, and that's what I'm telling the police."

"Are you going to turn me in, then?" she asked. She didn't say it pleadingly or like she was worried. She asked it calmly.

"I'll make you a deal," I told her. "If you leave me alone for the rest of the cruise, I won't say a thing." I could have left it right there, but my big mouth had other ideas. "But first you have to tell me what those passports are for. I have a right to know."

"You probably already guessed what they're for."

126

"I want to hear you say it."

"Why? Are you recording it?"

"Are you really that paranoid?"

She sighed. "I've been smuggling people into the United States."

"So, you're a coyote? That's what they call people like you, right?"

She looked at me like I had punched her in the stomach. "Coyotes do it for money—a lot of money. They take every penny they can from desperate people, and they don't even care what happens to them. But I don't charge people anything. I'm not making any money from this."

"Then why do you do it?"

"Because I can," she said.

"So who do you take? Criminals? Escaped prisoners?"

"No," she said calmly, and without any of the judgment my voice held. "I pick people who need to go."

She told me how she would make arrangements each week when the ship stopped in Cozumel, Mexico. She would smuggle one person on board and hide that person in her lifeboat.

"But it was only barely working—because I could get them on the ship, but I couldn't get them off. US Customs has the cruise port very secure . . . so they all had to leave the ship before it was docked."

"You mean . . ."

She nodded before I could finish the thought.

"They'd have to jump before we pulled into port. They would leap into the water just off the Miami shore, and I would never see them again. I would never know if they lived or if they drowned because of me."

And then something occurred to me, something I had pushed out of my mind since the beginning of the cruise. Someone jumping from the ship . . .

"This last time was the worst," Tilde said. "This man— he was too scared to jump until long after we were in port. Finally he got up the courage and jumped from the lifeboat. I couldn't bear to watch. He landed on the concrete, fifteen decks below. He died. Because of me."

I reached out and touched her hand, forcing her to look me in the eye.

"No, he didn't. I saw him fall, and he didn't hit the concrete. He fell between the ship and the dock."

She looked at me as if I'd just given her a new lease on life.

"You saw him?"

I nodded.

She took a deep breath and then let it out. It was filled both with relief and with a little bit of fear. "If you saw him, I'm sure you were not the only one. I'm sure he was caught by port security."

"No," I said. "Here's the thing: I went down to tell security what I saw, but no one believed me. I never saw him floating facedown in the water, so he must have gotten away."

Tilde closed her eyes and breathed slowly, still holding my hand. The Caribbean breeze tossed her hair this way and that. I wanted to reach out and brush her hair away from her face just so I could feel her hair in my fingers, but I didn't let myself do it.

"We won't have to worry about that again," she said. "Now we have authentic-looking passports, complete with a real microchip. Now we can slip people right past security, as long as they don't give themselves away."

It occurred to me that she was saying "we," and I didn't like that at all. It made me think again about Crawley's philosophy of self. *Me*, not *we*. Especially when "we" means being part of a criminal conspiracy.

"I think," Tilde said, "that you and I are bound together. I think there is meaning to these things. Do you believe in fate?"

"No."

"Do you believe in destiny?"

"No."

"You're lying."

"So what?" I told her, getting angry at all the conflicting feelings inside of me. "All you do is lie. Lie, and cheat, and steal. Why should I be a part of that?"

She grimaced, an expression I wasn't expecting. "Seven days," she said.

"What about it?"

"These cruises last for one week. Which means I have no friendships that last more than seven days. People get on the ship, and they get off. I never see them again."

And then something occurred to me. Something that made me feel . . . well . . . cheap.

"You have an accomplice on every cruise, don't you? You suck some poor bozo in and use them to help you."

She didn't deny it, yet still she held my hand. I pulled it back.

"Just to help me get money," she said. "I needed help breaking into cabins and getting enough money to buy those fake passports. But those other boys—they never knew what the money was for. They just thought I was a stowaway stealing money. They never knew about the secret people I brought on board. You're the first one to know the whole story."

"But those others boys—you took them to your secret lifeboat, didn't you? And you let them kiss you and hold you and whatever else you let them do. You let them do it just so they'll steal for you!" I was beginning to feel sick all over again.

"Yes," she said gently. "But it's different with you," she insisted. I could see tears in her eyes now. Maybe not like big Lexie tears, but tears all the same. But at this moment, I had absolutely no sympathy.

"You didn't want what the other boys did, but still you helped me . . . and it made me want you even more. I think I'm in love with you, Enzo. I know it can never be, you being who you are, but I think I'm in love with you. Isn't that crazy?"

I heard her words, but still I felt betrayed. "You'll say anything to get me to help you."

"Yes, I probably would," she admitted, "but now I'm telling the truth." And I believed her. She didn't have to lie, because the truth was so much more compelling, screaming so much louder than any lie could. The fact that she was so honest about her ability to lie just confused me even more. As for my feelings, I couldn't even tell what they were now.

They were all jumbled together and the only feeling I could pull out of that mess was a kind of dull anger that had no focus or direction. It shone its sorry light evenly on her, me, on the deck around us, on the whole stinking ship. Is this what Crawley feels? I wondered. A low-grade fever against the entire world? Is that how you protect yourself from feeling anything else?

I asked her something then. It was both a test and maybe even an accusation. Whatever it was, I felt I had the absolute right to ask it of her.

"If you love me," I said, very slowly, "then say . . . my . . . name."

She couldn't look at me. She just pursed her lips and scrunched her eyes closed like a little kid playing hide-and-seek. I knew there was pain behind it that I couldn't understand, and the fact that I didn't understand it made me more insistent that she pass my test. She knew my true name. She knew it from the beginning. I waited, but still she wouldn't say it, and I didn't know why. All I knew was that she had failed the test.

I stood up, leaving her there.

"Until you can say my name," I told her, "I don't want anything to do with you."

Because I knew it wasn't me that she loved; it was Enzo. And I was not Enzo.

My head swam that night as I tried to go to sleep. I still had no luggage, none of my familiar stuff; I had one friend who wanted to surrender to the not-so-neutral nation of Switzerland and a wild stowaway girl who was paving my personal path to hell with her good but fairly insane intentions. All I wanted to do at that moment was escape. I mean, isn't that the whole point of a cruise, trying to move fast enough to leave all your troubles behind? I never expected an "all-inclusive" vacation to also include its own troubles.

"I love you, Enzo," Tilde had said, and hearing that should have made me feel good, but instead it just made me angry, because the boy she thought she loved didn't exist.

Finally, the rocking of the ship put me to sleep, and the last thought I had before dozing off was that in the morning, I'd somehow make my escape from Tilde real.

CHAPTER 11

I'M AN ASS ON A HORSE TRAIL WITH OATMEAL IN MY SHOES

ESCAPE MEANS A LOT OF THINGS TO A LOT OF PEOPLE.

I heard about this guy who was so caught up in a dead-end life, he was ready to off himself. A bitter marriage, debt up to his eyeballs, hateful relatives, and a job he couldn't stand. So he leaves for work one morning, but he doesn't go to work. Instead he goes to a coffee shop to write a suicide note. Only he never finishes it, because the day just happens to be September 11, 2001—and I'll give you one guess where he worked. So what was, for everyone else, the most horrific tragedy in the nation's history became the answer to all his prayers.

With everyone thinking he was dead, he ran off to South America and started a whole new life and even had a new family. No one stateside knew he was alive for ten years, and it could have stayed that way if he hadn't tried to contact one of his old friends, who freaked when he got a phone call from the dead.

On the one hand, it was a horrible, selfish thing to do. But on the other, if he was gonna kill himself otherwise, can you blame him? So now he's in prison on like fourteen thousand counts of fraud—but in spite of it, he still seemed kinda happy and content in his *Sixty Minutes* interview.

That is not the extreme kind of escape I was talking about, but I did find myself busting into survival mode. There comes a point at which we all kick into survival mode. It's a natural fact of evolution—and evolution is all about dealing with extreme stress. Like when a comet comes and blows the hell out of the planet, who do you think survives? It's the various species that figure out how to adapt to a worst-case scenario. Those are the animals that get to serve their genetic soup to the next generation. And other species? It's like, "No soup for you!" and they go extinct.

So here I am, looking at a comet named Tilde who's barreling toward my world, about to kill off all my dinosaurs, and I decide it's time to embrace my inner Crawley and totally cut her off. Selfish? Maybe. But I think there's a difference between selfishness and self-preservation.

The next morning we awoke already docked in Grand Cayman—another Caribbean paradise—and I was determined to blast everything out of my mind and survive. More than survive, I was going to enjoy myself, and I knew exactly how to do it. It was time for Crawley's birthday kidnapping!

See, Crawley expected me and Lexie to abduct him on a regular basis and force him to do some thrilling activity that would make him scream and curse and threaten to have us arrested. This was his way of getting around his agoraphobia. Lexie and I had masterminded some great excursions for him, and I took great pleasure in watching him scream his way through them. There was the zip line through Prospect Park at sixty miles an hour and the ride aboard NASA's nose-diving cargo jet that simulates weightlessness; there was the death-defying drive through the south Bronx in a convertible.

This time I felt like I owed him something special for what he did for me last night, so I signed him up for the Parasailing Adventure. Parasailing is when they hook you up to a parachute, then pull you behind a speedboat like a human kite and hope you don't die. I figured with so many old people on cruise ships, a cruise line's gotta deal with enough expiring people already, so they're pretty good at not losing the ones that planned to live. In other words, survival odds on these adventure excursions were much better than they looked.

Lexie showed no interest in planning this particular abduction, so I got her a ticket to the dolphin encounter with Christina—my treat, with Crawley's money. Lexie, however, flatly refused to have anything to do with dolphins.

"I have no interest in touching something big and rubbery," she said.

"Really?" I replied. "Don't tell Gustav." (I swear, I could have flown a 747 through that setup.)

She ignored me and said, in a catty tone of voice, "As it so happens, I'm going with Gustav and his friends on the Island ATV Adventure."

"You can't drive an ATV," I reminded her.

"Of course not. I'm riding with Gustav."

"What a great idea," I said, clearly meaning the opposite. "And you won't even need to hold on; you can just Velcro yourself to his back hair."

What I didn't tell her was that my parents had also signed up for the ATV adventure. So whether she liked it or not, they'd be keeping an eye on her.

It was still early, so we had a couple of hours before our shore excursions. Howie dragged me into another search for the ghost of Jorgen Ericsson—this time on the pony trail. "Lance says someone saw him riding a dark, ghostly horse in the early morning light."

"Musta been a jackass," I said, but Howie didn't get it. I hadn't told him about the Viking ship, or anything else having to do with Tilde, and didn't plan to.

The pony trail wound through the higher decks of the ship and doubled as a hiking trail, so we weren't the only ones there. Considering that my head had been feeling so full of horse crap lately, it was the perfect place for me to be.

Howie's enthusiasm for the ghost hunt was tainted by other stuff going on in his head—only some of which I knew about at the time. I chalked his mood up to his unexpected financial crisis. He had been calling everyone in the world from his cell phone while on the ship because he thought it was so cool that his phone worked in the middle of the ocean.

"Howie," I told him, "your cell phone would probably work on Mars—it's all about roaming charges."

He looked at me like I just told him his grandma died. Then, when he checked his account, he had run up $643 in roaming charges. Now he was just kind of dazed, his head wobbling like a slow-motion bobble-head doll in short-shorts. "There's so much stuff that ain't fair, Antsy. And the phone companies just rub it in." I thought he'd go into one of his rants about global communication conspiracies and how Verizon is working on ways to control our minds through text messaging—but he didn't—he just got quiet, which is totally unlike Howie.

Then when we came around a bend, who did I see coming toward us down the path?

Tilde.

Survival mode, I think. *Save my dinosaurs.* I didn't want to talk to her or even devote a single brain cell to what happened last night. Suddenly I got this flash of stupidity disguised as inspiration.

"Quick," I say to Howie. "Hold my hand!"

"Huh?"

"Just do it. Don't ask questions, just do it!" And when he hesitates, I quickly remind him that he owes me more favors than he can ever pay back, but I'll wipe the slate clean if he holds my hand for ten seconds, fifteen, tops.

His head bobbles a little bit more. "Well, okay, I guess."

He takes my hand and our fingers intertwine.

I gotta tell you, it felt profoundly weird—like putting on someone else's shoes and those shoes just happen to be full of oatmeal—and not the instant kind. We're talking the cooked-for-an-hour-by-some-Quaker-dude-with-funny-hair oatmeal.

Tilde passes, making brief eye contact, sees our hands,

137

then continues on with a look on her face that I can't read, but that's okay because whatever the look is, I need to get away from it. In a moment, she's around the bend and out of sight.

In that moment, I realized that I had just broken my own promise to myself. Rather than refusing to act the part of Enzo, I played right into it. It was the one and only time I did, but it was done, and I couldn't take it back. I'm not proud of it, I'm not defending it, but I did it.

"You can let go now," I told Howie.

"Oh yeah, right." He pulled his hand away and looked at it like maybe his hand got splattered with some of the oatmeal in my shoe. Then he stopped walking and looked at me. I mean really looked at me, in a way that Howie never looks at people.

"You know, I'm not stupid," he said.

I took a deep breath, figuring I gotta give him the whole explanation about Tilde from day one—until he said, "There's no way you can get cell service on Mars."

CHAPTER 12

YOU SAY "STALKER"
LIKE IT'S A BAD THING

SINCE THE TEEN LOUNGE WAS CLOSED FOR emergency disinfection (don't ask, I don't know), Howie joined me on my Crawley kidnapping expedition.

"I think I'll enjoy making Crawley suffer for his own good," Howie said. "Other people's misery loves my company."

Once everyone else had left the ship for their shore excursions, I came up behind Crawley and blindfolded him with a fancy room service napkin. Crawley knew the drill. He resisted, complained, but in the end he got into the wheelchair we had brought for him since walking him around blindfolded was not a good idea. Even Moxie—who Lexie had been leaving behind since discovering her new two-legged companion animal—started thumping his tail excitedly when he saw Crawley blindfolded, because he knew it meant something interesting was about to happen. Unfortunately, this was one expedition where Moxie wasn't invited.

By the time we got down the gangway and onto the dock, Crawley was ranting about lax safety regulations in third world countries, still not knowing what sort of maniacal misadventure was ahead. But before we got on the tour bus, he peeked out from beneath his blindfold so he could read and sign the release form telling him what was in store. It proved that all his blustering was just for show.

"If I die, I will return from the grave and make your life a living hell."

"You already do that alive," I told him.

It was after we got seated on the bus that Howie said, "Don't look now, but that girl who's been stalking you just got on the bus."

I snapped my eyes up to see Tilde at the front of the tour bus. She sat down, pretending not to notice me, but I caught her sneaking a quick glance in my direction.

"Stalker? What stalker?" Crawley said. "Take this blindfold off."

I turned to Howie. "What makes you think she's stalking me?" No one had ever accused Howie of being observant. His life was like a long look through the wrong end of cheap binoculars. I don't know what surprised me more, the fact that Tilde was on the bus or that Howie had figured out that she and I had a brief but nutso history.

"How could I not know?" he said. "She's been stalking you since the first day," and he added, "Isn't that what the holding hands thing was all about? To get her to leave you alone?"

Gold star for Howie. Probably his first since kindergarten. "She's not stalking me," I told him.

"No? Then why does she always seem to turn up exactly where you are? Why does she just happen to be on the same shore excursion? Coincidence? I don't think so. Trust me. I've stalked enough people to see the signs."

I could just chalk this up to Howie's paranoia and love of conspiracy theories, but this time he was right on the money. I hadn't even realized it, but Tilde was stalking me. I thought back to last night, when she showed up on the sundeck. She must have followed me there, which meant she had been staking out my suite, which meant she had been tracking my moves for hours.

"Any girl that would stalk *you* needs to have her head examined," Crawley said.

"No argument there," I told him.

"If you like her," Howie said, "maybe you oughta stalk her back."

When I was in sixth grade, our history teacher, in order to force us to learn something about anthropology, had each of us secretly choose one person to "professionally observe," like we were studying the daily life of some weird urban culture. We all became juvenile stalkers. Our assignment was to log all that person's activities, then try to guess that person's habits and what they might be up to. It was a potentially dangerous thing if you ended up choosing the wrong person, like Davie McDougal did. He followed his neighbor and ended up being instrumental in a major drug bust. It made him a big hero, until his entire family had to go into the federal witness protection program. Now McDougal lives in, like, the armpit of wherever, and his name is McScrewed.

Fortunately for me, I wasn't so much of an overachiever. I followed a homeless guy. His activities were far more interesting than I expected. He had a daily routine meeting with various people in the neighborhood, he played a mean clarinet for spare change on a busy part of Coney Island Avenue, and he ended his afternoons reading the *New York Times* and the *Wall Street Journal* in the public library. I got an A on my oral report but a B minus on the written part, because the teacher couldn't read my handwriting.

What I didn't know was that one of my classmates had chosen to follow me. I didn't know until she gave her oral report. She kept referring to me as the "primate subject" and had very accurately logged everywhere I had been, right down to what I had had for breakfast that morning in my own home, which totally creeped me out. She even got me in trouble for ditching math class to go to the comics store. Of course she got in trouble, too, because she had to ditch a class to follow me there, so I got some satisfaction out of it.

As we sat together in detention, she told me she was now an expert on my "life," actually using air quotes around the word "life," and said that if I had represented an actual culture she was studying, she would advise scientists to nuke us. I told her, using air quotes, what she could do to herself.

This thing with Tilde was even creepier, because it was real. It was also kind of flattering, because people usually didn't give me creeped-out attention. I knew I shouldn't feel flattered by a stalker—I should only feel stalked—but I couldn't help myself. That's when I realized that there must be something seriously wrong with me—because I'd rather watch the world get blown away by an extinction-level event than save a single stinking dinosaur.

Crawley's parasailing misadventure hit a glitch once we got to the beach and the tour operator decided he was too old to do it. I don't think the blindfold helped in that decision. But the moment he was given the thumbs-down, Crawley ripped the blindfold off and ripped the tour operator a new bodily opening. His rage at being aged out of the event eventually forced them to give in and allow him to parasail. In fact, they let him go first.

He was hooked to the parachute, a speedboat started, and he was pulled from the beach into the air, where his rage against the system turned back into rage against me. Everyone else on the shore was forced to endure what may have been the foulest elderly mouth ever to visit Grand Cayman. Once Crawley returned to earth, he sat on a plastic beach chair and covered his eyes so he didn't have to see the outside world, mumbling that I was irresponsible, sadistic, and just plain evil.

Howie was the next of us to go. I went over to Tilde while Howie was up in the sky.

"What did you do, print up a counterfeit tour ticket?" I asked her.

"Maybe I just stole it," she said. "You lied to me about you and your friend."

I looked away, feeling more and more guilty about my underhanded hand-hold ploy. "Maybe not," I said, and waved the truth right in front of her. "Maybe what you saw was the lie."

But she didn't buy it for an instant. "Very funny—but I know you, Enzo."

"I guess you do know Enzo, but you don't know me."

She sighed and crossed her arms. "Must we fight?"

"Why are you even here? Don't you risk getting caught every time you get off the ship?"

"My risks are my problem," she said. "And I'm here because I want to make sure we're okay."

"There is no 'we' to be okay about."

"I know that. I just want to make sure you don't hate me."

"I'd have to know you to hate you," I told her. "And I don't know you any more than you know me. All I know is that you stow away on ships and you smuggle people into the United States."

"Shhh!" she said, looking around, but there was no one close enough to hear. "I thought we connected when we looked at the stars. I told you things; you told me things. I know that you and I could never be, but didn't you feel something?"

"Yes," I admitted. "But maybe it wasn't real. Maybe it was fake, like the stars."

Closer to the water, Howie landed on the beach, and the handlers grabbed him to keep the parachute from dragging him across the sand.

"Maybe we can just start our friendship over," Tilde said, gently touching my arm. It gave me goose bumps, and

I shuddered with a little bit of pleasure. I hoped she didn't notice.

"What's the point?" I told her. "The cruise is almost over. It's not like a few days is gonna change either of our lives." Famous last words, right? And since I was about to take a semi-dangerous soar over a beach covered with pointy umbrellas perfect for impaling, they might actually have been last words.

Since I lost my place in line talking to Tilde, I was one of the last to go. Tilde, it seemed, had no desire to parasail; she was just there to stalk.

I expected that I would get dragged across the sand and learn firsthand why it's called "sandpaper," but the second the speedboat started, I was lifted into the air like everyone else, and by the time I actually looked down, the entire beach looked pretty small. I was kind of scared and kind of not, because it was such an otherworldly experience. I think I was more scared when our plane hit turbulence, which is dumb, because I'm sure parasailing is far more likely to maim and kill.

Being dragged in a parachute across the sky was exciting, in an artificially thrilling kind of way, but it was also oddly calming. It was like meditating, being up there with nothing but curious seagulls looking at your eyes like they might be grapes and your own thoughts. Sure, it was only for a couple of minutes, but sometimes a few minutes of peace and perspective is all you need to bring things into clearer focus. I was in my own world. By the time they let me drift back down to the beach, I had an idea.

As soon as I was out of the parachute harness, I looked around for Tilde. She wasn't on the beach, so I went to check the tour bus.

"There was this girl," I said to the bus driver. "About this tall, long black hair, a little bit 'off,' if you know what I mean."

"Oh, you mean Tilde?"

"You know her?"

"Yeah," said the bus driver. "She come on de tour once and again. Sometime she join in, sometime she just help out."

It surprised me, but I guess it shouldn't have. "How long has she been on the ship?" I asked.

"Four, maybe five month."

"Did you say *months*?" Wow. I had figured she had stowed herself for maybe four or five voyages, but four or five months? This girl was a professional. If she'd been at this for that long, then it gave her plenty of time to hatch the whole passport scheme. She was a bottomless pit of surprises.

"She walk back by herself," the driver said. "Probably lookin' at shops."

I thanked him and went back to Crawley and Howie, who were happily sharing all the ways they almost died today. I left Crawley in Howie's hands. "I've got something to do. Make sure he gets back to the ship in one piece."

"Wait! You can't leave!" said Howie. "You're not allowed off by yourself!"

"What, are you my mother?"

"No, but your mother'll brain me if something happens to you."

146

"You gotta *have* brains to *get* brained, so you're safe."

"That's not technically true!"

But extending this conversation could only bring pain, so I left.

"The ship sails at five!" Howie yelled after me. "And be careful out there! Remember, Antsy—longpork! Longggggporrrrrrrk!"

The main street that wrapped around the bay was filled with touristy shops, selling everything from shell art and shellacked toads to diamond jewelry, which was definitely not mined in Grand Cayman. I wondered why would people come all the way down here to shop for things that came from somewhere else.

I found Tilde in a shop called The Blue Iguana, which had every type of thing you didn't actually need but would probably buy anyway and give as a gift to people who didn't need it either.

I pushed my way through a jungle of glass wind chimes (which, if you ask me, isn't a very well-thought-out product), and there she was, eyeing plush toy iguanas, only some of which were blue.

I picked up a lavender-sequin-covered iguana. "I'm no expert on amphibians," I said, "but I don't think this is very accurate."

I could tell she was surprised to see me, but she did a good job of hiding it. "For your information, iguanas are not amphibious."

"They're amphibious in the Galápagos Islands," I pointed out, pulling an actual fact out of my butt like freakin' David Copperfield. Thank God for Snapple caps.

147

I put my iguana down, because it was the last lavender one and a little kid was looking at it with planet-melting puppy eyes. He snapped it away before it was entirely out of my hands and ran off to his mother.

"Listen," I told Tilde. "I thought about what you said back on the beach, and I *do* want to start over. In fact, I want to do more than just start over."

"What is that supposed to mean?"

"In all those fake passports, is there one for you?" I asked.

She didn't answer me. I didn't expect her to. "What if there is?"

"Well, what if I told you that I can convince my family to take you home with us when we get off the ship? If you manage to get through customs and into the good old US of A, that means you won't be alone. You'll have somewhere to go and people to help you out."

It was a bold statement, even for me. Did I believe I could really convince my parents to do it? Maybe. Of course, it wouldn't be easy and would create arguments like you couldn't believe, but I've got decent powers of persuasion when it really matters. That was the decision I had come to while parasailing: I would offer Tilde political asylum, in the asylum that is my home. Now it was all up to Tilde.

She looked at me with eyes that were almost as planet melting as the little kid's. Then she looked back to the stuffed animals. "Why would I want to leave the *Plethora*?"

"Because eventually you'll get caught. You gotta know that, right? This can't go on forever."

148

"What about all the other people I want to bring in?"

"That's the catch," I told her. "You gotta give that up."

"No," she said. "I won't do that."

"It's too dangerous!"

Still, she just shook her head. So then I looked around, making sure no one was watching, and shoved one of the stuffed animals under my shirt.

"What are you doing?"

"Same thing you've been doing," I told her. "Smuggling. Yeah, sure, I might get away with it once, and maybe a second and third time . . ." Then I started grabbing iguanas, shoving them under my shirt, stretching it out until I looked like I was having triplets. ". . . but try to take a whole bunch at one time, and forget it. You'll get caught, and you don't even know how serious it'll be when you are."

"Can I help you?" said the shopkeeper who came up behind me. She looked at me, about to give live birth to a dozen colorful lizards, then crossed her arms, waiting for an explanation.

"Just making your day interesting," I told her.

"I don't need that kind of interest," she said, and sauntered back to the cash register. "Come over here if you want to pay for those. Otherwise, walk yourself to the police station and turn yourself in. I'll draw you a map."

Tilde grabbed my shirt and shook it so my litter of iguanas fell at my feet. "Thank you for the offer," she told me as we picked them up and put them back in the bin. "It's very, very nice of you. But I'll take my chances."

For the rest of the afternoon, we wandered through the

149

tourist shops and didn't talk about passports and human trafficking anymore. Instead we just made fun of the people buying stuff. Then Tilde took me to this little run-down shack that served the best Caribbean jerk chicken sandwich I'd ever had. Actually, the only one I'd ever had. Longpork was not on the menu.

When the clock tower by the port began to chime out the hour, I got a little nervous, but it only chimed four times. "Whew! For a second I thought it was five and we missed the ship."

Tilde calmly took a bite of her sandwich. "It *is* five."

"Don't even joke!" I said, laughing. But Tilde wasn't.

"*¡Es verdad!*" she said. "It's true—we're on ship's time. It's an hour ahead of island time."

You know that miserable moment when the curtain opens on your own idiocy? Yeah, you do. It's the moment your teacher says to turn in your fifty-percent-of-your-grade report on famed physicist Stephen Hawking, but by mistake, you did it on Stephen King. It's the moment you look out of your bedroom window in your underwear to see Ann-Marie Delmonico looking in from across the street, and you wonder what other things she's seen you doing in your underwear. It's the moment you wake up to a bright sunny morning on a friend's sofa after a non-parentally-supervised party and realize you've broken your curfew by nine hours, your parents are probably dredging New York Harbor for your body, and you know you'll be dead the moment they discover you're alive. I have been to all these places, and let me tell you, it's no pleasure cruise.

150

Christina, and we forgot about ship's time, that's all. We forgot. Easy mistake. And what would be the point of throwing us in the brig? Who needs that kind of grief? I don't need it, you don't need it—so let's just chalk this one up to experience, and let my sister and me get back on the ship, and forget about the whole thing, huh? Please?"

The captain was not impressed and spoke to Tilde instead of to me. "What is this one babbling about? Who is he?"

Tilde turned to me. "Enzo, I'd like to introduce you to Captain Fitore Pajramovic." Then she sighed and reluctantly said, "He's my father."

CHAPTER 13

NO PILLOW FIGHTS AT THIS
PAJRAMOVIC PARTY

THERE ARE ALL KINDS OF LIES. THE LIES WE TELL TO get out of bad situations, the half-truths, the lies we tell ourselves to keep us going on the worst of days. I'm not proud of the times I lie unless, of course, it's a really, really good one. The thing is, the more you falsify stuff, the more you've got to keep track of it and the more lies you need to tell to keep the first ones going. It's like the plate spinner at the circus. You gotta keep them going, or they all crash down.

Since stepping aboard the *Plethora*, I'd been involved in more untruths than I can remember, but when you're in the middle of it, you don't think about what a messed-up thing that is, because all your energy is spent keeping the plates spinning.

When it came to Tilde's grand game of deception, she was a much better spinner than I was.

The captain signaled the crewmen to pull in the gangway and close up the ship now that Tilde and I were on board, and as we strode toward the elevators, I stayed silent, trying to wrap my head around what I'd just heard.

"Would you mind telling me why you delayed our departure yet again?" Captain Pajramovic asked his daughter.

"Enzo got hurt," Tilde said, pointing to my still-bloody shins. "He was unconscious, and I knew if I didn't go with him to the hospital, the ship would leave without him—but I knew you wouldn't leave without me."

Her father looked down at my shins. "Those legs don't look like he's been to the hospital."

"We never got there," Tilde said. "Once he was conscious again, I made them stop the ambulance, and we came back to the ship. The ship has a better hospital anyway."

Then the captain looked at me. "Is this true?"

I might be able to lie in a pinch, but I'm not very good at backing up someone else's lie, so I answered by giving him a non-answer. "This is all very humiliating," I said, "and my head hurts." Since both of those things were one hundred percent true, he accepted it as if I had said "yes."

"Should I believe you?" he asked Tilde.

"No, you shouldn't," she told him, looking him in the eye. "You shouldn't believe me, because I am a worthless piece of street *basura* who can never be trusted to tell the truth."

The captain sighed, his shoulders slumping in defeat. Man, she was good.

"Come," he said to me, "we'll clean those wounds, check you for a concussion, and let your family know that you're all right." Then he led the way to the ship's infirmary. But before we got there, he turned to me and said, "Perhaps, if you're feeling up to it, you could join us for dinner."

"Dinner? At the Captain's Table?" I thought of my mother. "For my whole family?"

"Don't be greedy," he said. "The invitation is just for you." Then he threw a withering gaze at Tilde, which did not wither her at all. "It may be the only way I'll ever get my daughter to come to the dining room."

"I never said I was a stowaway. You just assumed I was."

We were sitting in the infirmary, waiting for my parents to come collect me. My shins were now covered with more bandages than were necessary, making my injuries look much worse than they really were.

"You could have said something!"

"Why? You were having so much fun helping the poor, poor stowaway girl."

I felt like the butt of a joke, and it just made me angry. Now that I had time to think about it, everything was falling into place. Why no one seemed to care when she was belowdecks, why so many people knew her, how she had the code to get into the Viking ship chamber—a code that only the captain knew. And as for the lifeboat, all those food stores weren't for her, were they? They were for the people she planned to smuggle on board.

"Does your father know about what you're doing?"

"Not a clue," she said, "so please keep it that way."

"Why should I?"

"Because, Enzo, whatever comes down on me comes down on you, too."

I grunted and stewed. "I don't like you very much right now."

"You'll get over it."

My parents showed up, their faces a deep sunburn red everywhere except around their eyes from their ATV extravaganza.

"Oh my God, Antsy, oh my God!" My mom came over to smother me in motherly anxiety. "Oh my God, they told us what happened, oh my God!"

"But you're okay," my father said. "That's all that matters."

"How high was the balcony? Did you hit your head? Oh my God, Antsy!"

"It wasn't high," I said, glaring at Tilde. She had told the doctor that I was at a restaurant, started choking, and fell from a second-story balcony. According to Tilde, a street vendor's umbrella broke my fall.

"How long were you unconscious?" my father asked.

"How should I know? I was unconscious."

My mother then proclaimed it was God's hand that saved me because Tilde's "eyewitness account" said the street vendor was selling silver crosses. "They have Mass on the ship every morning," my mom said. "You're going."

Finally, when they felt sure I wasn't going to bleed out or spontaneously combust on the spot, they looked over at Tilde.

"Is this her?"

She shook their hands. "Hi, I'm Tilde."

Then my mom looked at me sternly, pointing her

wagging finger. "You're lucky the captain has a daughter and that she knows the Heimlich maneuver!"

It's always formal night at the Captain's Table which is fine, I guess, if you actually have clothes—but my suitcase was still among the missing.

"You'll rent a tuxedo," my mother said.

"I don't want a stinking tuxedo," I told her.

"You're representing this family to the biggest big-shot captain of the whole Caribbean Viking fleet. You'll rent a tuxedo."

"I don't want a stinking tuxedo!"

My father came out of the bathroom. "What, are you trying to scare off the whales? Keep it down."

"*I'll* wear a tuxedo," offered Howie, but since he was as equally uninvited as my parents, no one took him up on his offer.

My mother took a deep breath. "Antsy," she said calmly, "of the nine thousand passengers on this ship, only a few dozen get to dine with the captain each cruise."

"Tuxedos are for old farts like Crawley," I said.

"I heard that," Crawley called from the adjoining suite.

My mother tossed up her arms. "Talk to your son," she said, without even looking at my father.

My dad shrugged. "Nothing to say. If Antsy wants to dress casually and stand out as different from everyone else at the Captain's Table, making himself the center of attention, he has every right to do that."

I glared at him, and he just grinned.

"Fine," I said. "Where do I go to get a tux?"

It wasn't the actual wearing of the tuxedo that bothered me; it was the reason I had to wear it. Everything surrounding this dinner was false. There were too many lies in the air, and me wearing a tuxedo was like a cherry on a hot fudge sundae of deception left melting on the counter while the waiters did the Macarena.

I didn't want to go. I was so furious at Tilde for lying to me, and yet, in a way I was relieved, because at least I didn't have to worry about her getting caught and thrown off the ship. It meant she was no longer my problem. She was officially the problem of Captain Feety Pajamas—which meant I didn't have to accept the dinner invitation at all; I could completely wash my hands of her.

So then why didn't I? I guess it's kind of like how sometimes when you've got a toothache that's not all that bad, you keep poking at the tooth and pushing at it with your tongue and maybe even chewing gum, which just makes it hurt more. Why do we do that? Maybe we want to make it worse so that we feel justified paying some dentist to fix it. Or when you shove a Q-tip into your ear, even though there are all these warnings about how never to shove a Q-tip into your ear, on account of deafness can occur, but we do it anyway, because we believe only imbeciles will break their own eardrums with a Q-tip, and besides, it's worth the risk to feel that mildly unpleasant, yet weirdly satisfying feeling of twisting a cotton swab around in your earwax.

So in the end, I got the tuxedo and chose to endure the discomfort of it all, even though I knew that poking at it would probably make it worse, and that this time the Q-tip wouldn't just puncture my eardrum, it would get stuck in my ear and I'd have to go through life with visual evidence that, yes, I was that much of an idiot.

I will say this once but will deny that I ever said it. Wearing a tuxedo was cool. I strutted onto the main floor of the dining room, and all heads turned—which I hoped was because of my overwhelming presence and not because maybe my fly was open.

As I approached that big round table smack in the center of everything, the waiter bowed to me slightly and said, "Mr. Benini, I presume."

"Something like that," I told him.

He led me to a seat that actually had a little formal place card for Enzo Benini. Around the table, various schmancies were already seated. There was a blatantly European couple with slick, perfect hair and slicker, even more perfect clothes. The woman was dripping diamonds the size of my eyeballs.

"*Buongiorno,*" the man said. "I am Lorenzo Something-that-sounds-like-Appletini, and this is my wife, Valentina." She put out her diamonds for me to grasp, or kiss, but I just nodded politely because I was afraid if I touched her hand, I might dislodge a diamond into her water glass, and it would get lost in the ice.

"It is a pleasure to make your acquaintance," Mrs. Appletini said. "We are Italian."

"Cool," I said. "I'm Italian, too."

The two glanced at each other, and Mr. Appletini looked back to me. "No," he said, "you are not."

Beside the Appletinis was a pair of really old identical twin sisters, dressed exactly the same and smiling exactly the same. They looked like old-lady versions of the creepy twins at the end of the hallway in *The Shining*.

"We always dine with the captain on Wednesdays," the starboard twin said. They were filthy rich and had retired on the ship. For a moment I thought of setting up Crawley on a birthday date with both of them and then smacked my brain for the thought.

Sitting next to them was the CEO of the hot social network Blather and a woman who was so beautiful it almost, but not quite, made up for how ugly he was. Personally I had trouble with Blather on account of I could never keep my bleats to 140 characters, so all my bleats ended like thi—

Finally, to my right there was a man in a kilt who spoke with such a strong Scottish accent, there was no hope of communication in this lifetime.

"Is the captain even coming?" asked the Blather guy's pretty wife/girlfriend/mail order bride.

"Captain Pajramovic likes to make an entrance," said the starboard twin. "Rumor is that his daughter will be joining him tonight."

"She never comes to dinner," said the port-side twin.

"We were beginning to think she was a ghost, like Jorgen Ericsson," said the starboard twin, and she added in a hushed whisper, "We've seen him, you know."

"Yeah, me too," I said, thinking about the coffin on the Viking ship.

The Appletinis had the best view of the entrance, and when they stood, everyone else at the table did. The captain approached, and beside him was Tilde—but this was Tilde like I'd never seen her before. She wore a sapphire satin gown and white gloves that went all the way past her elbows. She was also wearing makeup, which she didn't need, but wow! She could have been a goddess—but then the whole goddess thing was shattered when she tripped in her high heels and went sprawling like those fat guys at the belly-flop competition.

Gasps from around the dining room. I hurried to help her up.

"You okay?"

"I hate, hate, hate high heels," she said.

By now the entire dining room was looking at us.

"She refused to take my arm as we entered," her father said. "You see, Tilde, there are reasons for these customs."

Now she took my arm instead. I led her to her seat, and she said to me, like it was an accusation, "I wouldn't have fallen if I hadn't been looking at you and your tuxedo."

We quickly sat down, but her father remained standing, raising a glass of champagne. "A toast to my daughter," he said. "This is the first time Tilde has graced us with her presence in the dining room."

"Could it be," said one of the twins, "that she wanted to show off her boyfriend?" And both of them gave us creepy *Shining* grins.

162

I opened my mouth to deflect the question, but Tilde spoke first.

"Sorry, but no," she said. "Enzo and I are not interested in each other that way."

"Ah!" said Mr. Appletini. "I knew he wasn't Italian."

"Galicchh, galocchh McBroogie!" said the guy in the kilt.

And since I had no response to that, I took a long sip from my champagne—which, for Tilde and me, was just sparkling white grape juice. Fake, like everything else about this.

The attention mercifully shifted away from me to the Blather CEO, who answered every question about his social network with shifty eyes, like he had been cornered by investigative reporters.

"Oh, let's not blather about Blather," said his stunning wife/rent-a-babe/companion android. "After all, this is a vacation."

I busied myself eating bread, and Tilde stared at the spread of silverware before her, a little intimidated by it. "Where I come from, one fork, knife, and spoon is enough," she said, but only to me.

"Where do you come from?"

She leaned closer so the others couldn't hear. "I told you."

"No, you told me a pack of lies."

"Not really. I told you half-truths."

The captain, seeing that we were having a private conversation, tried to draw us back into the table talk. "So, Enzo, I understand that you hail from New York."

"Yeah. Brooklyn."

163

"Oh!" said one of the twins. "We have a nephew in Brooklyn. His name is Mike Last-name-in-one-ear-out-the-other. Perhaps you know him."

"Yeah, he's in my math class," I told them. "He owes me twenty bucks."

The twins were baffled by my response, and Tilde snickered but pretended it was a cough.

"Perhaps, Enzo, you and Tilde could be pen pals after your cruise is over." The captain had an annoying way of repeating my name every time he spoke to me, made worse by the fact that it wasn't actually my name.

"Maybe," I said. "What's a pen pal?"

"It's what people used to do before these hideous online social networks," said the starboard twin. The other twin cleared her throat and nudged her to remind her who was at the table with them, and when the first twin realized what she had done, she tried to backpedal, getting all red in the face. "Oh! Not that there's anything wrong with it. I'm sure Blather is perfectly wonderful for young people of today."

"Yeah," I said. "Everyone I know has the Blather app on their phone and bleats like fourteen thousand times a day."

To which the CEO guy said, "I'm glad to hear it. But please be advised that neither me nor my associates can be held responsible for the use and/or misuse of Blather and its subsidiary companies."

Dinner lasted forever, what with so many utensils. I guess the captain didn't just go down with the ship; he was also the last out of the dining room.

"I can't stand this," Tilde whispered to me. "Do something to end the meal!"

"What am I supposed to do?"

"You're smart; you'll think of something."

And I did. I reached over as if I was reaching over for the coffee creamer and "accidentally" knocked Mrs. Appletini's coffee onto her. Since she was already complaining that it was lukewarm, I figured it wouldn't burn much.

She stood up with a gasp, her fingers shaking so much her diamonds became like a disco ball shining tiny lights around the dining room, and she spouted the kinds of words in Italian that I actually knew.

I immediately apologized and tried to blot her breasts with a napkin, which, for some reason, only made her more angry.

The captain handled the whole thing calmly, the same way he might handle an iceberg strike.

"These things happen," he said, standing. "I will replace your gown at my personal expense if it cannot be dry-cleaned."

Now that he was standing, everyone else stood as well, and the meal mercifully concluded.

"You're a genius," Tilde whispered to me, then turned to her father. "Enzo and I are going to the Garden Deck. I'll be back whenever."

As furious as I was at Tilde, I didn't mind an evening stroll on the Garden Deck. As this was the only time in my life I'd ever be dressed like royalty, I figured I would take advantage of it. And now that we were alone, it was time for answers.

CHAPTER 14

DROWNING SHEEP, RUDE POCKETS, AND THE GUILTY CONSCIENCE OF A CAPTAIN

THE GARDEN DECK FEATURED A HUGE PARK WITH actual trees from around the world. A massive curved glass windshield protected it from the wind, so no matter how fast the ship was moving, the most you ever felt was a gentle breeze. They called it an arboretum, which sounds more like a place they stick dead people, but the only dead person would be me if my parents found out what I'd really been up to.

"I still don't understand why you're doing what you're doing," I told Tilde as we strolled through the arboretum. "Smuggling people on your father's ship? You're asking for trouble, and I don't get it."

"Things aren't as they seem," she said.

"Yeah, tell me about it."

She didn't say anything for a while. All I could hear was distant music from various parties and the rustling of leaves that had no business being this far from land.

"What I told you about my mother is true," she finally said. "Years ago, my father was a junior officer on a different ship. He met my mother, Beatriz Nuñez, in Cozumel, and saw her once every week, for many months. I do not know if they were in love, because my mother never spoke of those days. All I knew was his name and that he was Albanian. He was transferred to another ship, and she never saw him again."

"So he didn't know about you?"

"Oh, he knew. My mother made sure he knew. And he would send money to make himself feel less guilty."

"Hey, at least he did something. Some guys would just cut you off and pretend you didn't exist."

"Which is worse?" Tilde asked. "Having nothing honestly or surviving on blood money?"

I didn't answer, because I didn't know. I've never had "nothing." I mean, our family has had its share of money troubles, but "nothing" was never part of the bargain. If the restaurant ever fails, we could lose our house, but even then we wouldn't be left with nothing.

"My mother would give most of that money to the rest of her family," Tilde said, "but everyone knew the money was for me. People secretly resented it. Even though I took my mother's last name, my eyes were a little lighter, my skin was a little paler. From the time I was born, I felt like an outsider. So his money did not help me."

"Sounds like you really hate him."

She looked away. "No. Not hate him. But he has a lot to prove to me. After my mother died, I made the decision that it was time for him to start proving it. When I found out he was the captain of this new ship, I came to the port in Cozumel, and I demanded to see him. Even though the guards would send me away, I kept coming back, until finally he came down in his shiny white suit. I had never even met him before, but I told him who I was, and that my mother was dead, and that he was going to take me on his great ship and I would live there with him, and he did not have my permission to say no.

"He didn't say no, but still the ship sailed without me. I thought that was the end of it, but then two weeks later, he found me on the streets of Cozumel, doing what I've been doing since I was little. Selling silver crosses to tourists. He had gotten me an Albanian passport, probably the same way I got those passports in Jamaica, and he took me on board."

"So you're half Albanian, half Hispanic," I said. "So what does that make you? Alpanic?"

She ignored me. "He told me my last name was now Pajramovic instead of Nuñez and he bought me new clothes and said that this was my new life. Only it's not that easy. Because your old life is still there, and you look at your new clothes and you feel dirty for wearing them, and you think about all the people you know who don't have a ship's captain in a shiny white suit to save them. And then you realize that maybe you can do something about it. . . ."

She looked to me to say something then. What was I going to say? That I thought it was okay what she was doing? Part of me did think so, and part of me didn't, and part of me just wanted to enjoy being all dressed up with a beautiful girl, and part of me wanted to ditch it all and lose myself for the rest of the cruise on the waterslides and roller coaster and go-cart speedway.

"Well, I guess you'll do what you have to do, then," I told her.

"We are in Cozumel tomorrow," she reminded me. "I would like to show you where I come from."

"Show me?" I asked. "Or help you get people on board?"

She looked insulted and turned away. "I don't need your help for that. In fact, you'll only get in the way."

"Then why waste your time showing me around?"

She didn't have an answer for me, so I guess, amazingly, I had the last word—because at that moment, we were interrupted by another couple coming down the winding path.

There had been other people passing us in the arboretum, but we hadn't given them much attention until one particular couple wove their way toward us. It was Lexie and her walking wall of blond chest hair, although, as before, the chest hair was most hidden behind a shirt that was intentionally too tight. He stopped when he saw me.

"What is it, Gustav?" Lexie asked.

He struggled for the words. "I am see guy you knowing."

I spoke up rather than make Lexie suffer the embarrassment of having to figure out who it was—although I'd like to think that I'd be her first guess.

"Hi, Lexie," I said.

She stiffened a little. "Hello, Antsy. Would I lose my bet if I wagered that you are not alone?"

"I'm with Tilde," I told her.

"I guessed as much. Although not much of a guess—I could hear those wobbly heels from a mile away."

"Well," said Tilde, "we cannot all be born with a silver stiletto in our mouth, can we."

I took a step between them before claws started coming out. "Hey, we're all friends here, right? And who could be mad while surrounded by trees of the world?" I looked over at Gustav, who just stood there trying to decipher our English. He looked both neglected and intimidating, like a Rottweiler left tied to a tree.

"Are you still in your tuxedo?" Lexie asked, then, not waiting for an answer, she reached up, pressing her hands to my chest, and moved them up my lapel until she found my bow tie and straightened it. "Hmm," she said. "There are far better fabrics for formal wear, but it is a rental, after all."

"Lexie, vee go, ya?" said Gustav. He turned to me. "Vee go balls now."

"Excuse me?"

"Gustav is taking me bowling," Lexie explained.

"How does a blind girl bowl?" sneered Tilde.

I swear I could actually feel Lexie bristle. "I'll have you know that Dale Davis, a blind man in Iowa, bowled a perfect game! On the other hand, some people can have all their senses and still be completely senseless."

I tried to move Tilde away from Lexie before nuclear fission could occur. "Iowa! Imagine that! Isn't Iowa amazing."

"Lexie, vee go, ya?" said Gustav again, and came forward to guide Lexie away.

"Bye, Lexie. It's been fun," I said, but got no response.

I couldn't help but notice as they left that Gustav had slipped his hand into her back pocket and gave a little squeeze. Normally Lexie would have slapped several layers of skin off of anyone who did that, but this was not normal Lexie. Instead she slipped her hand into his back pocket, too.

Lexie wasn't the only one acting bizarrely on this cruise. When I got back to the cabin later that night, my parents had informed me that Howie hadn't shown up for dinner, and they sent me out to find him.

"Just make sure he hasn't drowned in the wave pool or gotten himself trampled on the horse trail," my dad said. "You brought him; he's your responsibility."

I went to the teen lounge figuring I'd find him there, but it was mostly empty.

Lance I'd-eat-my-own-thighs-in-the-wild was there, though, cleaning up after the international conglomerate of teenage slobs. Someone had spilled something sticky on one of the alien eggs, and the beanbags in the psychedelic section looked like they'd been cannonballed by fat kids.

"I'm looking for a kid named Howie," I told him. "My size but a little shorter. Talks like me, but more so."

"Howie . . ." said Lance with a pained little grin, making it clear he knew Howie all too well. "Yeah, he left a while ago. You're his friend Antsy, I'll bet. The one who forged his birth certificate."

Now it was my turn to give a pained grin. "He told you about that, huh?"

"Don't worry, I'm not gonna turn you in, mate."

I wondered if the "mate" was obligatory Australian, like

the Jamaican cabbie's "mon." Lance's accent wasn't quite as strong as the guy from Outback Steakhouse, though.

"So you haven't seen him?" I asked.

"He was here most of the evening, but he left a while ago." Then Lance looked at me thoughtfully, although I don't know what Australian survivalists think when they look at you. Maybe that you look like a turkey.

"You should talk to him," Lance said.

"I do all the time," I told him. "Believe me, it's no picnic."

"Maybe not," said Lance, "but you should definitely talk to him."

Then Lance got back to the business of cleaning other people's messes.

Howie, it turns out, had returned to the cabin while I was looking for him. He had spent the last couple of hours at the ship's salon, where he had his hair styled and colored—or I should say *decolored*—because now it was as blond as Lance's and cut the same way, too. Moppy on top, short on the sides.

"What the hell did you do to yourself?" I blurted out when I saw him.

Howie looks at me, all injured. "I'm going for a new look—you got a problem with that?"

I open and close my mouth like a fish. Then my mother comes in, takes one look at Howie, glares at me like it's my fault, then leaves, not wanting to know about it.

Her skill at removing herself from unwanted situations amazed me, and I thought maybe I could learn this behavior, too. *You should definitely talk to him*, Lance had said. Well, sorry, but my plate was already full from my trip to the international criminal buffet. So if Howie wanted to be Lance's mini-me, I wasn't going to stop him.

"It looks good," I told him, even though it didn't, then I dismissed it from my mind and got ready for bed.

I had trouble sleeping that night, and not even the gentle roll of the ocean could lull me. I tried counting sheep, but they kept jumping off the railing in my head and drowning in the open sea. It didn't help that my shins were still wrapped with a ridiculous amount of gauze from my seriously exaggerated "near-fatal fall." I tried to peel it off, but I think every single leg hair was caught beneath the tape, which got me wondering how girls can wax their legs and not go into immediate cardiac arrest. Who needs waterboarding when you've got body-hair waxing? So I'm lying there, in that very specific place between discomfort and misery that gets no sympathy from anyone, and the sheets are so over-starched that whenever I try to move, it sounds like I'm playing the maracas.

I forced myself to stay still, closed my eyes, and listened to the gargling bleats of drowning sheep in my head, beginning to wonder if maybe I oughta start "bleating," too. Just get online, sign on to Blather, and bleat out my own SOS, if I could figure out a way to keep it to 140 characters—but, of course, doing that would mean I'd have to slide out from beneath my covers, and the friction alone might set the room on fire. So I lay there, watching my flock of brain sheep leap into the Caribbean Sea, their bodies stretching out behind the ship like a trail of fluffy bread crumbs that, if I followed, might lead me back to where I started and maybe home to a normal Fourth of July.

Yeah, that's right, tomorrow was the Fourth of July. Independence Day for the USA and, if Tilde's plan worked, independence for a whole bunch of illegal stowaways, too. And if it didn't work, I suspected that the fireworks flying tomorrow would not bring joy to the masses.

With cotton on my legs and waterlogged fleece on the brain, my mind drifted to the time Wendell Tiggor insisted that cotton came from sheep and then beat up a kid who couldn't restrain himself from calling Tiggor a freaking imbecile, even though he knew it might lead to black eyes and tooth loss, because some things simply must be said, regardless of personal cost. Lately, though, I haven't been saying much myself, even though I probably should have been. And maybe that was the real reason why I couldn't sleep.

Somewhere in the midst of my cotton-wrapped legs and the trail of sheep, I must have fallen asleep, because the next thing I knew, my dad was shaking me awake, with far more enthusiasm than any parent has a right to have.

"Up, up, up!" he shouted so brightly I needed sunscreen. "Tulum! Tulum! Ancient Mayan ruins! Today's the day!"

I groaned. The clock said it was only seven thirty, but my dad was like a kid on Christmas morning, up and ready hours before the ruins tour.

"C'mon, Antsy!" My dad shook me again. "Expand your horizons! Experience a dead culture!"

174

"I like my horizons far away," I told him. "And I like my cultures alive and in my yogurt."

He ripped the covers off of Howie to wake him up and let out an uncharacteristic scream when he saw Howie's hair, which he somehow had missed the night before. My father looked to me for an explanation, but since Howie's new "do" was still lingering in the realm of science fiction for me, I just rolled over, pulling my covers around myself again.

I was still clinging helplessly to my blanket when my mother came out of the bathroom in full tourist uniform, complete with Hawaiian blouse, sun visor, and the same plastic Frida Khalo tote bag they sold in every port.

"Get up," she said. "'There are no couch potatoes at sea.'"

"I got a headache."

She looked at me with a motherly frown. "Were you drinking last night?" She sniffed the air around me, satisfied that I didn't smell like booze BO, if there was such a thing, but whatever she smelled made her wrinkle her nose and say, "Go take a shower."

The Exotic Tulum Ruins Adventure left promptly at eleven, so there was plenty of time. My parents and sister had already gone off to breakfast by the time I was out of the shower, and Howie had his own pre-ruins plans.

"Lance is giving a boomeranging lesson on the Lido Deck," Howie told me. "He says that on the last cruise, he actually killed a seagull!" For a moment Howie was lost in picturing the event, then said, "Oh, by the way— your stalker called while you were in the shower."

"What?"

"The captain's daughter. She says she'll be waiting at the gangway for you. She sounded impatient." Then Howie left to kill seagulls with Lance.

I was about to head to the gangway when Crawley came in from the next suite.

"Anthony," he said, "a word."

"Hemorrhoid," I responded. "That's a word. And an appropriate one, too, because everyone's being a pain where the grass don't grow today. Or does grow, depending on who we're talking about."

"Your impertinence freshens my day like bowl cleanser," he said, "but right now I'm not in the mood."

He sat down, already seeming worn out by the day. He waited for me to sit, but I stayed standing.

"This birthday cruise is not going as I had planned," he said.

"How did you plan it to go?"

"I don't know!" he snapped. "But I did not expect to be superfluous." Then he added "That means 'extraneous.'"

And since I wasn't one hundred percent sure of the meaning of either word, I said, "How so?"

"Lexie's gone every morning before I'm even out of bed. Your family plans shore excursions without me, and I eat most of my meals alone. You, Anthony, are the only one with the common courtesy to kidnap me for a Caribbean spree—but even so, I could tell your heart wasn't in it." Then he looked away. "And this was the first time Lexie wasn't a part of it."

I was getting antsy now—like I used to when I was little and I got the nickname. I knew Tilde was waiting for me. "Well, maybe Lexie just had other things to do."

"What could be more entertaining than tormenting me? Even you, with your blasted captain's daughter, found time for me." And then he got to the real point of this talk. "I'm worried about Lexie. Ever since she found out that her parents weren't coming, she's been acting . . . well . . . different."

I knew he was right, but I didn't know what to do about it. I had no experience with Lexie being off-kilter. I mean, she'd always been the most balanced, sensible person I knew. Okay, maybe sometimes she suffered from rich girl syndrome and expected some things handed to her, but she was not the kind of girl to make whoppingly bad decisions. That was *my* specialty—and, sadly, a tradition that was about to continue.

"I'm sure she's fine," I told Crawley, inching toward the door. "She just needs some space."

Crawley grunted. "She's growing up," he said, "against all my efforts to prevent it."

I thought to that back-pocket play I had seen between Lexie and Gustav yesterday. For a moment I thought to tell Crawley about Gustav but decided against it, because it would mean at least five more minutes of conversation.

A whole lot of things would have been different if I had given up those five minutes to help Lexie.

CHAPTER 15

RICHES TO RAGS TO RUINS, FEATURING IGUANA PHOTO OPS AND A STRIPTEASE BY YOURS TRULY

"ONE MORE MINUTE AND I WOULD HAVE LEFT without you," Tilde said as I came off the ship and onto the dock. She was dressed in regular clothes now: jeans and a T-shirt. She carried a backpack with her, which I knew was full of counterfeit passports, but it was also bursting at the seams with something else.

I followed her from the dock into the street, and once we came out from the shadow of the ship, we were blasted by the sun. The morning air in Cozumel was like breathing a bowl of soup. Oppressive. Humid—and I knew it would only get worse as the sun grew higher in the sky. I thought we might take a taxi like we did in Jamaica, but instead Tilde wove confidently through the streets. I had to remind myself that this was her home turf.

"I have to be back by eleven," I told her.

"Whenever," she said.

"No, not whenever. My parents are expecting me, and I've ticked them off enough already."

If she cared, she didn't show it, and I began to wonder as I always wondered when I was with Tilde, what was I doing here? She was like a Siren leading me to my doom. Not the ugly city type of siren, but the beautiful ocean kind—the kind that lured ancient Greek heroes to a watery death.

"Cerilla!" shouted a little boy selling silver on a blanket spread out on the sidewalk. He leaped over the blanket and gave her a hug.

"What did he call you?" I asked.

She became as cold as the morning was hot. "That's not your business."

"So they don't call you Tilde here?"

But she just ignored me.

As for the boy, he was as ragged as they come and had a look about him that was both innocent and yet seemed as old as Crawley. He said something to her in Spanish, but Tilde scolded him.

"English," she said. "English only from now on. Have you been practicing?"

"*Sí,*" he said. "I mean, yes."

"Enzo, this is Besso."

"Beto!" the boy corrected. "But she call me Besso. That mean 'kiss.'"

I grinned. "Do you ever call anyone by their name, *Cerilla*?"

She turned sharply on me. "I did *not* give you permission to use that name!"

"Why, what's the big deal?"

She glared at me like she would slap me, then just said, "You annoy me," and turned her back to me.

"You the captain's son?" asked Beto.

179

"Just a friend," I told him.

Then he turned back to Tilde. "They wait for you," he told her. Then he rolled up his blanket, making sure none of his wares fell out, and hurried off. "This way!"

We quickly left the tourist zone behind. No more jewelry shops and trinket booths. No more venders driving you nuts trying to sell island tours. Soon the paved streets ended. Now it was all dirt, like Jamaica, and the poverty all around me was this living, breathing thing looking at me, asking me what right I had to be here. Even dressed down, I was a schmancy in this place.

"Keep up," Tilde said to me. I hadn't realized I had fallen so far behind.

"I'm trying," I told her. "It's hard—it's so hot."

"Get over it."

We were still in the citified part of Cozumel, but it was more like a village now. Buildings were rarely more than two stories high. There was a lot of old "new" construction. That is, new buildings begun a long time ago that never got finished and now were slowly wasting away before they had the chance to be born.

People peered out of crumbling doorways. Some just seemed curious, some actually waved to Tilde and said "hello"—but there were others who scowled at her in clear disapproval and went inside like it was some sort of protest. I didn't know if they were protesting what she was doing or just who she was.

As we made our way through the town, dust from the street got all over my pant legs and into my lungs as I breathed. I kept having to cough. I never felt in danger. I never felt threatened the way I had in Hello-Hello, but, like that place, there was a certain lack of hope and an acceptance that the world was the way it was and it wasn't getting any better.

Tilde lagged behind Beto, letting me catch up with her. When she spoke, she didn't look at me.

"Tilde—short for Matilde—was the name of my father's mother. My own mother named me that to get his sympathy so maybe he would come for her and take us both away, but all he did was send money. I hated the name. So all my life I went by my middle name—the one my mother called me. Cerilla."

I almost saw a tear in her eye, but since she wouldn't look at me, it was hard to tell.

"Well," I told her, "I could call you Cerilla . . . and maybe you could call me Antsy. Or even Anthony."

She spared a single glance at me, all cold again. "If I am to be with my father, then I must be Tilde," she said. "Even though the name still feels false."

"Like Enzo?" I said, finally beginning to understand.

She didn't say anything to that, but she didn't have to. In all the time I'd known her, I'd never heard her call anyone by their actual name. Why should others have that right if she didn't?

"This way," Beto called back to us. "They're in the hair store, like you said."

He led us into a local beauty parlor—a concrete building painted a shocking color of pink that I think only exists in Mexico. A bell jangled as we went in, and I found myself faced by about fifteen people, all with dark Indian skin. They ignored me and made a fuss over Tilde when she came in. That was fine with me. I was more than happy to be just an observer. Tilde kept trying to get them to speak English but finally gave up. She spoke in English but let them answer any way they wanted.

"What's going on in here?" she asked.

One proud women turned around a salon chair to reveal a boy with freshly bleached hair as blond as Howie's new hairdo—like maybe blondness was contagious like one of those cruise ship viruses the news makes such a big deal about. There were other people in the salon whose hair had also been bleached. Kids mostly. One girl still had the bleaching solution in her hair.

"Who told you to do this?" asked Tilde.

The woman smiled proudly. "My idea. To look American."

"No! That's not why I wanted you to meet here! You might as well just put a sign on your heads that you're sneaking onto the ship!"

"No, it might be okay," I said. "Kids always dye their hair and stuff. Just as long as it's just a few and not all of them. Then it will be like *Village of the Damned*," which is this old movie about really creepy kids with blond hair, like from California.

Now everyone was looking at me, and I suddenly realized that I was now the official authority on how to pass for American. I took a deep breath.

"It's not about your hair or even your skin," I told them. "It's an attitude."

Then one kid gave a belly-bulging exaggerated strut. Everyone laughed and I thought, *Is that what the world thinks of us?* But that was too big a question for a crowded pink salon on a hot Mexican morning.

"No," I told them, "it's like this," and I gave them my best Brooklyn walk. "It's like . . . it's like you got something to show off, but you're not quite sure what it is. All you know is that you've got it."

One guy walked the walk, and he could have been right out of my neighborhood.

"That's good," I said. I pointed to someone else. "Now you—walk like you've got somewhere important to get to, but you forgot where you're going, and you don't want anyone else to know you forgot." He took a moment to process the English, then did a pretty good impersonation of a New Yorker on the way to work.

"That's fantastic," I told him. Then I pointed to a middle-aged woman. "You! You want something really, really badly, but you don't know what you want—all you know is that you want it." And she did an uncanny impersonation of my mom that made me shiver. Then I felt a tug on my shirt.

"How about me?" asked Beto.

"Easy," I told him. "You've got to be really cute and really irritating at the same time."

"He's good at that," said a man who must have been his father. Everyone laughed, and suddenly I realized that I was no longer observing this. I was a part of it.

"Okay, enough fooling around," said Tilde. "We don't have much time. First of all, no luggage." She kicked over a

183

woman's ancient-looking suitcase for emphasis. It thudded on the floor and rocked itself still. "Whatever stuff you have, you have to leave it behind. The most you can carry is a purse or a small plastic bag. You've got to look like a tourist."

The woman with the suitcase stood it upright again and looked at Tilde pleadingly, about to say something, but Tilde offered no pity.

"Either leave it behind or don't come."

The woman swallowed whatever it was she was going to say.

Tilde opened the smaller pouch on her backpack and spilled the passports out on a counter, about forty of them— almost three times the amount we needed.

"These passports are for each of you. There are men, women, girls, and boys. The pictures are all Hispanic and so are the last names. But the first names are American. That's on purpose. So look through them and find someone you think you look like and memorize the name. From now on, that's you."

"You really think that will work?" I asked.

"I watched them at the cruise port," Tilde told me. "At customs in Miami, they have so many people coming off the ship, they don't look too closely. They just scan the passport through their machine, then go on to the next person—and I paid a lot to make sure these passports would pass the scan."

Everyone crowded around the table, sorting through the passports. Watching them move around that table, looking at the faces in the little booklets, was like watching a game of musical chairs where everyone's future rested on whether or not they found a seat. Even with that many passports, what were the chances they could match themselves to a face?

"What if they can't find a passport that looks like them?" I asked.

"Then they don't come," said Tilde.

"That's a little harsh."

"You don't know harsh." Then, of all things, she took out a camera and began to line them all up for pictures.

"Not exactly a good time for a Kodak moment," I said.

"The passports are for US Customs in Miami," Tilde told me. "But to get on the ship, they need a cabin key. And when they scan the key on the gangway, it pulls up a picture on the security monitor. I have keys for them, but I have to get their pictures into the security computer."

"So, they're just going to walk right up the gangway with the rest of the passengers?"

"If they have a key and a picture to go along with it, then, as far as security is concerned, they *are* passengers. They won't doubt their own system unless we give them a reason to."

I looked at the group, and it struck me that if nothing else gave security a reason to doubt, their clothes would.

"You need to dress differently," I told them. "What you're wearing, it just doesn't say 'cruise.'"

Tilde gave me a grin and opened the main compartment of her backpack, pulling out shirts and blouses courtesy of the Caribbean Viking onboard store. People began to browse through the clothes, but there was this one kid who kept his distance. He looked doubtful about the whole thing and stood toward the back of the salon. He seemed about my age and was the worst dressed of all. His shirt was faded and discolored, the threads barely holding together. His jeans were badly frayed, like the ones I had first seen Tilde wearing: not fashionably worn, just worn. He scowled at me suspiciously when I approached.

"You got a name?" I asked him. He looked at the passport he was holding.

"Kyle Hidalgo."

"No, your real name."

"Jorge. Jorge Garza."

"Do you really want to do this, Jorge?" I asked him.

The scowl never really left his face. "That is not the question to ask," he said. "The question is do I really want to do *this*." Then he reached over and lifted something up and shoved it toward me. It took a second until I realized that he was shoving a two-foot-long iguana in my face. I flinched and backed against the wall, knocking over a blow-dryer.

He smiled at my reaction. "Do you like him? This is Ignaçio."

The iguana was wearing a little red sombrero that was strapped with elastic around his neck. He looked bored and resigned to the fact that he would look ridiculous for the rest of his days.

"I take pictures of people with Ignaçio," Jorge said, "and they pay me a dollar per picture. My father started with Ignaçio when he was my age, but this iguana outlived him.

He died last year of a heart attack right there on the pier."

Jorge put Ignaçio down. "I don't want to die on the pier. I don't want my son to inherit Ignaçio."

I had no idea how long iguanas lived, but I know that's not what he meant. There would always be another Ignaçio.

At that moment I made a decision—the kind of decision you make without even realizing you're making one. It's only when you look back that you realize how huge it was.

"Take off your shirt," I told Jorge.

"Why?"

"Just do it."

Then right in front of everyone there, I stripped down to my underwear and switched clothes with Jorge. We were about the same size, so our clothes fit each other. Usually I feel embarrassed stripping down in front of people—at the doctor's, even in gym class—but for some reason I couldn't care less about it now.

Once our clothes had been switched, I looked at myself, feeling funny in someone else's ragged clothes but also knowing that no matter how I was dressed, no one was going to question me getting back on that ship, even if I didn't have a key. They'd just send me to guest services to get another one.

I reached over and took the little hat from Ignaçio. "I'll keep this," I told Jorge, "and you can set Ignaçio free."

Jorge just looked at me and, shaking his head, he asked, "Why do you do this for me? I know why Cerilla does this, but why you?"

Good question. Why would I give the clothes off my

back to a total scowling stranger? Well, maybe it was because Jorge's father died of his heart attack and my father hadn't.

It takes a certain mix of courage and desperation to be willing to leave everything you know in search of a completely new life. Take my great-grandparents. They each came over from Italy with nothing. They just boarded a boat, waved good-bye, and bam! They're in Brooklyn thinking, *I left Italy for this?* But I guess it was worth it for whatever opportunities they weren't getting back where they came from.

I don't know if I could ever do that. It's kinda like skydiving with your life—and half the time, these people didn't even know if they had parachutes.

That's what America is, I guess. A country of skydivers, starting way back before there were planes you could hurl yourself out of. It started with the Puritans, then the colonists, then the Sooners, then the waves of immigrants in the early 1900s to now. Legals, illegals, it's all the same. Everyone in America is either a skydiver or is descended from skydivers.

Which kind of explains why everyone's nuts.

For the rest of the morning, Tilde gave orders like she was the ship's captain. The blond kids' hair was all to be dyed back to its original color. Everyone got haircuts, shaves, and waves put into their hair to match their passports—*that's* the reason why Tilde had them all meet in the salon. I pointed out that the pictures Tilde took for the key cards wouldn't work now that they had new looks, and she got all mad at herself for not thinking of that.

"See why I need you?" she said. "I can see the big picture, but I make stupid little mistakes." Then she took all their pictures again.

I continued my mission of Americanization, giving them each something to do while they went through security—something that would make them blend in.

"Fuss over your daughter's sunscreen and have her whine about it."

"Talk to each other about how you can't get cell phone reception."

"Be amazed by the low price of tequila."

And to the ones who didn't speak English well enough to pull it off, I told them to just yawn a lot.

The plan was for Tilde and me to get back to the ship alone, break into the security computer using whatever magic password Tilde had gotten her hands on, then go back into Cozumel to gather all the new passengers. We'd give them their key cards and let them trickle on board with everyone else.

That was the plan.

But as Tilde and I got back to the dock, I felt a hand grasp my shoulder with such force it hurt.

"Where have you been?"

I turned to see my father glaring at me, with Howie and Christina beside him.

"Do you have any idea what time it is? It's a quarter past eleven!"

The ruins! I totally forgot!

"Do you have any idea how much I paid for these shore excursion tickets? How could you be so irresponsible?"

I looked at Tilde, then back to my father. "Dad, I'm sorry, but I can't go."

"Like hell, you can't!" he shouted. Then when I glanced at Christina, she shook her head with what we call "the Deadly Head Rattle." That rapid head shake was family code. It meant that it didn't matter if the sky opened up and the heavenly host was heralding the Second Coming. The Deadly Head Rattle meant that if Dad says we're going to the ruins, then we're going to the ruins.

"Dad, you don't understand . . ." I tried to explain.

"I understand that you have been a selfish little bastard since the moment you got on this ship!"

I reeled at that. My father *never* used the *b* word with me. Something was wrong. Really wrong. Tilde must have sensed it, too.

"You go," she said. "I'll be fine by myself."

"No, you won't."

"Yes," she said calmly, "I will." She turned to go onto the ship. I tried to follow, but my dad grabbed my arm. I spun on him.

"You have no idea what you're doing!"

"Oh, I know exactly what I'm doing," he said. "I'm taking my daughter and my son and his no-good fool of a friend to the ruins at Tulum!" Then he stormed off and we had no choice but to follow.

"What's his problem?" I said. And my sister told me something that made it all crystal clear:

"Crawley's closing Dad's restaurant."

THE RACE TO RUINATION AND EXPANDED HORIZONS, NOW IN 3-D

COZUMEL IS ACTUALLY AN ISLAND THAT IS ABOUT twenty miles off the coast of mainland Mexico, so to get to the ruins, you gotta take another boat. Problem is, the tour boat left five minutes ago.

"So, so sorry," said the girl organizing the tour groups, "nothing we can do about that now. How about a nice snorkeling trip instead?"

"No," my father said. "We are going to Tulum."

"Well, you could take the public ferry . . ." Then the girl pointed to a pier about a mile away. "The ferry will take you to Playa del Carmen. From there you can take a taxi to Tulum if you like." And then she looked at her watch. "Of course, you'll have to hurry—the ferry leaves in five minutes."

We sprinted toward the ferry pier in the full heat of the day.

"Dad!" I said. "Its not worth it. Your heart . . ."

"My heart is fine. I'm in shape now."

"But Dad . . ."

"Do you see me huffing and puffing!"

But he was out of breath by the time we reached the

pier. We all were. And we got there just in time to see the ferry leave.

My father threw up his arms in frustration, but not in defeat. He strode to a guy who ran the pier—or at least acted like he did.

"When is the next ferry?"

"Not until this evening, señor," the pier guy said.

"We need to get to Tulum."

"It's too late for that, my friend," the pier guy said with a smile. "How about you go snorkeling instead?"

"NO!" my father insisted. "We are going to Tulum."

I looked to Christina, who just shrugged, not willing to get involved, and Howie looked about ready to crawl under a rock.

"Dad, maybe we should just forget it . . ." But I don't even know if he heard me. He was looking out at the many small boats in the marina.

"These are fishing boats, right? You take tourists out fishing?"

"*Sí*, señor," said the man. "Would you like to go fishing? I can rent you a boat and poles?"

"How much to charter one of those boats to take us to the mainland?"

Ten minutes and two hundred dollars later, we were all in a little boat that barely held the four of us and the fisherman piloting it. The fisherman didn't speak to us either in Spanish or English; he just drove that boat. We each held a rented fishing pole because it was illegal to shuttle passengers to the mainland—the port police had to think we were going fishing. Then, as soon we were in the open sea, we put down the poles and tried to keep from getting seasick as the boat rode up and down the waves. My father was about as silent as the fisherman piloting us. I could only imagine how much he was hurting from Crawley's bombshell.

"Listen, Dad . . . about the restaurant—"

"I don't want to talk about it," he said. "We are going to Tulum. We are going to be amazed, and we are going to make a memory that will last a lifetime. This is probably the only chance we'll ever get to do this, and we are not going to blow it. We *will* make this memory."

Then he looked me over, noticing for the first time. "What is that you're wearing?"

I looked at myself and remembered I was still wearing Jorge's clothes.

"What do you want from me?" I said. "They still haven't found my suitcase." I looked back toward Cozumel. We were miles away now, but the *Plethora* still towered above the rest of the island. I suspected we'd still be able to see it once we got to the mainland. I wondered if Tilde had managed to get into the security computer. I wondered about all those people whose futures now rested firmly on her shoulders.

And I wondered if it was more important for me to be there . . . or here.

Once the boat dropped us off, we had no problem finding a taxi. The problem was that Tulum was an hour's drive from there, and the ferries back to Cozumel didn't exactly leave like subway trains. If we missed the return ferry, good luck finding a fishing boat at that time of day to take us back. Long story short, by the time we got to Tulum, we only had twenty minutes to do the ruins before having to turn around and go back. Dad decided to go all in for this since we were mostly there already, and he hired a private tour guide to whisk us through. She told us her presentation took forty minutes.

"Talk fast," my father told her. "*Hablas rápido.*"

Until that moment I didn't know my father knew a single word of Spanish. We sprinted ahead of all the other tourists, squeezed our way through the narrow stone passageway, and found ourselves before a series of towering ruins you couldn't even see from the jungle around it.

My father was right about the ruins—they were pretty amazing: a walled city of Mayan temples on a cliff overlooking a stunning white sand beach.

Our tour guide took her instructions very seriously. She spoke really, really fast. I don't think she knew much English, but she had memorized her spiel. It was kind of like listening to a kindergarten teacher on speed.

"The Castillo is to your left. Do you see the Castillo? It is the tallest building in Tulum. Over here is the Temple of the Wind God. Do you not see the round base? Do you not see how the walls slant inward? This was of deep religious significance to the Maya."

We darted from temple to temple, scattering the hordes of iguanas that laid claim to the ruins. Our tour guide called them Mexican chickens; however, unlike Ignaçio, none of them wore a sombrero.

"Here now is the Temple of the Descending God. Will you look inside? The painted walls have original pigment. Do you not see the original pigment?"

I think she gave us her entire forty-minute presentation and in under twenty. When she was done, I felt liked I had just crammed for an exam, and Howie looked like his brain had been removed in a human sacrifice—which our tour guide claimed was blown way out of proportion and was more Aztec than Mayan anyway.

My sister, who used to travel with a notebook everywhere she went, had long since discovered the "notes" feature on her iPhone. She tried to keep up with the tour guide, but her thumbs gave out halfway through, so she resorted to taking pictures until her memory was full. As for my own memory, I had no idea how much or how little I would remember. I don't know if my horizons were expanded, but my father looked deeply satisfied, and I guess that's what mattered most.

"Let this be a lesson to you," he said as we hurried back to the parking lot. "Everyone told us we couldn't get here, but we did."

"Where there's a will, there's a way," I said, then pointed. "And look, there's the taxi. Do you not see the taxi?"

We caught the ferry with ten minutes to spare. Howie and Christina went to the top deck to enjoy the view, while my dad and I sat on the lower deck on chairs that looked kind of like really old airplane seats. There was no air-conditioning and more locals than tourists on the public ferry. I was much more okay with that now than I would have been a week ago.

Now that we had successfully done the ruins and the ferry was on its way back to Cozumel, my dad began to get lost in his own thoughts again. I knew that if his restaurant closed, it wouldn't just be the end of a business, but the end of my father's dream . . . so the real ruins that he was looking at today were his own.

It seemed too much was at stake for a day that was supposed to be about celebrating independence.

I thought about what Tilde might be doing at this very moment. Were the people she was trying to help being cooperative? Were they so scared that they would give themselves away? Did they really look enough like those people on the passports to pull it off? I thought of Jorge and Ignaçio, then pulled out the tiny sombrero, which was still in my pocket, and considered it. We all complain that we hate school, but do we really? Would you trade school for a life standing every day in the hot sun, getting people to take pictures of your iguana?

I realized that I was more worried about those people in the salon, who I didn't even know, than I was about my dad's business. Was that wrong? I mean, it's like I said before, even if we lost everything, we wouldn't really lose *everything*, would we?

"Souvenir?" my dad said, noticing how intently I was staring at the little sombrero.

"Sort of," I told him. And I realized that, of all the junk I collected on my shelves back home, this one might be both the junkiest and the most valuable at the same time. It made me think of this kid I knew in grade school who had a glass eye—but I think that wasn't the only reason he came to mind.

See, they kept having to redo the eye, and so he kept the old ones, collecting them on a shelf, like some people collect shot glasses. I don't know how he could sit at his desk and do his homework with a bunch of eyes looking at him. Anyway, the last eye I saw him with was the best match to his real one, but you could still tell it wasn't real. I once asked him if it would pop out if he sneezed real hard.

"It could, because my head's still growing," he told me. "Worse, though, is if I get socked in the face and it gets lodged in my brain." Which I guess is one of the warnings they ought to put on the box when you buy a glass eye.

He said the problem with having only one seeing eye is that you don't have depth perception. The world looks flat. The rest of us don't really notice it much when we close one eye, because our brains compensate—but try closing one eye while you're watching a 3-D movie, and you'll know exactly what I mean.

I think they call that *parallax*: being able to know the distance of something because you're seeing it from two separate points—and the farther apart those two points are, the more accurate you can be. Put one eye here and one eye fourteen feet away, and you know a whole lot more about the world you're seeing. Of course no one has a head that's fourteen feet wide, unless you're a Cyclops. But since a Cyclops has got only one eye anyway, you're pretty much screwed.

The thing is, if you go through life with just your own point of view, you're like that kid with the glass eye. If there's something that's right up in your face, it looks really big—overwhelming even. But if you've got that parallax—if you've got that other point of view—you realize that there are bigger, much more important things that are far off toward the horizon. Once you focus on *those* things rather than the stuff way up close, that close-up stuff becomes nothing more than a nuisance blocking the view.

And now, as I looked over at my dad, I suddenly realized that, hey—maybe my horizons had been expanded after all.

"Y'know, it's not the end of the world," I told him. Which, according to the Mayan calendar, already happened.

"I really don't want to talk about this, Antsy," my dad said.

But I wasn't leaving it alone. "I don't care if you don't want to talk about it; I do. Because I'm not sure Crawley really wants to close your restaurant at all."

"Why would he say it if he didn't mean it?"

Then I thought of something my dad said to me earlier today and, finding a little of my own parallax, I realized the truth. "Because," I told him. "You've been a selfish bastard since you got on the cruise."

He looked at me in disbelief.

"What did you just call me?"

I looked him in the eye, unflinching. "The man invited you on this cruise for his birthday—HIS birthday—all expenses paid. But have you spent even five minutes with him since you got on the ship?"

199

He didn't answer, because we both knew what the answer was.

"Have you invited him on any of the shore excursions you and Mom went on? Did you even try to get him out of his suite to come to dinner with the rest of us?"

My dad waved his arm, trying to dismiss it. "Aw, you know Crawley. He's a recluse; he doesn't like people. He doesn't like going out."

"That's true . . . but did you ask him?"

"Why should I ask him if I know the answer is going to be no?"

"Because," I said, "it allows him the dignity of actually saying 'no.'"

My dad let out a long slow breath. "So what am I supposed to do now? Kiss up to him for the rest of the cruise?"

"I don't know," I said. "Is there a difference between kissing up and just being decent?"

He gave absolutely no response to that, but after a few moments he said, "Why don't you go check on your sister and see that she hasn't fallen off the ferry?"

"I'm more worried about Howie making other people jump off the ferry," I told him. Then I left my dad alone with his own thoughts and maybe some of mine, too.

CHAPTER 17

YOUR OBSTRUCTED VIEW INCLUDES A GUY FROM BROOKLYN DOING A SPIDER-MAN IMPERSONATION, BUT YOU'RE TOO IN LOVE WITH YOURSELF TO NOTICE

WHEN WE GOT BACK TO THE *PLETHORA*, IT WAS close to the "all aboard," so there was a long line of people trying to get through security. I scanned the line looking for Tilde and maybe some faces I would recognize from the beauty shop, but I didn't see a single one. Once I was on board, I wandered the ship, searching through the crowds for signs of her and the others. Then I finally realized I wasn't going to find her that way. I went to the suite and fished through the dresser drawers until I found the passkey that Tilde had given me.

I was going to have to pay a visit to Bernie and Lulu.

Bernie and Lulu's door had a Do Not Disturb sign hanging on the knob. I paced the hallway, trying to figure a way to get onto their balcony, and then realized that maybe I didn't need to. Each of the *Plethora*'s lifeboats covered the length of maybe half a dozen "obstructed view" cabins, and each of those cabins had a balcony.

I knocked on the next door, but that cabin was occupied, too. I wasn't surprised. It was that time after everyone was back on the ship but before dinner: the time when everyone was either dressing or napping. Finally, four doors down from Bernie and Lulu, I knocked and no one answered. I used the passkey to get in and immediately saw steam coming out from underneath the bathroom door. Someone was taking a shower and singing a really bad cover-your-ears karaoke version of "Mack the Knife." I knew as long as I heard the shower and the singing, I was safe. So I made my way to the balcony as fast as I could, slid open the door, and stepped outside.

When I looked to the lifeboat, I could see why Tilde had chosen Bernie and Lulu's cabin. Because of the tapering design of the lifeboat, all the other cabins had a larger gap between balcony and boat. The balcony where I stood was toward the far end of the lifeboat, and the gap was pretty huge.

The ship hadn't set sail yet. If I jumped and missed, I'd either fall about fifteen feet to the next deck and break a few bones or my momentum would be enough to miss the ship completely, in which case I'd splat on the concrete of the dock ten stories down—because there was no gap between the ship and this dock the way there had been in Miami. Behind me, the guy in the shower stopped singing, the shower turned off, and the bathroom door began to open.

I've done a lot of things in my life that my teachers would call "ill advised," but few things could be iller advised than leaping like a maniac from a balcony to the very end of a lifeboat.

I landed halfway on, halfway off, with the boat rocking from the force of my jump—which made me start to slip.

202

Panicking, I kicked my legs up. Thank God, I got new sneakers for this cruise and wasn't wearing the treadless wonders I usually wore. One foot found a grip and then the other. I pulled myself up and lay sprawled facedown on the bright yellow roof of the lifeboat, my fingertips spread out, clinging like Spider-Man, until I felt sure I wasn't going to slide off. Inside the cabin, a guy in a towel was admiring his physique in the mirror and had no idea I was now the key feature of his "obstructed view." Carefully I crawled the length of the boat to the little roof hatch, pulled it open, and dropped in.

I found myself in the company of a whole bunch of very serious people.

"About time you got here," Tilde said.

It was pretty dim in there. There were lights, but Tilde said they'd know on the bridge if a lifeboat's electrical system powered up, so we all sat in darkness with nothing but the faint light coming from a few small portholes.

"Did everyone make it on?" I asked.

Tilde shook her head. "A few people panicked at the last minute and ran away."

But there were also success stories.

"There was a guard as I was getting on," said one man. "He was staring at me until I start to talk to my wife about the price of tequila. Then he just checked our cards and let us on." The man smiled and gave me a thumbs-up.

Beto was there with his parents. Jorge was there. The woman who dyed people's hair was gone. All told, we had nine new passengers. And now that the reality of the situation had hit them—the truth that in just a few minutes they'd be sailing away from their old lives—they looked, well, scared. Like they had no idea what to do now. Like maybe they had made a wrong decision.

"You did good," I told them, trying to be positive. "The hardest part is over."

"They still have to make it through US Customs," Tilde reminded me. "*That's* the hardest part."

"Yeah, but they have two days until then, right? And it is the Fourth of July. Time to celebrate."

A few people began to cheer and applaud, but Tilde shut that down real fast.

"*¡Callate!* No one must hear you. You can't talk; you can't move. If someone sees the lifeboat rocking, or hears a voice, or notices an open hatch, or looks from their cabin to see a face in a porthole—then it's over."

Through everything, I'd never seen Tilde this stressed. I realized with all of her planning, there were parts of this she was flying blind. Now the others weren't looking at her; they were looking at me for guidance and comfort. To tell you the truth, it made me feel like pissing my pants, so I tried to take the attention off of me. I looked over to all the food that Tilde had stockpiled: big cans of tuna, vegetables, even olives. Like what were they going to do with a ten-pound can of olives?

"Is anybody hungry?" I asked.

"Yes," someone said, "but we have no can opener."

I looked at Tilde and grinned. "Big picture, bad with details?"

She stuck her tongue out at me.

"Okay, I'll get you a can opener," I told her, "but there's no way I'm going out the way I came. We'll have to wait until Bernie and Lulu leave before I can jump to their balcony. I just hope they don't lock that balcony door."

"That door doesn't lock," Tilde said. "I made sure of it four cruises ago."

Suddenly the entire lifeboat began to vibrate, and people braced.

"It's just the thrusters," I told them. "The *Plethora's* pulling away from the dock. We're on our way."

Then one of the men—one I hadn't even spoken to before—reached out and grasped my hand, firmly shaking it.

"*Gracias,*" he said. "*Gracias por todo.*"

I didn't know his name; he didn't know mine. And yet it was the most heartfelt handshake I'd ever received.

Thankfully, Bernie and Lulu were big gamblers, so as soon as the ship was at sea and the casino opened, they were off, and so was I.

I got a can opener from the buffet line. All I had to do was ask, "Hey, you got a can opener?" And since, on this ship, passengers got what they wanted with no questions asked, the buffet dude gave me a can opener with a smile.

"Yes, sir! Here you are, sir! Did you have a good day in Cozumel, sir?"

"The best!"

It was pretty easy to make my way back into the lifeboat

now that I had access to the right cabin, but I knew that each time someone came in or out of the hatch, it was like pulling a Russian roulette trigger. If we kept doing it, eventually someone would notice. So once they had the can opener, Tilde told them they were on their own until the ship reached Miami. Then she would come for them. I could tell Tilde didn't want to leave them, though.

"Trust us," Jorge told her. "We know what we have to do. Keep quiet. Keep still. Think American thoughts." Then he gave her a warm hug, and I realized that they had probably once been more than friends.

"Remember," I told her as we left Bernie and Lulu's cabin, "you have to act normal for the rest of the cruise. Skip out on dinner, turn up in places you're not supposed to be. Be a general pain in your father's aft."

Tilde sighed. "This is going to be a very long two days."

And then we went in opposite directions. I realized at that moment that if all went smoothly, I might not see her again.

But the *Plethora of the Deep* wasn't bound for smooth sailing. And neither was I.

CHAPTER 18

UNTIL YOU'VE HEARD A SALSA BAND PLAYING "GOD BLESS AMERICA," YOU DON'T KNOW THE MEANING OF FREEDOM

I HAD THIS REALLY ANNOYING CONVERSATION WITH Howie once.

"I saw this thing on TV about something they call 'the cosmic theory of chaos strings,'" he told me. I think he'd gotten two different things confused, but when you're dealing with Howie, you gotta be willing to roll with it.

"According to a bunch of brilliant scientists," he said, "random events tend to clump."

"That doesn't make sense," I told him. "If they clump, then they wouldn't be random, would they?"

"Hey, don't blame me. Blame the scientists." Then he went on to talk about the Super Bowl and the Academy Awards. "Do you know they have this random number generator at some college somewhere? And they noticed that when like a gazillion people are focused on a single event, like the Super Bowl or the Oscars, the numbers that were generated were less random."

"Where did you hear this?"

"Cartoon Network. But it was a very serious cartoon."

It would have been easy to just dismiss this as classic Howie, but it bugged me enough that I went to check it out. Not on Cartoon Network, but on actual online sources. I even avoided Wikipedia. My teachers would have been proud. And you know what? It's true. Somewhere out there are these scientists who believe that random events clump together and that human focus makes stuff less random. Call me nuts, but isn't most religion based on the idea that stuff ain't so random?

Thinking about science and God sharing the same bathroom was enough to make my head explode or send me to hell or wherever—but isn't it both cool and creepy at the same time that randomness might not be all that random?

So the next time you got nothing to do all month except for six random events that all fall on the same Tuesday, think about those brilliant scientists and maybe send them some hate mail.

For me, my random events all came down on the Fourth of July, rolling in like a perfect storm that I wouldn't wish on my worst enemy. Well, okay, maybe my *worst* enemy, but no one else.

At eight o'clock that evening, with the lights of Cozumel like a distant line of fire on the horizon, I went up on deck with most everyone else on the ship. The Independence Day party had started, and a salsa band had taken the main stage on the pool deck, launching into a set of rousing yet highly danceable patriotic songs with a Latin beat.

Then the fireworks started. Sure, my parents' clothes iron was confiscated from their luggage as a fire hazard, but they could still do fireworks. I guess you could call that "ironic." Anyway, these fireworks, unlike mine from last year, did exactly what they were supposed to do. I could only imagine what the folks in the lifeboat were thinking about all these explosions. It made me think about Tilde and where she might be. I kept trying to remind myself that the whole thing was no longer my problem but still felt way too connected to it, and to her.

I was surprised to find Crawley in the corner of the Lido Deck—but maybe I shouldn't have been surprised, because my parents were the ones who had brought him out.

"I detest fireworks," he complained, "and all these gyrating people on the dance floor are making me sick to my stomach. I demand that you take me back to my cabin now!"

My father patted his shoulder. "In a few minutes," he said.

"Things will only get worse for you," threatened Crawley.

"How could they possibly?" answered my father.

Crawley saw me and turned to me for help. "Do you see this, Anthony? Your parents have chosen to torture me on the day before my eightieth birthday. They're probably hoping I don't survive to see it."

"They kidnapped you," I said, and winked at him. "What a novel idea."

He grabbed his cane and tried to whack me with it, but I was out of range.

My mother brought over a huge plate of french fries for everybody to share, and to my utter amazement, rather than complain about the grease, Crawley ate them along with the rest of us—although he did throw one at a guy who passed with a lit cigarette.

"Far too many smokers on this cruise," Crawley said. "They should all get cancer and die."

With all the things going down today, it was a relief to have a few moments to relax, without worrying about stuff that was out of my control. I thought that maybe, just maybe, I might be able to let go for the rest of the cruise and enjoy myself.

Then Crawley asked, "Have you seen Lexie?"

To be honest, I hadn't even thought of Lexie for most of the day. My brain could only juggle so many knives without cutting my hands off. From experience, I knew that Lexie did not have a love of fireworks either. "The sound of fireworks," she once told me, "and the feel of the concussive blast is far less pleasant than the visual spectacle must be."

Up above, the sky exploded with color. The crowd oohed and aahed.

"She's probably off with Gustav somewhere," I told Crawley.

"Who?"

I realized that I slipped something Lexie may have wanted to keep secret—but then again, she never specifically asked me not to tell.

"Just this guy from Switzerland," I told him. Then I thought about what Gustav's stated goal was and realized there was only one day left of this cruise to accomplish it, and I started to get worried, like I maybe should have been two days ago. It had been easy to tell myself that Lexie knew what she was doing and that she could take care of herself—but she was not herself on this cruise anymore than I was myself.

The band finished up something that sounded like a cross between "America the Beautiful" and "Low Rider," and the fireworks reached their grand finale. The crowd applauded, and the party continued, but I went inside, where you couldn't quite hear the music, just the rhythm of the drums. I went to all the places Lexie might be. The teen lounge, the arboretum, the bowling alley, the roller coaster, but there was no sign of her or Gustav anywhere. I couldn't even be sure she was still on the ship, and I started to think, how well did I really know this Gustav guy?

I knew I was probably making a mountain out of a molehill, but at this particular moment I had no parallax, and now that it was in my face, this molehill might as well have been the Matterhorn—which I'm sure Gustav could see from his stinking Swiss chalet.

I paused in a stairwell, trying to think this through. If I was Lexie and Gustav, where might I be right now? I didn't like any of the answers I came up with. That's when I heard the distant barking of a dog.

"It's Jorgen Ericsson's ghost hound," said a kid passing me in the stairwell.

I knew for a fact that aside from the goats and llamas in the petting zoo and ponies on the trail, there was only one other four-legged creature on board: the one who belonged to that bark. In all my years of knowing Lexie, I had never heard Moxie bark like this. Sure, he'd whimper and whine from time to time, but Moxie, as far as dogs go, was the mellowest of the Crawleys' fifteen dogs. Now I was getting really worried.

"Moxie!" I called out, as loudly as I could. The bark came again, but this time it came from a different direction, like maybe it really *was* Ericsson's ghost hound. "Moxie!" I went from deck to deck looking down each hallway, but there were so many decks and so many hallways, and he didn't sound like he was staying in the same place.

I finally found him down a hallway on Deck Five, way aft. "Moxie!" He came to me, panting and yipping and more freaked out than I had ever seen him before. I knew that fireworks messed with his head, like they did with most dogs—but I also knew that on the Fourth of July, Lexie made a special point of sitting with Moxie, stroking him to calm him down. So why wasn't she doing that now? And why was he still wearing his guide harness? Lexie never left him in his harness when he wasn't guiding her. That must mean that he took her somewhere and somehow got shut out or forgotten about. There was something about all this that had me about as freaked as Moxie.

"Do you know where Lexie is, boy? Take me to Lexie."

But Moxie was not like one of those ridiculous TV dogs. He wasn't going to lead me to Timmy in the well. He was just a dog—a smart one, but also confused and scared. He whined a bit and circled around me, then took off. I followed him upstairs and downstairs, down one hallway and up another. Finally he ended up at the door of Lexie and Crawley's suite—the only place he really knew how to find. I let him in and he went out onto the balcony and did his business in the sand box that the cruise line had provided for him. Then he came in and lay down about as low as a dog could get, with his jaw pressed to the floor, and just whimpered.

I let him out of his harness. I knew Crawley would be down soon, once his protests got real and my parents had to give in. I swore to myself that I would find Lexie first and have her here before he got back.

On a hunch I went up to the loft bedroom. Lexie's bed looked like it hadn't even been sat on since the cabin steward made it this morning. Next to her bed was a little pad that was completely blank to anyone who didn't know what to look for.

I turned on the side-table lamp and tilted the pad at an angle. The sideways light revealed a bunch of tiny little bumps—exactly what I was looking for! Lexie would sometimes use the tip of an empty ballpoint pen to make notes for herself in freehand Braille. She prided herself on it, even though she had blind friends who thought it was weird.

"The sighted can handwrite, so why can't I?" She would make the symbols backward, pressing the pen tip firmly into the pad, then flip the page and voila! Instant Braille. Much more convenient than the Braille typing machine she used.

I ran my fingers over the bumps. I couldn't read Braille by touch, but Lexie, in one of her own attempts to expand my horizons, had taught me numbers and letters in Braille, if not by touch, then visually. I still remembered most of them.

I sat down and began to decode the messages on each slip of paper. Most were times and places around the ship. Something about her aromatherapy massage. And then I came across a single capital G and four numbers. Eight. One. Three. Four.

I took off for cabin 8134.

CHAPTER 19

LIFESTYLES OF THE RICH, THE FAMOUS, AND THE FILTHY GOOD-FOR-NOTHING PIECES OF HUMAN SLIME

EVEN BEFORE I GOT TO THE HALLWAY OF GUSTAV'S cabin, I heard someone yelling and a door banging open. Then, when I looked down the hallway, I saw none other then Gustav himself storming in my direction. With his shirt open, he looked like this wall of meat barreling toward me. I balled my hands into fists and dug in my heels, ready for whatever fight I could put up.

Then as he got closer, I saw that his shirt was not open; it was torn. Not just that but there was blood on his forehead and a weird look in his eyes that I couldn't make out, but it kinda reminded me of Moxie.

He saw me and said, "That girl's a nut job!" in perfect English without even a hint of an accent. "I'm so totally outta here." Then he pushed past me and was gone.

I hurried down the hallway until I came to the open door of cabin 8134 and went inside.

Lexie was there all right, sitting on the bed, her knees to her chest. Her hair was a mess, but I couldn't see her face because her head was down into her knees. I pushed the door open a little wider, and it gently tapped the rubber stopper.

214

Her head popped up. "Go away!" she yelled.

"Lexie . . ."

"I said, go away!" She reached beside her, grabbing the only thing on the end table—the TV remote—and hurled it at me. I ducked, and it hit the wall. Now it was just one more thing on the floor of a messy room—and I mean messy. There were dirty clothes everywhere. Clearly Gustav and his friends or brothers or whatever were slobs—but there was more going on here. I also noticed a cracked mirror and a shattered cell phone on the floor.

"Lexie, it's me. It's Antsy."

"I know who it is!" she screamed. But this time, she didn't reach for anything to throw.

"What happened here?" I asked. "Did he hurt you? Because if he hurt you . . ."

"He didn't hurt me," she said.

"Are you sure?"

"I told you, he didn't!"

I carefully went toward her and sat at the far end of the bed. "Well, that's good, then, right?"

She didn't answer for a while. One of Gustav's friends or brothers or whatever looked in, caught my gaze, and ran off. I turned back to Lexie. "Tell me what happened."

"It's none of your business."

"Fine. Don't tell me; I don't care. Just as long as you're okay."

"I'm *not* okay! Can't you see that I'm not okay?"

I shut up then, because I knew anything I said would be the wrong thing. I just sat there in Gustav's messy room, and after a couple of minutes Lexie spoke.

215

"Gustav—if that's even his name—brought me down here when the fireworks started," she told me. "I know what he was thinking. I've known since the first day. Once we heard the fireworks, we started kissing. Actually, we've been doing that a lot."

"Yeah, you can skip that part," I told her.

Now it started to get hard for her. I could see tears building in her eyes. "And then . . . and then he told me that he really liked me."

"Yeah?" I said.

"He said it in perfect English! I guess he didn't mean to, but he slipped. Antsy, he's not Swiss at all—he's an American exchange student living in Zurich. Everything about him is a lie."

"Yeah, I kinda got that. I'm sorry."

"The thing is, I was lying, too. I told him I didn't speak German so I could spy on the things he said to his friends and always have the upper hand." She wiped her tears, but they kept coming. "I think that at a different time and in a different place on the ship, we could have laughed about it. Two stupid liars, trying to pull the wool over each other's eyes. But it wasn't a different time and place. It was here and now, and I guess I got a little upset. He backed off, and I got mad that he backed off, and that just made him back off even more. So I grabbed him and I kissed him harder and he pushed me away and I pulled him by his shirt onto the bed—I think I ripped it off of him."

"Not completely," I told her. The thought of Lexie being so aggressive that Gustav freaked . . . well, it shattered everything I thought I knew about the universe.

"He got away from me . . ." By now, her sobs were overtaking her words, and she had to fight to get them under control. ". . . and he . . . and he . . . and he called me horrible things, Antsy. Words I don't even want to think about. That's when I started throwing things. I couldn't stop myself. One of them hit him. I think another broke a window."

"A mirror," I said.

"He rejected me, Antsy. I threw myself at him like some back alley slut, and he just threw me away like garbage."

Now I wished I *had* hit Gustav as he passed me or at least given him a swift kick in a place he wouldn't forget. "You don't need a guy like that."

Lexie got quiet then. "Maybe I do," she said. "Maybe I'm all the things he called me and worse."

"No," I told her, "never say that. Never even *think* that."

Finally I reached out and put my hand gently on her knee. See, Lexie was all about physical contact, and as a friend—although not a very good one lately I wanted her to know I was here. Not just in words, but in *presence*. That hand on her knee was a promise that I wasn't going anywhere.

"From the moment I got in the room with him, all I could think about was how shocked my parents would be, and it made me want to be here even more." Then she got quiet. "I would have done it, Antsy. If things didn't go so wrong, I would have. So what does that say about me?"

"That you're sixteen and just as screwed up as the rest of us?"

She had no response to that. Like I said, Lexie is masterful at concealing what she doesn't know. It had never occurred to me that she could be hiding how little she knew herself.

"C'mon, let's get out of here," I told her. I found her shoes in the mess and knelt down, slipping them on her feet like she was Cinderella. Then, with my arm firmly around her waist, I led her out of Gustav's dirty little playpen and back to her suite. She completely relied on me, as if she had lost all sense of direction. The counting of strides, stairs, and turns that had always been as easy to her as breathing was gone, as if her own blindness wasn't an old familiar thing, but new and unsettling. I could only hope that she'd find her confidence again, because it defined her. I didn't want to imagine Lexie going around without definition.

Crawley, who was already in the suite, came into the main room the second I opened the door, and Moxie came running over to Lexie, tail beating. The moment Crawley saw her, his cane began to tremble.

"She's had a really bad day," I told him.

"Are you hungry, Lexie?" he asked. "The steward brought these canapés, as if I could digest them."

Lexie knelt, giving her attention to Moxie instead of her grandfather, because I guess it was easier.

"I'm tired," she said. "I'll see you in the morning, Grandpa." Then she went up to her bedroom. She didn't even take Moxie, which meant she really and truly needed to be alone for a while.

Crawley turned to me. "Anthony, a word."

"Exhausted," I said. "In fact, it's the word of the day."

He ignored me and gestured to the other suite. No one else was there at the moment, which I really wished wasn't the case, because it meant we could talk in private. Right now I didn't want to talk to Crawley in private, but I guess I had no choice, because he closed the door between the suites, making sure Lexie couldn't hear us. Then he threw me a solar flare of a gaze.

"This is *your* fault!" he said.

"What?"

"Where were *you* when she was having this 'bad day'?"

And that's when I lost it—which surprised me, because I didn't even know I had anything inside me left to lose.

"I AM NOT THE GUARDIAN OF THE WHOLE STINKIN' WORLD!" I yelled. "I got enough going on without babysitting you and my parents, Lexie, and Howie, so maybe you oughta just thank me for actually finding her and bringing her back and then just leave me the hell alone!"

Crawley did not respond by yelling back at me like I expected, and maybe I wanted him to, because it meant I would get to yell even more. Instead he got all calm. "Hmm," he said. "Struck a chord, did we?"

I took a deep breath and tried to lower my voice but wasn't too successful. "You have no clue what crazy crap I'm dealing with, and trust me, you don't want to know, so get off my back!"

He studied me for a few seconds, then said, "To whom much is given, much is expected."

"Given?" I screeched. "What have you ever given me besides a hard time?"

"How about a cruise?"

"Fine! What have you ever given me besides a cruise and a hard time?"

"A controlling interest in my restaurants," he said.

"Wh . . . what?"

You know how in the first *Star Wars*—not that lousy Episode One, but the one that they now call Episode Four—when, right at the last minute, Han Solo shows up out of nowhere, blows up a couple of bad guys, and sends Darth Vader tumbling into the next movie? Well, what Crawley said was kind of like that.

"It's in my will," he told me. "Lexie gets all my money, but controlling interest in the restaurants goes to you."

My head was still tumbling in space. "Why would you do that?"

"Because it will infuriate my son," he said. "It's bad enough that he didn't come to my eightieth birthday, but what he did to Lexie—skipping out on his own daughter— that's unforgivable. He deserves all the misery I can heap on him from beyond the grave."

"So you're doing it for spite?"

"Don't oversimplify."

"What if I don't want it?"

"So sell the restaurants and make a fortune," he said. "What'll I care? I'll be dead."

I stood there annoyed at my own speechlessness, and that just made him laugh.

"Don't worry about it," he said. "I intend to live a very long time, and I'm sure you'll give me plenty of reasons to cut you out of my will between now and my demise."

Then he turned, opened the door, and went back into the other suite.

"Wait," I said, realizing something. "You said restaurants plural. So does that mean you're not closing my dad's?"

"The jury is still out," he said.

"You're the jury," I reminded him.

"Right," he said. "And I'm out." Then he closed the door behind him.

The seas got rough during the night on account of we were moving so fast. According to the captain's announcement, there was a "tropical depression" to the north—which was code for an angry storm that was trying to decide if it wanted to go postal and become a hurricane.

"Not to worry," he told us all over the ship's loudspeakers. "These things happen—and the best place to be is in a ship at sea, because we can always outrun the storm. Especially in a ship as fast as this one."

Anyway, since the storm was blocking the shorter path back to Miami, we had to take a southern route, slipping under Cuba, and really book to make it back to Miami in a day and a half.

The ship let off all these weird but perfectly normal creaks and groans. "The hull is like a big steel drum," our cabin steward told us. "A wave hits it, and boom-boom-boom!"

My parents and Christina got annoyed that the ship's motion made all the hangers in the closet clatter, so they took them out and laid them on the floor. Meanwhile on the sofa bed across the room from me, Howie was obsessing about the current entry in his million-ways-to-die list.

"Metal fatigue, Antsy!" he kept saying. "It's why things crash and blow up! The *Titanic* split in half, you know!"

"It hit an iceberg first," I pointed out. "There are no icebergs in the Caribbean."

"There are other things."

Right. And less than twenty-four hours later, we were going to discover one of those "other things."

CHAPTER 20

I AM NOT LOOKING FORWARD TO THE TASTE OF LLAMA AND SPAM, ALTHOUGH I THINK I MIGHT BE ABLE TO STOMACH THE FIRST ONE

COZUMEL HAD BEEN OUR LAST PORT, AND THE next day was a sea day again. It was July fifth—Crawley's birthday—and that afternoon we had his big birthday banquet. It was held in his suite by his request and held early, because he wanted it to have a Thanksgiving-in-July kind of feel, since we were all supposed to spew gratitude at him as well as acceptable presents. The concierge staff decorated the whole suite with streamers and balloons. It's impossible not to feel festive when there are balloons, and I was able to, at least for a little while, forget about the big yellow time bomb of stowaways.

We ate filet mignon and sea bass—Crawley's favorites—then right before dessert, Crawley got up to give himself a toast, because he didn't trust anyone to do it for him.

"You people," he said, "have gotten under my skin like deer ticks."

I held up my glass. "Here's to parasites!" I said.

He glared at me. "I cannot begin to understand what possessed me to bring you all on this trip. Perhaps senility.

223

Be that as it may, it is my birthday, and you're here, so I would not be opposed to you drinking to my health."

"Have you poisoned it, Grandpa?" Lexie said, and the steward pouring the champagne laughed.

Crawley frowned at the laughing steward. "There goes your tip."

He began to open his presents. Since he showed neither disgust nor appreciation for most of them, I assume they were acceptable. Howie got him a pair of high-end binoculars for spying on people from his windows. Lexie got him fourteen gold dog collars, engraved with the sins and virtues, as those were the names of the dogs. My family's gift was the most interesting—and my parents didn't even tell me what it was, just that they had it covered. My father handed Crawley a small piece of paper, rolled up and tied with a bow. A piece of paper? I cringed, figuring he would be furious.

Crawley looked at it, more worried than curious; then he opened it.

"It's a recipe I'll be adding to the restaurant when we get home," my dad said. "That is, if there *is* a restaurant."

Crawley examined it through his bifocals, and his chin began to quiver in anger. But when he took off his glasses, I could see it wasn't anger—there were tears in his eyes. Real tears. Crawley had tear ducts!

"How did you know?" he asked, his voice all warbly.

My mother smiled at him. "We have our sources," she said kindly.

He wiped his eyes until the tears stopped. I didn't

224

get a glimpse at the recipe, but whatever it was, it melted Crawley's heart like the Grinch for an entirety of twelve seconds. Then he folded the paper, put it in his shirt pocket, and said: "I expect to see it on the menu by next week."

It was as they brought dessert—a huge baked Alaska with enough candles to melt a glacier—that something happened.

The whole ship was shaken by a weird vibration that was different from all the others. This one was really jarring, knocking over all our champagne glasses, and with it came a creepy metallic groan from beneath us that sounded like something dying.

Howie instantly turned to me, his death meter twitching and his jaw dropped in silent terror.

"Uh . . . I think we hit a whale," I said.

No one said anything, but the steward who brought in the baked Alaska politely excused himself and hurried out.

The *Plethora* was quiet now. Too quiet.

"I'm sure it's nothing," my father said.

"Maybe we should get our life jackets anyway," said Christine.

Then Crawley slammed his fist on the table, and said, "Isn't anyone going to sing 'Happy Birthday'?"

Everyone on the ship had heard it and felt it. The lower decks got it even worse than we did. People were out in the hallways exchanging theories—I wasn't the only one who thought that maybe we hit a whale—but that wasn't what had happened. The truth was a whole lot simpler:

The *Plethora of the Deep*, the largest, most advanced, most luxurious cruise ship in the world, had just fallen for one of Mother Nature's oldest tricks.

We were stuck on a sandbar.

I remember hearing in the news about a cruise ship that got stranded off the coast of Mexico. Engine fire or something like that. The fire got put out, and no one was hurt. In fact, the damage wasn't even bad enough to abandon ship, but with no engine, the ship floated like a cork, with no electricity, for days. The food all went bad; the showers didn't work; the toilets wouldn't flush. Basically the thing became like a Brooklyn apartment building.

So after a couple of days, they send out helicopters to that stranded ship—but are they rescue helicopters? No. Instead they air-drop SPAM and Pop-Tarts, I guess to trick the passengers into thinking they had somehow sailed into hell.

Eventually they managed to tow the ship into port, and all these smelly SPAM-fed refugees got free cruises for life.

Even worse than that was some Italian ship that got a massive hole ripped in its side by rocks and keeled over sideways in a bay that was shallow enough to keep it partway above water but deep enough to drown about a dozen people. When the media asked the captain why he abandoned ship with people still on board, he told them he "tripped into a lifeboat." Right.

Knowing what happened on those other ships, people onboard the *Plethora* were understandably worried. A sandbar, however, is not like a hole in the hull. A hole is a crisis. A sandbar is an embarrassment.

"These things happen," Captain Pajramovic was quick to announce, although he was a bit sheepish about it. "We have determined that there is no damage to the hull, so it is only a matter of time until the tide rises and the sea graces us with a wave large enough to dislodge us and send us on our way."

Yeah, good luck with that. We were already at high tide, according to some know-it-all on deck. As for waves, the sea was like a bathtub, and that so-called storm was so far away there weren't even any clouds in the sky. Bottom line, we could be stuck here for days.

Howie had already gone into survivalist mode. "If we run out of food," he said, "we could always eat the petting zoo."

The cruise director had quickly wrangled one of the ship's bands. They took the main stage on the Lido Deck and played classic songs with newly tweaked lyrics, like "Run-a-ground Sue" and "Beached Baby."

I decided to go looking for Tilde, because this was a monkey wrench I knew she didn't need. I found her pacing in the hallway outside of Bernie and Lulu's cabin.

"We've got to get in there," she said. "I've got to get to the lifeboat, but none of these people are leaving their cabins!"

"Maybe it'll be okay—it's not like we're abandoning ship."

"No, you don't understand. On this ship there's a

procedure for everything—even running aground. Each lifeboat is lowered to the muster stations and checked for seaworthiness. They're almost done with the port-side boats, and in a few minutes they'll be coming to this side. We have ten minutes to get everyone out."

CHAPTER 21

THE SHEEP IN THE PETTING ZOO
AND IN MY HEAD AREN'T THE ONLY
THINGS THAT BLEAT

THE PLAN TILDE AND I CAME UP WITH, WHICH WAS
no plan at all, was to draw Bernie and Lulu out of their cabin
in a way that wasn't suspicious, and if we couldn't do that,
we'd try the cabin next to theirs, then the next, then the
next.

"Then we've got to hide every single stowaway," Tilde
insisted.

"Why not just hide them in plain sight?" I suggested.
"They've got fake keys, right? They could sit on deck with
everyone else, drinking mimosas and dancing to "Sand by Me."

She shook her head. "Security found their pictures in
the system. Right now the security chief thinks it's just
a computer glitch—people who didn't get wiped off the
system from a previous cruise—but if they start seeing the
same faces around the ship, then it's over."

I thought that maybe I could hide them in my suite . . .
but to do that, I would need everyone's cooperation. Howie,
I wasn't worried about. I could tell him I was an undercover
operative in a government conspiracy—and Christina was
always bribable. But breaking the news to my parents that

I was involved in an international smuggling operation? I might as well just bury myself at sea right now.

Then I realized that I *did* know a place we could hide them—and so did Tilde. A place that no one would go looking. Except for maybe a certain ghost . . .

"Hello. Dis is guest service desk on phone. Is dis Mr. Bernard and Miss Lulu?" I didn't do a very good unidentifiable foreign accent on the phone, but if I was lucky, Bernie was not too sophisticated.

"That's us. What y'all want? Are ya gonna ask me to do my contest-winning belly flop off the ship and splash us off dat dere sandbar?"

I guess I was in luck. "We are needing you both to sign signature, please. To prevent fraud in casino, please."

"Fraud? Whatcha mean, fraud?"

"Is just precaution. Please come, or fraud will result."

"Yeah, yeah. We'll be right there."

I hung up the phone, and Tilde and I waited by the elevator bank until they came out. Bernie was a large guy with a belly that could win any competition, and Lulu had such big hair it wouldn't fit on a smaller cruise ship.

The second they were in the elevator and the doors closed, Tilde and I went into their cabin. I stood guard, shielding my eyes from the sun, which was now low on the horizon, shining through the tiny, unobstructed part of Bernie and Lulu's obstructed view. Tilde went over the railing and into the lifeboat, then a few moments later the first stowaways started to come out, while inside the rest were probably scrambling to hide the stockpiled food beneath the benches, leaving no evidence that they had been there. I climbed over the railing to help them onto the balcony one by one. In less than a minute, they were all in Bernie and Lulu's room, with Tilde bringing up the rear. It would have all been fine except that she left the hatch open.

"I'll get it," I told her. I jumped to the lifeboat, quickly closed the hatch, and took a moment to look down the line of lifeboats. The setting sun was making their bright yellow shells glow even brighter . . . and just a few yards away, the next boat over was being lowered for inspection. We had made it with minutes to spare.

Once we were out in the hallway, the group looked kind of conspicuous, but only to someone who was looking for something unusual. Everyone stayed quiet. We passed Bernie and Lulu, who were already on their way back to their cabin, complaining about the guest services agents, none of whom had a clue about any sort of fraud.

"These people don't know their arse from their elbow," Bernie complained to anyone who would listen. "Can't even sail the boat right."

Once we reached the stairwell, Tilde made a quick decision. "We can't take the main crew hallway to get to the Viking ship," she told me. "Too many crewmen. We'll have to go through the galley."

We went down to Deck One, then through a pair of swinging doors and entered a surreal stainless steel hallway. Even the ceiling was stainless steel.

Tilde checked ahead and told us all to crouch low so we'd

stay out of view. We made it down the hallway and into one of the food preparation stations. The food prep area was huge, and although there was galley staff preparing food, they were so absorbed with what they were doing, they didn't know we were there. The roar and rattle of the huge industrial dishwashers masked the sound of our footsteps.

We quickly went down a food service escalator that wasn't moving and out onto a crew deck. Now we were in a narrow corridor that led to the main crew hallway, but we only had to cross it to get to the series of narrow, winding passageways that led to the Viking ship.

We broke into groups of four, hiding until the coast was clear, then darting across the hallway like it was an interstate.

Once we were all across, Tilde breathed a huge sigh of relief.

"Thank you, Enzo," she said, and gave me a peck on the cheek, which Jorge snorted at. "I'll take it from here. You can go now."

"Go? Where can I go? I'm in the crew area."

"Don't worry," she said. "It happens all the time. If someone sees you, just tell them you're lost and they'll take you back to the passenger decks." Then she disappeared down the winding passageways with her nine stowaways.

The sun was below the horizon when I got back to the passenger decks. Now that everyone was convinced they wouldn't die, the entire ship seemed to be in this wild sandbar tailgate party. Waiters were handing out free drinks, and every band, whether they were scheduled to perform or not, was somewhere on the ship making music. It was all so well organized, you'd think getting stranded on a sandbar was just part of the *Plethora* experience.

I found Lexie lying on a lounge chair with Moxie by her side, even though the sun was long gone from the sky. "Starring herself" she called it. Because "sunning" was too harmful to her delicate skin, she much preferred to lie out in starlight and feel that "sultry" Caribbean breeze. I thought Lexie might still show signs of her encounter with Gustav—kind of like post-traumatic schmuck syndrome—but she seemed back to her old self.

"I'm beyond it," she told me, and offered nothing more.

"So, then . . . you're okay?"

She sighed, pretending to be irritated. "Yes, I'm okay, thank you for asking; now can we just move on?"

"Nope, we're on a sandbar," I said.

I wasn't entirely convinced that she really was okay, but I knew she didn't want to revisit that uneasy place inside, where parents forget you exist and you throw yourself at slimeballs in muscle shirts. I suspected she needed some of her own parallax before she could think about it again. If not visual, then a sort of mental 3-D perspective on the situation. For now it was best to leave her alone.

I had to admit that my stress bomb meter was dropping from the red into the yellow. Things were finally starting to calm down. Lexie was bouncing back, the lifeboat crisis was averted, and my parents were even getting along with Crawley. I was beginning to think being stuck on a sandbar was not such a bad thing after all . . . until I got back to the suite and saw Howie looking like he had just seen Jorgen Ericsson's ghost.

"Antsy, I think you gotta look at this."

"I'm not really in the mood, Howie," I told him. "You kept me up half the night talking about shipwrecks, giant squid, and the Sydney Opera House. Now I'm taking a nap."

"No," he said, "I think you really need to see this." He turned up the TV to reveal a CNN news report. Vanderbilt Hooper, the big shot CNN reporter, was on screen with a picture of our ship on the screen behind him, taken in happier days.

". . . and sources have confirmed that the *Plethora of the Deep* is in fact lodged on a sandbar off the coast of Cuba."

I grinned. "No way! We made the news. How about that?"

"Yeah," said Howie. "Keep watching."

"We've been receiving bleats from people on the ship all day, including images and videos," continued Vanderbilt. Then the screen behind him began to show those bleated videos.

"Ha," I said, amused, "that's instant communication for you. Using the ship's own satellite link to send out the SOS."

"Keep watching," said Howie again.

"This is what you might expect from a ship stranded at sea," Vanderbilt said, "but there's one bleat we found particularly interesting, and more troubling each time we look at it. Here it is again."

Then the screen filled with a video of one of the *Plethora*'s

234

lifeboats—a video taken from a deck somewhere above it. I watched with that special brand of horror reserved for slasher films and life-altering moments as the long line of stowaways climbed out of the lifeboat and were helped over a balcony railing by a boy whose back was to the camera. The image was shaky. Faces couldn't really be made out, but it was very obvious what was happening. I stared in disbelief, trying to wrap my head around the fact that our secret wasn't just out to some guy with a phone camera—it was now being broadcast to millions of homes across America. For all I knew, it was on the Jumbotron in Times Square.

"It appears to us," said Vanderbilt, "that these people are being smuggled into the United States via Caribbean Viking lifeboats—and there's already speculation that this is not an isolated incident, but part of a much larger smuggling operation."

Like everyone else, the last person out of the lifeboat could not clearly be seen. But it was obvious that it was a girl, and she had left the hatch open. Then the boy by the railing jumped onto the lifeboat to close the hatch, and, like the idiot that he is, he looked up. Not high enough to notice the camera, but high enough to clearly show his face.

"Antsy," said Howie, "I don't know how to tell you this . . . but I think that's you."

CHAPTER 22

"ATTENTION! ATTENTION! THIS IS CAPTAIN PAJRAMOVIC. WILL ENZO BENINI PLEASE REPORT TO THE BRIDGE IMMEDIATELY."

I HAVE A LONG, SAD HISTORY OF BEING CALLED into the principal's office. Stupid stuff, mostly. Cracking a joke at a teacher's expense. Smacking somebody who truly deserved to be smacked. I've even had the occasional fistfight, although those were pretty rare.

But having your international crime broadcast on national television and then moments later being called to the bridge by the captain of a ship takes it to a whole new level. I mean, a captain can perform weddings, right? Which means that at sea, he has the legal authority of a judge, so he could also probably pronounce the death penalty, like maybe they still made people walk the plank.

Regardless, this was definitely going on my permanent record.

CHAPTER 23

A HUMORLESS BROUHAHA OF GLOBAL PROPORTIONS MAKES ME THE MASTERMIND OF A DRUG CARTEL ACCORDING TO SOME TOOL IN OMAHA

IT TOOK ME A WHILE TO FIND THE BRIDGE, NOT just because I was freaked and frazzled, but because there was no way to get there from the passenger areas. I had to first figure out which deck it was on and which of the No Admittance doors would lead me there.

When I got close, there was a bridge officer in the hallway who looked at me with this cool judgmental I'm-all-dressed-in-white-and-you're-not kind of gaze.

"Enzo Benini, I presume?"

"Yeah, something like that," I said.

"Captain Pajramovic is waiting for you." Then he opened the door and let me in.

The bridge was this huge, glass-fronted room as wide as the ship. It was full of navigational computers and stuff that didn't really look like it needed human beings to operate—and yet it still couldn't keep the ship off a sandbar. Must run Microsoft programs, I guess. `Warning! Sandbar Error! Reboot Cruise Ship Now!`

With so much technology, there weren't many officers

on the huge bridge, and when the captain saw me, the bridge officers left, like townsfolk hiding from a shoot-out.

As I came around a computer console, I saw he was standing in front of Tilde, who sat in a chair, looking at her toes. CNN was playing on an overhead TV screen. Vanderbilt Hooper was having a phone conversation with an immigration expert in Nebraska (like, why would they even have an immigration expert in Nebraska?). She said this whole cruise line smuggling operation was clearly masterminded by one of the big drug cartels.

Tilde looked up at me sadly. "Hello, Enzo."

But her father didn't let her say another word.

"First of all," he said to me, "there is no Enzo Benini on the ship's roster. It doesn't surprise me that you're using an assumed name, considering what you've been up to. Your real name, please?"

"Anthony Bonano, but . . ."

"Well, Anthony, it seems you and my daughter have created quite the international brouhaha."

"Uh . . . does that mean it's funny?"

"It couldn't possibly be more serious."

No matter how much he tried to wilt me with his gaze, I refused to look down at my toes. What is it they say? Never let 'em see you sweat? But in this humidity, it was a losing battle.

"With all due respect," I told him. "We're not the ones who landed us on a sandbar."

Point for me. He shifted his shoulders uncomfortably, like he'd just been stung in a place he couldn't reach. "Yes, it would be bad enough if this ship was just the laughingstock of the fleet, but now thanks to you and my daughter, it's at the heart of an international scandal."

"It's not his fault," said Tilde.

"He chose to help you! That makes him equally to blame."

"These things happen?" I offered.

The captain was not amused. "It would be better for all involved if you told me right now where the stowaways are."

"Don't tell him, Enzo!"

"Tell me, Anthony."

I looked up at the TV screen. They were playing the video of the stowaways climbing out of the lifeboat again—this time with the expert from Omaha giving commentary, like it was a football game.

"I'm waiting, Anthony."

And so I said what my brother, Frankie, told me to say if I ever found myself in an impossible situation.

"I want to speak to a lawyer."

The captain let off a growl that was eerily werewolf-like, then ended with a resigned sigh. "Did either of you even once think of the consequences of what you were doing?"

"It is all I thought about!" said Tilde. "And I decided a long time ago that it was worth the risk."

"Was it?" said her father, "Well, let me be the first to inform you of the real-world consequences, because I know a little bit about international law." He turned to me. "You, Anthony, will be looked upon by your country as a victim and will be given a slap on the wrist in the form of six months to a year in a juvenile detention center."

"What? I'm going to juvie?" Somehow, that didn't seem like a slap on the wrist to me.

"You, my darling daughter, who I knew even less than I thought I did, will be stripped of the Albanian passport I struggled so hard to get for you, then you will be sent back to Mexico and will probably end up back on the streets."

"You would do that to me?"

"I will have no control over it, you see, because I will be in prison."

Both Tilde and I were silent.

"Do you honestly think they'll believe that two kids masterminded a smuggling operation?" He pointed to the TV hanging overhead like an anvil ready to fall on us. "They're already talking about conspiracies and drug money and corruption at the highest levels."

"But . . . but it was just us," I said.

"Which do you think people will believe?" he asked "That two teenagers managed to sneak a boatload of people onto this ship under everyone's noses? Or that the ship's captain was being bribed to look the other way?" He turned away from us and looked out of the grand windows to the twilit sea. "Today," he said, "the sandbar is the least of my problems."

He ordered me back to my suite, telling me that I was under house arrest.

"Be happy I haven't sent you to the brig." He didn't press me again for where the stowaways were, and I realized that he already must have figured it out—and had decided that for the time being, it was the best place for them to be. They couldn't be on any more videos as long as they remained unseen.

Two security guards were waiting for me at the door of the bridge.

"I'm sorry," I told the captain, as if "sorry" could possibly mean anything at this point. He didn't look at me or his daughter. He just looked out at the sea, like maybe he was imagining going down with his ship—and I realized what he was thinking. No matter what happened now, this would be the last voyage he would ever take as the captain of this or any other vessel.

Everyone was in my suite when I got there. They all knew. They had all seen the video, and I swear it was like walking into a room of strangers. My parents just stood there staring at me. Howie kept his distance. My sister tried to take some video, but my father stopped her. Crawley was the first to actually speak.

"Well, this has certainly been a birthday to remember."

Lexie came up to me and said, "You really should have told me about this from the beginning."

"Why? Would you have helped?"

"No," she told me, "but I think I would have successfully talked you out of it." She gave me a hug and went back to her suite, making her grandfather go with her.

I thought my parents might yell at me, but this was even beyond yelling.

"Why don't you tell us everything from the beginning?" my father said.

And so I did, and they listened and asked all the questions you might expect them to ask. When it was over, they actually seemed relieved.

"Well, it's obvious," my father said. "She used you."

"No, it wasn't like that," I insisted.

"Antsy, please," said my mother. "It wasn't your idea. You don't even know those people. Honey, you're just a victim."

"You're wrong!" I stood up, and I thought about what the captain had said and realized he was dead-on. The spin was already taking hold right in this very room.

"Can I sell Antsy's autograph on eBay?" asked Christina.

"No!" my parents said in unison.

"Listen," said my father. "All we can do is let this thing play out." Then he turned off the TV. "I don't want to watch that anymore."

I don't know what compelled me to do what I did next. Maybe I just knew I couldn't live with the thought of Tilde back out on the streets selling silver crosses and her father on trial for being part of a conspiracy that didn't exist.

"Hey, Howie, do me a favor and get your phone."

"What for?" he asked, all full of suspicion.

"Don't look at me like that," I told him. "I'm still the same guy I was before."

"I know, Antsy," he said. "I just got more stuff than I planned to think about today. I mean my head was already kinda full. It's been hard making more room, you know?"

"Full of what? More giant squid?"

242

"Hey," he said, "you're not the only one with stuff going on." Then he went to go get his phone.

With Howie's help, I made a little video. Nothing too long, but probably the most important video of my life. When it was done, I told Howie to bleat it out to Blather.

"What? At these roaming charges?"

"I'll pay the charges. Just do it."

"It won't do no good to put it up on Blather," he said. "I don't got any followers."

"How could you have no followers?" I asked. "Inanimate objects have followers."

"It's intentional."

I was not willing to go down that path today. "Just bleat it right to CNN. They'll know what to do."

"Okay," said Howie. "I really hope you know what you're doing."

"I don't," I told him. "If I did, I'm pretty sure I wouldn't be doing it."

CHAPTER 24

I GOT YOUR DRAMATIC
CHIPMUNK RIGHT HERE

"Hello. My name is Anthony Bonano on the Plethora
of the Deep. *For a while, I've been seeing all this
stuff about how poor they are in Mexico—not at
the fancy hotels that got pools and Jacuzzis up the
yin-yang—but like the real places that we usually
don't wanna know about. When I found out I was
going on the* Plethora, *I decided to do something
about it. I got a bunch of fake passports in Jamaica,
then connected online with some people in Cozumel,
on accounta they got Internet everywhere. I even
cracked the ship's security system so it would think
the stowaways were passengers—pretty easy if you
know anything about computers and passwords.*

*"Sorry, but there ain't a conspiracy like those
moron 'experts' think. It was just me. I did it because
I wanted to see if I could—and you know what? It
worked. Almost. Anyway, I just want to let everyone
know that I'm sorry for the trouble that I caused. To
be honest, I never actually believed I could get this
far working alone."*

· · ·

There's a reason it's called viral.

Smallpox, for instance, is a virus. People think the Europeans conquered the New World, but they didn't. Smallpox did it: a virus that wiped out entire civilizations in its path. One week a native village is there, the next week, it's gone.

Sure, when something goes viral on the Web, it doesn't exactly wipe out civilizations, but it does get the attention of a whole lot of people with too much time on their hands— and all that human focus is bound to alter some randomness somewhere.

The video we bleated was on TV within ten minutes, and a minute after that, it had fourteen thousand hits. Not "*like* fourteen thousand" but *actually* fourteen thousand, then a minute later fifty thousand, then one hundred thousand, and then after that, I stopped checking because numbers that big get scary real fast.

That's when the *Plethora of the Deep* conveniently lost its satellite signal and all communication in and out of the ship stopped. Passengers couldn't send out eyewitness accounts from their phones, and no TV signal could get in.

I was okay with that, though. It was weird watching myself on TV and listening to people who didn't even know me analyze me and pick apart my words like I was speaking in secret code or something. The video was sincere enough that people believed it, and the conspiracy theorists crawled back under their rocks where they belonged. Not all of it was about picking me to pieces.

245

See, they had already figured out that I was the same guy who dumped a pitcher of water over the head of an obnoxious blowhard senator at my dad's restaurant six months ago. I just did it because he was an idiot and he deserved it—but a picture of me dumping that water had made the news on account of everybody hated that senator and wished they coulda poured that water themselves. I hear they even made mugs with that picture now. So the media brainiacs connected the dots from the water-dumping incident to the stowaway incident, and suddenly they're painting me like I'm all political.

It was a good thing that the TV signal got cut off when it did, because sitting on a sandbar out in the Caribbean Sea, I could pretend that this wasn't any bigger than the ship—which was pretty big, but actually kind of small when you compare it to the whole freaking world.

And luckily the signal got cut before my parents got to see my video up on TV. Christina saw it, though, and she promised not to tell if I agreed to sign autographs for her to sell on eBay.

"I believe it may fund my college education," she told me, because she knew the only way to get rich off of an Internet meme was through merchandising.

We stayed in our suites all night and half the next day, in total radio silence with the outside world. On deck and around the ship, bands were playing and food was being served and the cruise director came on the loudspeaker to announce various activities, in a weird pretense that everything was normal.

Then, right around noon, I was brought up to the bridge

again. My father wanted to come but was told I had to come alone, which really ticked him off.

"You're a minor! They can't interrogate you without parental supervision!"

"Don't worry, it's okay," I told him. "If they ask too many questions, I'll swallow the cyanide pill."

He looked at me all worried for a second. "That's a joke, right?"

Two silent guards led me to the bridge, where the captain waited for me alone. Tilde wasn't there. She was still under house arrest in their quarters, so it was just me and the captain.

"Either you're very stupid or very smart," the captain said to me. "I can't figure out which."

"I know the answer," I told him, "but I'm not sayin'."

"Do you have any idea what's going on out there?"

I looked out over the bridge window. "Looks pretty calm to me," I said.

He didn't dignify that with a response. "While communications are down on the rest of the ship, we do have a satellite connection here on the bridge. Would you like to see the commotion you've created over the past sixteen hours?"

"Not really," I told him, a little troubled that he had actually measured the time since I bleated my video to the world.

"Well, that answers my first question," he said. "I was wondering if you were doing this for attention. I can see now that you're not. Why, then, did you send out that video and take the blame if it wasn't for the attention? Clearly there's nothing in it for you."

So I told him the truth. "I did it because the worst that could happen to me is nothing compared to what could happen to you and Tilde."

He shook his head, looking at me with this weird combination of being both disgusted and impressed. Kind of like I must have looked when I ate snails the other night. Then he turned on the TV and made me watch the fallout from my little nuclear video.

First off, I couldn't believe how many pictures they found of me online to slap up behind newscasters. A "digital footprint," they call it. There were school pics with plastered hair that made me look saintly and other ones that made me look like the devil's spawn, depending on the point they were trying to make. There were polls. Forty-five percent of those people polled liked me, forty-five percent hated me, and ten percent were undecided.

"You're not a person anymore," the captain told me. "You're an idea."

"When do I get to be a person again?" I asked, but he had no answer.

Meanwhile on the news, they had somehow dug up everyone who ever knew me and were getting quotes from them, like the quotes they get from a serial killer's neighbors that say he's friendly, quiet, and has no friends except the people in the freezer.

"He was always an excitable boy," said my fourth-grade teacher. I still don't know whether that's a good or a bad thing.

"Bonano's a psycho with a capital *S*," Wendell Tiggor said.

"He peeks in my room," said Ann-Marie Delmonico.

"One thing you can say about Antsy, he's got guts, right?" said Hamid.

But the best quote came from my aunt Mona, who I couldn't stand until the moment she said this:

"Antsy's got a combination of street smarts, conscience, and confidence that could make the world his oyster if he had half a brain. Most of the time you want to strangle him, until you step back and realize that the irritating grain of sand has become the pearl."

So thanks to that, I don't hate Aunt Mona anymore. Except for the way she smells.

As for the stowaways, the media was calling them "the Caribbean Nine." I suppose, like me, they were "ideas" now, too.

"It only gets worse," said the captain, flipping stations. As it turns out, the ship was stuck fairly close to Cuba, and since Guantanamo Bay was the closest bit of US territory, some bozo in Washington announced that the ship would be sent there once it got off the sandbar, for "debriefing." The idea that the Caribbean Nine were going straight to Gitmo was met with public outrage, and people were rallying in major cities, holding huge protests.

All this in the course of sixteen hours. I guess the captain was right when he said if there's going to be a storm, it's best to be at sea, where you can outrun it. But this storm was gonna catch up with me no matter what I did.

I grabbed the remote and turned off the TV. "I don't feel so good," I said.

"I'm not surprised," said the captain. Then the bridge phone rang and he picked it up. "Yes," he said into the phone. "Yes, I understand."

I was still grappling with my rolling stomach, which could not be seasick since we weren't moving, and then the captain shoved the phone into my hand.

"It's for you."

I took the phone, figuring it was my parents calling me from the suite. But the voice on the other end wasn't anyone I recognized.

"Is this Anthony Bonano?" said an official-sounding woman on the other end.

"Yeah?"

"Good," she said. "Please hold for the president."

CHAPTER 25

I CAN'T EVEN BEGIN TO TELL YOU
HOW FREAKED OUT I WAS,
SO I'M NOT EVEN GONNA TRY

"HELLO?"

"Hello, Anthony. Do you know who this is?"

"Yeah," I said, my voice all shaky. "Although you sound different on the phone than you do on TV."

He cleared his throat. "This is Kyle Ericsson, president of Caribbean Viking cruise line."

"What?"

"I said this is Kyle . . ."

"I heard what you said." I sucked in a deep breath, realizing that for the longest time I hadn't been breathing. "You don't go telling people to hold for the president and then get on the phone and say 'hello this is Kyle Freaking Ericsson'; you could give a person a coronary!"

"I'm sorry if my assistant was unclear."

"And not only aren't you the president, you don't even sound Norwegian!"

"My father was from Norway— I was born in Miami. And you are in no position to be talking back to me, young man."

"Actually, I am," I told him. "Because things couldn't

251

possibly get any worse for me, so I can say anything I want and it won't make a difference." Then I realized the whole "Please hold for the president" thing had triggered my fight-or-flight response, and there was so much sudden adrenaline shooting through my veins I probably could have lifted this ship off the sandbar myself while doing a one-handed push-up.

I handed the phone to the captain. "Talk to him for a second. I gotta go find my brain." I sat down and put my head between my legs like they tell you to do when you feel like fainting. Finally I found my brain lodged way up my butt. I sat up, took a few deep breaths, and asked for the phone back. Instead, the captain just put it on speaker, so Kyle Not-Exactly-the-President Ericsson boomed out like the voice of God.

"Can we try this again?" he said.

"Yeah, yeah, sure. I'm good now."

"Captain Pajramovic has explained to me the entire situation. And when I say entire, I do mean entire. We know about his daughter's involvement in all this."

"Got it."

"I want to make sure you understand the consequences of taking full responsibility."

I swallowed hard. "I'm not going to Gitmo, am I?"

He actually laughed. "I doubt that."

I looked at the captain, who showed me no readable response, and I thought of Frankie's advice again. "I'm not saying anything else until I speak to a lawyer."

"Of course," said Ericsson, way too calmly. "We have plenty for you to choose from."

"Excuse me?"

Ericsson sighed. "I still don't think you understand the position you're in." He spoke slowly as if to an imbecile. "By taking full responsibility for smuggling these people on board, you've cast the blame off Caribbean Viking cruise line and its employees. Thanks to you, the worst we can be accused of is a vulnerable security computer—and if we spin you as a computer genius, that would be even better."

I was silent. In my mind, I tried to spin myself as a computer genius and got hurled off the ride.

"So . . . I'm not in trouble?"

"Oh, you're in a world of trouble," he said. "But it's in the cruise line's best interest to help you out of it. After all, we are a family-friendly company. If we paint you like a saint, offer you our forgiveness, and provide you with legal counsel, our clientele will eat it up."

Suddenly this whole thing was like the grand buffet. It was coming at me too fast to swallow. "Don't most saints gotta be burned at the stake first?"

"Well," he said, "that's what's happening right now, isn't it?"

I guess it was. I knew the media was having a field day with all of this.

"The fact that our illustrious captain got our flagship stuck on a sandbar could have been the worst negative publicity we've had in years," Ericsson said, and the captain shifted uncomfortably, "but thanks to you, no one's even talking about the sandbar anymore."

Then he told the captain to call for my parents.

"Do we have to do that?" I asked.

"I'm afraid so."

"Will you at least repeat that part about me being a saint? Because then my mother might not disown me."

"Of course."

"Oh, and by the way, I saw your father's Viking ship. I think it's really cool."

A pause on the other end. "I don't know what you're talking about," Ericsson said in a cold, flat voice. "There is no Viking ship hidden within the *Plethora of the Deep*. To even suggest such a thing would be a violation of my father's last wishes."

"My mistake," I said. "I never saw a thing. Nice Viking ship, though."

My parents were already shell-shocked by all of this, so hearing news of the world and of my freshly trending meme was like pouring salt in a wound that was already brain dead. They just kinda "dealt." They talked calmly on the phone to the cruise lawyers and spin doctors, giving brief little sound bites about me that could be used to my benefit and would make the cruise line look good, too. They did decline to do a satellite interview with Vanderbilt Hooper, though.

"I'm far too sunburned to be on TV," my mother said, although I knew the real reason was that it was simply too much to take. Now she kept looking at me like she had never seen me before—and sometimes she simply couldn't look at me at all.

"I honestly don't know whether to be proud or ashamed of you, Antsy," she told me, a little teary-eyed.

"Maybe you could be part of the ten percent undecided," I told her.

My father just stared at the news coverage there on the bridge, trying to wrap his head around it. I was worried on account of I didn't want to give him another heart attack, but this time it seemed more likely he'd have a stroke. I'm not sure which is worse.

"Can you believe this?" he said. "There are people out there calling you a criminal and saying you should forfeit your citizenship. I oughta give them a piece of my mind!"

"Do you think I'll lose my citizenship?" I asked my father.

He shook his head. "People like to talk out of their behinds," he said. "They'll say anything if it gets them in the spotlight, too."

"Are you mad at me?" I asked, and immediately regretted asking. "Stupid question. Of course you're mad at me."

But he didn't answer right away. He thought about it, and then he said, "Remember that time Frankie got drunk and drove his new car into the duck pond?"

"Yeah?"

"Well," he said, gesturing out to the Caribbean Sea, "this is your duck pond."

BOARD GAMES, BOOMERANGS,
AND A BAG OF BODY PARTS

MY PARENTS STAYED ON THE BRIDGE WITH THE captain, and I was returned to the suite, where my missing suitcase was waiting at the door. There was a pre-printed note on it that said *To our valued guest: Your luggage has been located. We apologize for the inconvenience.* I brought it in and pretended for a moment that I was starting this cruise all over, that I could rewind it to day one and just have a normal trouble-free vacation.

My sister, who had been anxiously awaiting my return, began nagging to interview me on her iPhone. "I can't believe you went to Howie to do your video! I won my school's junior journalist award! You should have come to me!"

But I think it was a good thing that just this once, I kept Howie connected to what currently substituted for my life. Because right then Howie was about as disconnected as Mr. Potato Head with all his parts still in the Ziploc bag that accidently got shoved in the Trivial Pursuit box, so good luck finding it.

Howie was out on the balcony sitting by himself, fiddling with a boomerang that he had engraved his name on. Something about it made me sad, and I didn't know why.

"Hey," I said. But he didn't say "hey" back. I wondered if he was mad at me or maybe just freaked out about what I had done. It had not yet occurred to my steel trap of a mind that this wasn't about me at all.

"Why do I do this stuff?" he asked.

I shrugged. "I don't know—what stuff are we talking about?"

He still wouldn't look at me. "Everyone at home's gonna make fun of my hair. And I got no pants anymore on account of I cut 'em all short. And then there's the tattoo I got in Jamaica."

"Tattoo?" I looked him over but saw no visible sign of it. "Where is it?"

"You don't wanna know."

We looked out over the sea for a few moments, because looking out over the sea makes you feel wise rather than just awkward. Wise enough to think you got ahold of the bag with all your friend's missing pieces . . . until you discover that it's not in with Trivial Pursuit at all. Instead, it's Boggle.

"I get it," I told Howie, thinking I had him all figured out. "You got all obsessed with the Australian survivalist, and you want to impress him, or be him, or both, but then you realize he couldn't care less, he's just some loser collecting a paycheck, so you end up like two ships that pass in the night. Or don't pass, considering our current sandbar situation."

"Yes and no," Howie said. "See, Antsy, here's the thing . . . Remember that time you made me hold your hand so Tilde wouldn't know you actually liked her?"

"Yeah?"

"Well . . . I kinda sorta . . . didn't hate it."

This I was not expecting.

"So . . . do you mean *my* hand in particular or just the general concept?"

"Nah, your hand was clammy. Just the concept."

I looked out at the sea again, trying to find more wisdom, but all I got was an ocean of WTF. See, the thing you need to know about Howie is that he's always been predictable. I mean, even when he says stuff that comes out of left field, we totally expect it, because left field is where Howie lives, although he usually forgets his mitt.

"So, what are you saying, dude?" I think this was the first time I'd ever used the word "dude" when talking to Howie. But somehow that high level of formality felt necessary here.

"I don't know," he said, all frustrated. "I don't know what I'm saying. That's the whole thing. See, Antsy, it's been a really confusing year. What with my dad in prison and my mom failing anger management and our cat being diagnosed with feline obsessive-compulsive disorder and now this hand-holding thing. It's all kinda topsy-turvy, you know?"

I didn't know what to say except, "Sorry about your cat," which was the only Howie-related drama I had not heard. I thought back to the time Lance told me I should talk to him, but did I? No. Instead, I pretended like nothing was going on, because I didn't want to be bothered with it.

Now I started to get mad. Not at Howie, but at myself. If I was half the man Enzo Benini was, I would have checked in with Howie sooner rather than just checking out on him.

Howie saw the look on my face, and he read me all wrong.

"You hate me now, don't you?" he said, looking away. "I knew it!"

So I reached out and put my hands firmly on both of his shoulders so he couldn't turn away. "Howie, listen to me— because with all that's going on, I don't know if I'm going to get a chance to say this again, so I want you to hear it now. I really don't care who you like holding hands with, okay?"

I could see his eyes getting a little teary, which was making my eyes get teary, too.

"I was afraid you'd think I was an idiot, and you wouldn't be my friend no more."

"Gimme a break," I told him. "I'll always be your friend, and I already think you're an idiot. I promise you, those two things are never gonna change."

He smiled, immensely relieved. "Thanks, Antsy. You don't know how much that means to me. Unless you got telepathic abilities."

I took the boomerang from him and looked at it. Although it said "Made in China," it couldn't have been more Howie if he had cut down the tree and carved it himself. "So," I said, maybe getting the slightest handle on some of the stuff going on in Howie's head. "Lance has quite the thighs, doesn't he?"

"Don't get me started."

We laughed—and for once I was laughing *with* him rather than *at* him—which I think was a weirder experience for both of us than holding hands. Until today, I had thought the extent of Howie's inner struggles maxed out at "paper or plastic." It was actually good to know there was something more going on in there.

I handed Howie back the boomerang. He looked at it, then out toward the horizon. For a second I thought he might hurl it into the sea the way Lexie hurled her flute, but he didn't. I suspect he'll be pondering that boomerang for a long time before he ever throws it.

"Howie, I'll make a deal with you," I told him. "You got my express permission to be confused about stuff for as long as you want as long as you promise to tell me what's up once you get it all figured out."

"You'll be the first to know."

"Honestly, I'd rather be the second or third."

"Deal." He held out his hand and I shook it, then I pulled him into a spontaneous hug because I knew it would make him feel better and maybe me, too.

After our non-traditional bonding moment, I felt a little bit better about this "duck pond" I had driven my life into. Yeah, the world was crashing down, but I had this protective layer of mildly tweaked people around me who cared enough to keep on caring no matter what happened. Thinking about that brought back some of the conscience and confidence my aunt Mona accused me of having.

"There's somewhere I need to go," I told Howie. "Why don't you come with me?"

"Where we going?"

Then I whispered ". . . To visit the ghost of Jorgen Ericsson. . . ."

As it turns out, the guard at our suite door was not authorized to physically restrain me if I tried to leave the room. All he could do was intimidate me with mean looks. Frankly, I'd seen meaner looks on Don't Walk signs. When Howie and I left, wheeling my suitcase with us, the guard tattled on us into his earpiece and yelled about all the trouble we'd be in—but in the end, all he could do was follow us like a dog, calling it "close personal surveillance."

We reached the captain's quarters, where Tilde's guard gave me another round of mean looks. I knocked on the door anyway, and Tilde let me in.

She was alone, since her father was still on the bridge with my parents, trying to beat my brouhaha into submission while also trying to get the ship off the sandbar, maybe by mental levitation, because I didn't see any anti-sandbar equipment at work all day.

"My father won't talk to me!" Tilde said furiously, beginning to take out her frustration on me. "I don't know anything that's happening."

I gave her the gist, and that just made her angrier. "You made everything worse! I should never have involved you."

And then Howie stepped forward. "Excuse me," he said, matching her tone, "but this is your screwup, and you're lucky you have Antsy to fix it for you!"

I got between them before it could escalate. "I'm not here to argue. I'm here because we gotta bring food and water to the Caribbean Nine if they're gonna survive the rest of this voyage."

She turned to her guard, who was still standing at the open door. "I know! I would do it myself, but this *pendejo* won't let me go!"

I approached her guard, who actually looked like he might physically restrain us if glares failed. "If the Caribbean Nine drop dead of starvation, it won't look good for the cruise line," I told him. "Or for you."

Now he looked a little worried.

He did some talking into his earpiece, strings were pulled, and room service, who did not quite grasp the concept of feeding fugitives, sent us appetizer trays and nine bottles of Perrier.

Our guards carried the trays and bottles down with us to the narrow winding hallway that led to Jorgen Ericsson's star-filled alternate universe while I tugged my suitcase behind me.

At last we found ourselves in front of the unremarkable iron door. The guards looked worried. This was beyond their security perimeter.

"So," asked Howie, "what are we gonna see?"

"Best if I don't tell you."

Tilde punched in the code and pulled open the door. The lights were already on, because people were moving, which relieved Tilde because it meant they hadn't suffocated.

"*Hola,*" Tilde called out. "*Todos están bien?*"

Jorge stood up and looked over the railing of the Viking ship. "What about English only?"

"It doesn't matter anymore," Tilde told him. "And neither do the passports."

Now everyone was looking over the edge of the Viking ship, waiting for an explanation and concerned by the strange sight of security guards holding platters of mini-quiches and sparkling water.

"Better tell them what's going on," I whispered to Tilde. So she gave them the bad news. All of it, from the bleated video, to the media frenzy, to my public crucifixion, as if I had anything in common with Christ beyond the occasional bad hair day.

After hearing the whole story, the nine mumbled to one another, troubled.

"So we're going back?" asked Beto.

"Maybe yes, maybe no," Tilde told him.

Jorge smashed his fist onto a railing. "I knew this wouldn't work."

"Careful," I told him. "That wood's like a thousand years old."

Meanwhile, Howie and the guards just stared at the Viking ship. "Oh, wow," was all Howie could say. "Oh, wow."

"It's Jorgen Ericsson's tomb," I told him. "He's buried in it. But you can't tell anyone."

"So it's true!" said one of the guards, looking less intimidating than before as he passed around his tray of quiches to the hungry stowaways.

While everyone ate and drank, I opened my suitcase. Inside I saw a neatly packed miniature version of my life. I held the image in my mind for just a moment, and then I started to give everything away. "Here," I told the Nine, "wherever you're going, at least you'll have clean clothes."

Beto looked dejected and scared, so I gave him my iPod, and I whispered to him, "Here's a secret. If everyone's really, really still, the lights in the room go out, and you can see the stars."

When there was nothing left to give out, I handed my empty suitcase to the woman who had to leave hers behind.

"I don't understand," said Jorge. "If they know about us, why are we still here? Why haven't they taken us away?"

"It's complicated," I told him. Although he didn't want to accept that, I didn't want to give him any more.

Howie, meanwhile, was looking for a way to pry open Jorgen Ericsson's coffin.

"I really don't think that's a good idea," I told him.

"Yeah," he agreed. "Maybe not."

"I'm sorry, Enzo," said Tilde as we were about to leave. "I think I have ruined your life."

"Don't beat yourself up about it," I told her. Because maybe the ruins of my life could be cool, like Tulum.

Just then the entire Viking ship began to rumble. The lights flickered, the wood of the old ship creaked, what was left of the mast quivered back and forth, and the steel hull of the *Plethora* let out a ghostly moan so loud, it could have been the end of the world.

"It's him!" shouted Howie. "It's Jorgen Ericsson's ghost! We raided his tomb, and now we're cursed!"

Then the door to the chamber—which we had left ajar—swung open, and standing silhouetted in the open hatchway was a nasty, gnarled figure—the very shadow of death itself, and Howie and I both screamed like little girls . . .

. . . Until the figure stepped through the hatchway, and said—

"What's all this about? It's still my birthday, why aren't we celebrating, and why is there a Viking ship down here?"

I recovered from the scream fest, and the moan in the ship around us faded into echoes. "Your birthday was yesterday," I reminded Crawley.

"I've extended it," he said. "Do you have a problem with that?"

The passengers of the Viking ship were chattering among themselves, laughing a little bit from their own panic at the *Plethora*'s great metallic complaint. Crawley took in the scene. "So this is the Caribbean Nine?"

"Yeah, that's them," I told him.

"And what's with the old boat?"

"Jorgen Ericsson's tomb."

He glared at me, then said, "And people think *I'm* eccentric."

I felt a gentle rocking motion that I hadn't felt for more than a day, and I suddenly realized what all that noise had been about.

"We just got off the sandbar!" Tilde said, realizing it the same moment I did.

"I guess we're going home," said Howie, kind of disappointed by the thought.

Tilde and I told the Caribbean Nine that we'd be back for them and not to worry, even though there was plenty of reason to worry, but worrying makes you want to eat, and the quiches were already gone.

As we left, I turned back to take a wide look at the scene again and realized something. This is probably the same kind of boat that Leif Ericsson sailed when he discovered America. So maybe the Caribbean Nine would get there after all.

FREUD, SCHADENFREUDE, AND BRAIN FRIED

HOWIE MIGHT NOT HAVE ALL THE ANSWERS, BUT HE definitely knew the right question:

Why do we do this stuff?

And there's so much stuff, they don't make luggage big enough.

For Howie it's a head of Lance hair and an unmentionable tattoo. For Lexie it's an all-expenses-paid trip to the Land of Douchebag Beef. For me, it's a secret criminal life that's not so secret anymore.

Let's face it, we all got issues. Most of the time we can deal with our own overstuffed baggage, but every once in a while a few marbles bust out of the bag, go rolling down the aisle, and we got no choice but to chase after them.

Chasing after our lost marbles is like an out-of-body experience. For a while it's like we become someone else—someone we don't recognize. It scares us and gives us new and bigger headaches—which is why there's no Excedrin anymore, just extra-strength Excedrin.

They got shrinks to analyze why we do weird crap. Sometimes they tell us it's all because of our parents, which makes us happy, because we all want to blame our parents for everything, right? If it's a good deed we've done, maybe we can say we were touched by the Holy Spirit, or if it's bad, we can say "the devil made me do it." No one ever seems to take responsibility themselves—because if we don't blame it on our parents, or the devil, or the government, or the freaking position of Venus in relation to Mars, then we're still left with that big ugly "why?"

Most of the time all we know for sure is *what* we did, *when* we did it, and *where* it happened. Which means we're not playing Boggle anymore; now it's Clue. But does anyone ask *why* Colonel Mustard killed Professor Plum with the lead pipe in the ballroom? No.

When we look at our own lead pipes and ask ourselves why, the answer never really comes, so we find someone or something to blame, because "I don't know" is not an acceptable answer.

Well, I won't tell this to the media, or to the lawyers, or to the nine people down in the Viking ship, but here's the truth.

I don't know.

For a week I lied to my friends and to my parents; I broke tons of international laws; I helped smuggle people onto a ship illegally. And why did I do it? Sure, maybe some of it had to do with being intrigued by Tilde and maybe some of it had to do with my American guilt, at having so much when others have so little, and maybe I even got off on the danger of it all. But is that why I did it? I don't know.

So, if you gotta have an answer, you might as well go back to Freud and blame it on my parents. Just don't tell them I said so.

After spending more than a day on the sandbar, the *Plethora* made up for lost time, racing at full speed the rest of that day and through the night. I slept the sleep of the dead that night, and by the time I woke up, the sun was already high in the sky.

I looked across the room to see Howie still asleep, too, gripping the boomerang like a teddy bear.

From my bed I could see we were pulling into port, but it sure didn't look like Miami. It looked like the bay of another island.

I got up to get a better look, and that's when I saw I had an audience. In the main part of the suite, my parents sat with worried expressions. Their suitcases were already packed beside them. Crawley was at the wet bar making himself a bloody Mary, Lexie was stroking Moxie—but that wasn't all. Tilde and her father were there, too.

That's when I realized I was in my underwear.

This kind of thing happens to me on a regular basis—although usually it's in dreams. I'm reading an English paper to the Dallas Cowgirls. In my underwear. I'm at my father's restaurant, busing a table for George Washington, Cleopatra, and SpongeBob. In my underwear. So, having been in this position before, I knew exactly what to say.

"Sorry, I've been time traveling."

Somehow it makes much more sense when I'm dreaming.

"I laid out some clothes for you," my mother said. "Come back when you're decent."

"That could be years," said Christina, bumping down from the loft with her own suitcase.

I went off into a corner that wasn't as hidden as I would have liked it to be and slipped on my pants and a shirt. Oddly I felt more uncomfortable in front of Lexie than anyone else, because, sure, she couldn't see, but from the smirk on her face, I knew whatever she was imagining was far more embarrassing than reality. By now Howie had woken up and was looking at everyone with a boomerang impression on half of his face, trying to make sense of what was happening.

"Did I sleep through breakfast?" he asked.

I came back from my corner, fully dressed and as decent as I get. "What's this all about? What's going on?"

"We're being put off the ship," my father said bitterly. "That's what's going on."

"It was a long haul at top speed—but we are about to make port in St. Thomas," Captain Pajramovic told me. "It's been decided that your cruise ends here."

"Decided? By who?"

"Please, Antsy," said my mother, sounding beaten, "don't make this any harder than it has to be."

"What about the Caribbean Nine? What happens to them?"

The captain sniffed, clearly irritated that even I was calling them that. "Their trip ends here, too."

"No! That's not fair!"

I looked to Crawley—the man who complained about everything—only to find he had nothing to say. I turned back to Pajramovic, furious. "What about them?" I said, pointing at Crawley and Lexie. "You're just going to kick a feeble old man and his blind granddaughter off the ship?"

Lexie stiffened when I pulled the "blind" card, but I didn't have much else up my sleeve at the moment.

"No," said the captain, far more calmly than me. "Your friends can return to Miami. But you and your family have to go."

I looked for an ally in Tilde, but after all her big talk, it was like she had switched sides. It made me angry. "So you're okay with all this?"

Her father put a hand on her shoulder to keep her from answering, but there was still some fire left in her, I guess, because she broke free and came up to me.

"This is the way it has to be, Enzo."

"Don't you care that all those people you worked so hard for will never get to America?"

"St. Thomas *is* America," Tilde said.

"It's part of the US Virgin Islands," her father told me, "a United States protectorate. And the lieutenant governor of St. Thomas has graciously offered to take them in, which means they will automatically be US nationals."

"They'll be legal immigrants, can travel to the US, and can eventually become full citizens," Tilde said.

"Why can't they just do it in Miami?" I asked.

"And face all those protesters and news crews?" the captain scoffed. "I think not. By taking care of this quickly

271

and on our own terms, we avoid all the unpleasantness. Everyone gets what they want."

"Not everyone!" I said. "Not me! Because I just want to go home."

"I imagine you will," said the captain, ". . . eventually." Then he grinned, taking great pleasure in my suffering. I think there's a word for that in German. I'll have to ask Gustav.

There was a knock at the door, and my father let in one of the guards who carried food trays last night. Today, he carried handcuffs.

"Turn around," he told me.

"You've gotta be kidding!"

My mother crossed herself, and I started to wonder if maybe it was time to start saying the Lord's Prayer. Handcuffs meant business.

"Is that really necessary?" my father asked.

"Your son has confessed to an international crime," Pajramovic said. "And there are protocols."

Then Crawley got up and jabbed the captain in the stomach with his cane so hard, the captain went, "Oooof!"

"You can stick your protocols where the sun don't shine!" Crawley said.

I laughed, and then he shoved the cane into my gut as well.

"Oooof!" I said.

And he smiled. "Who's feeble now?"

Just outside of the suite were half a dozen more guards, like maybe they thought they were dealing with King Kong or the Incredible Hulk. I was flattered that they thought I'd put up a superhuman struggle.

Then my mother's phone started to ring, surprising her as well as me. She fumbled to get it out of her purse.

"There's service here?" I asked no one in particular.

The guard who handcuffed me said, "US territories have US phone service. It's just like back home."

To which I said, "Oh. You mean there ain't no service."

Turns out the call was from my brother, Frankie, who had been pulling his hair out trying to get through to us since he first saw me on the news.

"Hi, Frankie, how are you? How's work?" my mother said, unable to deprogram her small-talk instinct. ". . . Yeah, Antsy's right here. You wanna talk to him?"

But since I couldn't conveniently hold the phone, I told her to just relay any brotherly advice Frankie might have.

"Frankie says, 'Hang in there.'"

"Tell him he's useless."

"He already knows."

At this point, you would think that the captain might want to slip me down a back staircase so as not to draw attention, but Caribbean Viking works in mysterious ways. Before they walked us down the hall, they got us all organized. Two guards took the lead, followed by Tilde and those of us who weren't getting thrown off, then my family, then more guards, then me and the captain and the rest of the guards behind us. The whole thing resembled a wedding procession or a human sacrifice, depending on your cultural persuasion.

I thought we were heading toward the nearest elevators, but instead we went right past them and out onto the Lido Deck, crossing the entire length of the ship, toward the farthest possible elevator bank.

There were hundreds of passengers out there lounging around the pools. When they saw the procession, they all stood up and took notice. Half of them started to pull out cameras and cell phones. If I had been at the front of the line, they might not have gotten them out in time, but with me bringing up the rear, they had plenty of warning.

I turned to the captain, who walked beside me like the father of the bride.

"Bad move," I told him. "No way to control the flow of information now. Videos are probably already streaming right onto the Web."

The captain didn't seem bothered. "These things happen."

All around us, people snapped pictures like paparazzi. Then I heard someone call, "Hey, Antsy," and I looked up to see this guy I didn't know looking down at me from the sundeck with a fancy-looking camera.

"Say '*queso*,'" he said, which is "cheese" in Spanish if you didn't get his stupid joke. But instead of saying cheese, I did something else. On a whim, I raised my handcuffed hands in the air making fists with them in a show of inner strength and stared proudly into his camera lens. It's the pose you probably remember, on account of it made the cover of *Time Magazine* the next week. The guy sold it to them for like a gazillion bucks, but did I see any of that money? No. There ain't no justice.

The crowd around us applauded and cheered when they saw my pose of solidarity. Then, like thunder after lightning, came a rumble of "boos" also. I guess even on the ship, it was a love/hate relationship.

We finally got to the aft elevators, but the walk of shame wasn't over because these were glass elevators—so I was forced to descend into the pit of despair with eyes watching from every single deck of the ship. It was only now that I realized that there was nothing accidental or poorly planned about our trek from the suite. This was a show. The cruise line *wanted* those pictures bleating and those videos streaming. What is it they say? There's no bad publicity. This is what Pajramovic meant by "on our own terms." Maybe you can't stop the media from chewing you up, but sometimes you can spoon-feed them exactly what you want them to eat.

I let out a little chuckle, and the captain looked at me sternly.

"You find this to your amusement?"

"Daddy, leave him alone," said Tilde.

"I'll have you know that because of this fiasco, I'm being forced into early retirement."

"You're welcome," I told him—because we both knew that if I hadn't come forward to take the blame, it would be a whole lot worse for him. "So what happens to Tilde?" I asked.

"I will be taking my daughter with me to Albania, to meet her relatives." Then he added, "That will be punishment enough."

The elevator doors opened on Zero Deck, where the

gangway was. Waiting there were the Caribbean Nine, looking scared and worried. I singled out Beto and gave him a smile, but he didn't smile back; he just looked away.

"We've docked," an officer told the captain.

"Good," he said. "Lower the gangway, and let's make this quick. I want them off the ship before the local news crews arrive."

That left me just a minute to say my good-byes as they swung open the huge iron door and lowered the gangway. Lexie gave me a hug and whispered a thank-you into my ear. She didn't have to say what it was for. I knew.

"I'll see you soon," I told her, although I had no idea if it was true. "Stay away from guys who look at you like you're longpork."

"Without you around, how will I know how they're looking at me?"

"You'll know," I told her. "Some looks you can smell."

Crawley glared down his nose at me, which was getting increasingly harder to do now that I was taller than him, and said, "I will make a sensible statement to the media on your behalf upon our arrival in Miami."

"You?" I said. "What about your crowd anxiety?"

"It's amazing what sufficient medication will do."

Howie grabbed me and gave me a sobbing bear hug like I was going off to war. "I'll never forget you, Antsy," he said. "Unless I get Alzheimer's."

He wanted to give me advice about ninja techniques to withstand torture, but I told him it was best not to divulge ninja secrets.

Captain Pajramovic gave me a courteous nod—I guess the closest thing I would get to a thank-you from him. "You, young man, are a thorn that I am most grateful to have removed from my side."

"Yeah," I told him, and glanced over at Tilde. "But you've got an even bigger thorn that ain't going nowhere."

The gangway was out now, and I didn't have much time left so I turned to Tilde. She looked into my eyes, beginning to tear up.

"Enzo, I . . ."

I didn't give her time to say a thing. Instead, I leaned forward and planted on her lips the best, sloppiest kiss I had in me. And you know what? I surprised myself! I mean, I'm not one to brag, but this kiss was for the record books. It was the kind of thing that makes you spend the rest of your life bouncing through relationships because you just can't match the absolute intensity and sheer perfection of that one all-consuming facial fusion.

I pulled back, leaving Tilde bleary-eyed and breathless. She looked at me, her eyes practically spinning in shock, knowing without question that the feeling I put behind that kiss was real.

"Antsy!" she said, like she was seeing me for the first time, which I guess she was.

"That's right," I told her. "Enzo don't live here no more."

Then my mother whacked me on the head, and we were hustled down the gangway.

A PLACE WHERE A PERSON COULD
DISAPPEAR IF THEY'RE NOT CAREFUL

I'LL ADMIT THAT I WAS SCARED.

I mean, here I was, thrown off the largest cruise ship in the world in handcuffs, and in front of me are two dark vans with darker windows and a team of beefy guys in suits, looking like Secret Service wannabes.

The Caribbean Nine were all whispering to each other in Spanish, and my parents were whispering to each other in Italian, thinking I didn't know what they were saying, but I did because I knew how to curse in Italian, too.

"Stay calm," my father said, and I'm thinking maybe these guys have concealed weapons, and that's why we need to stay calm, because what if one of 'em is trigger happy or just plain psycho?

So the dangerous guys in suits directed the Caribbean Nine into the first van. They looked even more scared than me.

"Where we go now?" asked the woman with the suitcase, which was now popping at the seams, and I wondered what she found on the old Viking ship to fill it with, hopefully not the body of Jorgen Ericsson, because that would be really bad.

"It will all be explained to you when you get there,"

said a guard with a gaze that had seen combat and a jaw that looked like it was chiseled in stone. It was the kind of face that could say "your mother loves you," and it would sound like a death threat. Needless to say, the Nine were not comforted by anything the Jaw said.

"It'll be okay. Trust me," I called out to them, even though I didn't trust anything myself, but I figured at this point what mattered most was cooperation. These were guys you didn't want to tick off. Meanwhile, behind us, the *Plethora of the Deep* pulled in the gangway and prepared to set sail. I knew there was no going back.

Once the Nine were in their van, my family and me were next. The second van was the same as the first, but there was already someone inside, although I couldn't see a face through the dark windows.

"So what happens now?" my father asked the Jaw.

"Please step inside," he threatened. "The president will brief you personally."

"What?" said my mother. "What did you just say?"

I savored the look of absolute shock on my parents faces until the Jaw swung open the van door and out came a short man with reddish hair, graying at the sides.

"Hello, I'm Kyle Ericsson, president of Caribbean Viking cruise line."

My dad let out a breath like maybe he'd been holding it for a whole minute, and my mother turned to the Jaw, suddenly more intimidating than him.

"What's wrong with you?" she said. "My husband has a heart condition—you don't go telling someone 'the

279

president will brief you personally' and give them Kyle Ericsson."

"See, that's what I said," I told them, but nobody cared.

Ericsson sighed, like he dealt with this on a regular basis. "Be that as it may, I came here to personally resolve this situation." Then he turned to me. "Anthony, I presume."

"You presume right."

He snapped his fingers, and the Jaw obediently got out a key and removed the handcuffs. "You won't be needing those now."

I had been in handcuffs for maybe ten minutes, but it felt like hours.

"So, then I'm free?"

"Yes and no," Ericsson said. "Mostly no."

Then he hustled us into the van and we sped off, because, like Captain Pajramovic predicted, an island news team was hurrying down the pier, microphones and cameras in hand.

Some skillful maneuvering got us out of the marina without any unwanted photo ops.

"Well, at least you can't say your experience on the *Plethora of the Deep* wasn't unique!" Ericsson said. He smiled with teeth so perfect, I figured his dental work probably cost more than our house. I guess winning teeth are important for a CEO.

"Is anyone going to tell us what happens now?" my father asked, no patience for Ericsson's polite corporate ways.

"Yeah—and where are they taking the Caribbean Nine?" I asked—noticing that we were no longer following the other van but had turned in a different direction.

"Your concern for the stowaways is admirable, but unnecessary," Ericsson said. "They are being taken to the embassy for processing. They'll each be given a visa, so their presence here will be official."

"You're giving them credit cards?" said Christina. "Can I get a Visa, too?" I'm glad she said it and not me. It was time someone else around here felt stupid.

"He means a permit to stay here," my mother told her. "A green card. Although I don't know if they're actually green."

"Oh. I knew that," Christina said, even though we all knew she didn't.

"That still doesn't answer my question," my father said. "Are we being held here, or can we go home?"

"The truth is, you can do whatever you please," Ericsson said. "The cruise line itself isn't pressing charges against Anthony, and until the US State Department officially puts out a warrant for his arrest, you're free to fly home. In fact, I can tell the driver to take you straight to the airport if that's what you *really* want . . ."

There was a huge "but" hanging in the air, and I didn't like the way it smelled, so I asked the obvious question.

"Why wouldn't we want to?"

"Because," said Ericsson, "if you go home now, you'll find news teams camped at your front door and the government will be forced to take action against you, Anthony. More than likely you'll go to a juvenile detention center for a very long time . . . and maybe prison after that." He paused, waiting for that to sink in, but he didn't have to wait. It sank like a Mafia informant in the East River. ". . . *But* . . . if you agree to wait here in St. Thomas until this whole thing blows over, the media will forget you, and our lawyers will be able to negotiate you a milder punishment."

"And how long might that take?" my father asked.

Ericsson pooched out his lower lip and shrugged. "A few weeks, a month, the rest of the summer perhaps. Certainly by September."

My father shook his head in disbelief. "No! I won't do it!"

"Mr. Bonano, one of the island's finest resorts, in addition to offering jobs for the Caribbean Nine, has graciously offered a place for your family to stay while you're here, so your comfort won't be in question."

"I don't need comfort," my father yelled. "I have a business to run!"

My brain was still sleeping with the fishes, stuck on the concept of endless juvie, but it was Christina who helped us all see the bigger picture, making up for that "visa" gaff, which I will tease her about for the rest of her life.

"Hold it," Christina said. "Mr. Ericsson, are you telling us that we are being handed an all-expenses-paid vacation . . . at a five-star Caribbean resort . . . for as long as we want to stay?"

"Well, yes," he said, "but our lawyers prefer to call it 'protective exile.'"

"Okay," said Christina, "whoever wants to be in protective exile in a tropical paradise for free, raise your hand."

I swear, the cruise line should fire their spin doctors and

hire my sister. I raised my hand even faster than she did. My mother's hand went up next, and we all looked to my father, who still held out.

"Joe," my mom said, gently clasping his hand. "After that cruise, don't you think we need a vacation?"

He reluctantly nodded and put his hand up, too.

"Splendid," said Ericsson. "I think you're going to like this place; I've stayed there myself—it's something special."

Exile's a funny thing. Ask any overthrown dictator. No matter how much people want to get rid of you, you're better off to them alive than dead, because if you're alive, all you get to be is a memory, as in, "hey, what ever happened to that ex-dictator guy?" But once you're dead, there's a good chance people might see you as a martyr, having died for your cause. Then they'd start healing people in your name, making graven idols to you that get on the news when they cry blood, like this lawn gnome on our block. The guy who owned it claimed that it was a manifestation of the Holy Spirit, but no one believed it, because, come on—it was a lawn gnome. Everyone knows lawn gnome blood is blue.

My own exile began down an overgrown dirt road that didn't look like it was leading anywhere good. When we stopped in a clearing in the middle of nowhere, I had a dark little flashback to Hello-Hello, but there weren't any crumbling buildings around us. There was nothing but rain forest.

"Here we are," said Ericsson, and opened the door of the van.

When we stepped out, we saw nothing but a sign that said LOBBY, pointing toward a bunch of trees.

"Uh-oh," said Christina. "Now comes the firing squad."

Then from somewhere right in front of me I heard a voice that was familiar and yet wasn't. Like it had changed a little from the last time I had heard it.

"Hi, everyone," the voice said, "Welcome to Peekaboo Cove Resort!"

My heart missed a major beat. Not just because of the voice, but because I couldn't see who was talking, even though I knew he must have been right in front of my face. That could only mean one thing!

"Schwa?"

I blinked, and there he was, my old friend Calvin Schwa, wearing a leaf-print shirt that blended in perfectly with the background and with eyes the same exact color as the sky.

"Hi, Antsy," said the Schwa. "It's good to see you."

MY LIFE AS AN INTERCONTINENTAL
BALLISTIC MISSILE

CALVIN SCHWA, IN CASE YOU DIDN'T KNOW, IS famous for being supernaturally unnoticeable, functionally invisible, observationally challenged. He's the kid whose picture never shows up in yearbooks, the kid who never gets called on to answer questions, and you know when you buy a picture frame at the store? I swear, his is the face that comes with the frame.

Most people ignored him, but he didn't go unnoticed in my life—and if it wasn't for him, I'd never have even been on that cruise and my dad wouldn't even have a restaurant. That's because I would never have met Crawley or Lexie had it not been for the one, the only Calvin Schwa. Funny how it's the small, seemingly insignificant things that end up changing your life. And funny how it all comes back around.

A couple of years ago, the Schwa went off in search of his long-lost mother, and he found her hopping around the Caribbean, lost, you could say, in the Bermuda Triangle.

He introduced us to her in the lobby. She was a wholly indescribable woman. I mean that literally. You couldn't describe her. She was so ordinary, the best you could do was to say that she looked like someone's mother.

"I've heard so much about you," she said as she shook my hand. She said hello to my parents, but they were so busy looking around, they didn't notice she was there. Apparently the Schwa's suspicions had been correct: His mom suffered from "the Schwa Effect," too, although to be honest, neither of them was suffering.

While my parents checked in, the Schwa gave me a tour of the grounds.

"My mom won this place in a poker game," he told me as he led me down a path that seemed to go nowhere until it opened up on a series of beautiful island villas. "But the guy who lost the game asked if she'd settle for marrying him instead. It was much more romantic than it sounds."

"So what about your father?" I had to ask.

The Schwa shrugged. "He spent Christmas with us. Then once he got home, he wrote me a letter saying 'Sorry I missed seeing you.'"

"Typical."

"Yeah, some things never change. Anyway, since my mom and I got here, business couldn't be better."

As it turns out, the Schwa effect was stronger when he and his mother were both together, and they found a way to turn it to their advantage, creating a little niche business for themselves.

"We make famous people disappear," the Schwa told me. "Just for a week or two—however long they need a break from the world. No tabloid headlines, no photographers, no fans. They get to be normal people while they're here, and thanks to my mom's and my 'special touch,' the outside world doesn't know this place exists. Believe me, some people will pay a lot of money to not be noticed!"

As he led me around, it amazed me how every single building of the resort was hidden by the forest around it until you were right next to it. If you weren't looking, you wouldn't even know the resort was here, and it occurred to me that all of us, no matter how bizarre our personal set of skills is, manage to find a place in the world.

"So what famous people are here now?" I asked.

"I'm not allowed to say," he told me, "but I'm sure you'll meet some of them."

"You should tell me who they are," I insisted. "'Cause what if I meet them and I don't recognize their famousness and they get all insulted?"

"No need to worry about that," he said with a smile. "I guarantee you'll recognize every single one of them."

Just then a guy with long hair who looked remarkably familiar, even without his guitar, came down the path.

"Pardon me, mate," he said very Britishly, "d'you 'ave a clue where the pool's at?"

"Keep going straight, then turn right at the next path," said the Schwa.

He backed up, a little freaked. "Whoa! Where'd you come from?"

"Same place as him," said the Schwa, pointing at me. "But I've been here longer."

He gave the Schwa another funny look, then went off in search of the pool.

I was speechless. "W . . . was that who I think it was?"

"Yep," the Schwa said. "Like I told you, you'll recognize everyone."

After the grand tour, we rested in a couple of hammocks down by the beach, drinking virgin mango-ritas out of coconuts and watching catamarans sailing by in the distance.

"I gotta admit it, Schwa—you know how to disappear in style."

"It's an art form."

I took another sip of my drink and thought for a moment of all I'd been through. I wondered if Tilde knew that this was the plan, or if she thought I was still under arrest, or if she had already moved on and was looking for her next "Enzo." I could only hope she'd miss me as much as I'd miss her.

"So are you really going to give jobs to the Caribbean Nine?" I asked.

"At first they'll be guests like you," the Schwa said. "But to stay in St. Thomas, the adults have to have jobs and the kids have to go to school. It's part of the deal. They'll probably go to the same school I do. It's small, but it gets the job done." He slurped the bottom of his drink. "Anyway, we pay a fair wage, and our guests are very good tippers. So they oughta do fine."

Farther down the beach, my parents were walking hand in hand, my dad finally relaxing. Behind us, in an open-air café, my sister was having an in-depth conversation with a kid actor who wasn't as acne free as the poster of him in her bedroom back home. I thought of my dad's backyard Zen garden and realized that this place wasn't all that different. Whatever was going on in the outside world didn't matter. Here, all was calm, all was balanced, all was well.

"So how about you, Antsy—do you know what happens when you finally go back?"

I nodded. Ericsson had told me a bit more of the plan before he left. "Well, the cruise line's lawyers feel pretty sure they can get the charges against me dropped if I agree to go to military school."

The Schwa stopped rocking. "Military school? *You?*"

"I know, crazy, isn't it?"

"Yeah, like putting a monkey on a moon mission!"

I laughed at that. If anyone else had said that, I would have been mad, but I couldn't get mad at the Schwa. "So are you insulting *me* or the monkey?"

Military school was not something I was looking forward to. I mean, back home, I tended to make fun of the ROTC kids, and now I'd be one of them. I tried to imagine myself in a uniform and couldn't.

"My parents say the discipline will build character— which I need like a hole in the head—but hey, there are worse things."

"Maybe you'll like it," suggested the Schwa.

"It'll be different," I said. "I can handle different." And that much I knew was true, because I was handling it right now. I mean, if you told me a month ago that I'd go on a cruise, create an international incident, and wind up drinking mango-ritas out of coconuts with the Schwa, I would have had you committed. But fate is a freak when it comes to messing with your future in ways you don't see coming.

Teachers, and parents, and those self-help books my

mother always reads—they're always saying "visualize your future." I never had luck with that. I never could see much at all. When I thought of the future, all I saw was my street, my neighborhood, Brooklyn, and more Brooklyn after that, because there ain't no end to the place. You can think you've seen it all, and suddenly you'll take an unexpected turn into some twilight-zone neighborhood you never knew existed, where all the street numbers got square roots.

Somehow looking at my future is different now, though. Sure, I still can't see much—but now the stuff I can't see goes way beyond where it used to. Now I'm like last year's fireworks fiasco, taking on gravity's rainbow—and I'm not coming down on the poor slobs on East 53rd Street. For all I know I'm going intercontinental, like some kind of missile, ready to take out a poor unsuspecting city. Or at least mess with it a little.

But there'd be plenty of time for that. Right now I had nothing pressing, unless you counted the hammock strings digging a pattern in my back you could read like a road map.

"You know what, Schwa?" I said, realizing this for maybe the first time. "It doesn't suck to be me."

"Yeah," he said, "I know the feeling."

And there we stayed until sunset—me, for once, happy to just sit still.

Oh, and by the way, the president—the REAL president—actually did say something about me, in his next press conference, although he never actually mentioned my name.

"We need to put this event in perspective," he said. "We

290

mustn't exaggerate the importance of one well-meaning but misguided youth."

Leave it to the president to sum up my whole life in a single sound bite. I'd put it on a T-shirt, but I'm sure it would get lost with my luggage.

ACKNOWLEDGMENTS

This ship could not have sailed without the help and support of quite a few skilled ship builders. First and foremost, I'd like to thank my editor, Julie Strauss-Gabel, as well as Don Weisberg, Lauri Hornik, Eileen Kreit, Scottie Bowditch, and everyone at Penguin for believing in this book, and letting Antsy take this voyage. Thanks to my agent, Andrea Brown, for not just being a great agent, but a great friend. Thanks to my kids, Brendan, Jarrod, Joelle, and Erin for their love and input, and for our research cruises on several of the world's largest cruise ships. A dirty job, but someone's gotta do it. Many thanks to my tireless assistant, Marcia Blanco, without whom nothing would ever get done. A shout-out to Wendy Doyle for her work on my newsletter, and for transcribing my various mad ramblings. Thanks to Chris Goethals for being so supportive, and giving me notes on my early draft. Endless gratitude to my critique group, the Fictionaires, for their wisdom and friendship. And finally a heartfelt thanks to all the fans who screamed for another Antsy story. I think this is the best one yet—I hope you find it to be an epic sail!

293